THEIRS WERE THE TRIUMPHS AND
TRAGEDIES, THE ~~LOVES AND~~
BETRAYALS T~~HAT FORGED A~~
NATION—AND A ~~LEGEND RISING~~
OUT OF THE FL~~AMES~~

David—Israel's belove~~d warrior-king,~~ he
stands on the brink ~~of his~~ ultimate triumph: the
capture of Jerusalem. But his victory could turn to
ashes in the heat of love—and murder.

Bathsheba—Wife of a Hittite mercenary, she is the
most sensuous and desirable woman in all Jerusalem. Her beauty has inflamed Israel's great king,
who has vowed to possess her, even if it costs him
his soul.

Sunu—Fearless and indomitable in battle, he is one
of David's most courageous and loyal young warriors . . . until the suspicious death of a comrade-
in-arms plants a dark seed of doubt in his valiant
heart.

Leah—A girl of quick intelligence and beguiling
charm, she will grow into a woman of striking
beauty. But her power to see into the hearts and
minds of others could prove to be a dangerous and
unwanted gift.

Kaptar—Chief adviser to his half brother Sheshonk I,
the Egyptian king, he has the chance to journey to
the land of the Hebrews in search of the father he
has never met . . . a quest that will put his loyal-
ties to the ultimate test.

Nefernehi—Kaptar's devoted wife, she remains behind on the banks of the Nile awaiting her husband's return. But in the time of his absence she
will discover that the man sworn to protect her is
the one man who can destroy her.

From the Creators of Wagons West

The Children of the Lion

THE CHILDREN OF THE LION
DEPARTED GLORY
THE DEATH OF KINGS
THE SHINING KING
TRIUMPH OF THE LION

Volume XIX

TRIUMPH
OF THE LION

PETER DANIELSON

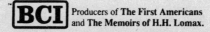

BCI Producers of **The First Americans**
and **The Memoirs of H.H. Lomax.**

Book Creations Inc., Canaan, NY • Lyle Kenyon Engel, Founder

BANTAM BOOKS
NEW YORK • TORONTO • LONDON • SYDNEY • AUCKLAND

TRIUMPH OF THE LION

*A Bantam Domain Book / published by arrangement with Book
Creations Inc.*

Bantam edition / January 1996

*Produced by Book Creations Inc.
Lyle Kenyon Engel, Founder*

ISBN 0-553-56148-0

Published simultaneously in the United States and Canada

*Bantam Books are published by Bantam Books, a division of Bantam
Doubleday Dell Publishing Group, Inc. Its trademark, consisting of the
words "Bantam Books" and the portrayal of a rooster, is Registered in
U.S. Patent and Trademark Office and in other countries. Marca
Registrada. Bantam Books, 1540 Broadway, New York, New York
10036.*

PRINTED IN THE UNITED STATES OF AMERICA

OPM   0 9 8 7 6 5 4 3 2 1

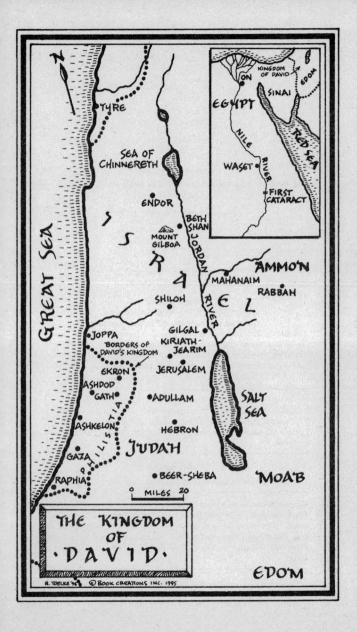

THE KINGDOM
OF
· DAVID ·

TRIUMPH
OF THE LION

Prologue

The old man slipped through the rear door of the tavern just as a three-legged stool sailed past his head and crashed into the wall. He ducked away from the splintering wood and bolted into the alley outside with the alacrity of a wise man—if not, perhaps, the dignity of an elderly one.

After he had turned several corners and put the commotion well behind him, he paused, drew a deep breath, and combed his fingers through his white beard. A frown of indignation creased his high forehead. He had stopped at the tavern on his way home from the temple, intending to have a cup of wine before returning to the bosom of his family. Certainly he had had no inkling that a brawl was about to erupt.

None of it would have happened, he thought, had that sword-wearing wanderer not come into the tavern, trailed by a disreputable-looking spotted dog. Looking askance at the traveler's ragged cloak and the dog, the tavern keeper had made the mistake of judging him to be a mendicant and saying as much. An instant later the peace-loving old man had found himself in the middle of a fray that soon engulfed the entire tavern.

So, with the wisdom of his years, he had left as quickly and unobtrusively as possible. Now he heaved a regretful sigh. His cup of wine, still almost full, had been left behind.

Ah, well, there was nothing he could do about it now. He straightened his robe and looked around. He would proceed to his home, as he had originally intended, and

1

put this incident behind him. If only he could spot some familiar landmark . . .

The old man's frown deepened. True, the back streets of the city resembled a rat's warren, but he had lived here for many years. A few twists and turns while he was not paying attention should not have been sufficient to make him lose his way, and yet he saw nothing he recognized. People came and went on the street, but he knew none of them. Nor did any of the buildings look familiar. He craned his neck, thinking that perhaps he might spot the king's palace on the hill and orient himself from that.

Nothing. He might as well have been dropped down in ancient Ur, where he would have been as well and truly lost.

Frustration welled up inside him. He did not like making such an admission, even to himself. And most assuredly he was not going to stop any of the passersby on the street and ask for directions. To do that would be to invite snickers and jeers behind his back. "See that pathetic old man?" they might say. "I had to tell him how to find his way home!"

No, he would not—could not!—risk such an indignity. He squared his shoulders, straightened his robe again, and began walking down the street. If he kept walking, surely sooner or later he would encounter something or someone familiar.

For a moment he considered trying to retrace his steps to the tavern, but he knew that he was just as likely to find his way by going ahead as by doubling back. As he muddled on, he suddenly recalled his father counseling him not to spend too much time looking back over his shoulder; something unpleasant might be gaining on him. The old man knew what his father had meant: It was a mistake to dwell on the past. But at his age he had much more past than future, so it seemed only natural to ponder the people and events that had come before. He snorted. He had lived in an age of heroes once, of men unafraid to grapple with destiny and bend it to their own will. Now it was a time of merchants and traders, men who spent their days in the market counting beans rather than slain enemies. In many *ways, of course, this was better. But there were times when the old man longed for those other days. And they were not so far behind, not really—*

"Ho! Old man!"

He looked up, jolted out of his reverie by the arrogant hail. It had come from one of a group of youths standing shoulder to shoulder in the narrow street, blocking his way. The old man blinked, uncertain whether to be angry or frightened. The youths had a rough look about them and might be intent on stealing his purse, even though it was almost empty.

"Where are you going in such a hurry, old man?" asked the lad who had first addressed him. He was tall, broad-shouldered, full of the confidence of his years.

"I am on my way home," the old man replied quietly, his deep voice betraying little of the rumbling power he could summon up when he wished.

The youth waved a hand at the paving stones under his feet. "On our street?" he asked.

"This is a public street."

The youth shook his head. "No longer. It belongs to us, and you must pay us for its use." He took a step forward, menace in his stance. "You must pay us, one way or another."

"I . . . I am an old man. I have few coins." The quavery, pleading tone in his voice grated on his ears. Just moments ago he had been regretting the passing of the age of great heroes. Now he was being as timid as any lowly beggar in the market. He was nothing more than a mendicant himself, begging these callow youths to let him pass unmolested rather than demanding his rights as a citizen. Well aware that he might be placing himself in danger— and at the moment not caring a whit—he drew himself up and went on, "And I have no intention of sharing them with the likes of you."

At his sharp, angry tone, the mocking smiles on the young men's faces fell away. They exchanged glances; then the leader stepped even closer, his hands clenched into fists. But the old man stood firm.

Unexpectedly the lad stopped short. A strong hand fell

on the old man's shoulder. "There you are," a man's voice said. "I wondered where you had gone after that fight broke out."

The old man turned and saw the hot-tempered wanderer from the tavern. His swords were sheathed now, and he was smiling. The spotted dog stood nearby, wagging its tail.

Although this man's presence was clearly deterring an attack by the youths, the old man was not going to pretend a friendship where none existed. He said formally, "Do I know you, sir?"

"No, but I know you," the swordsman replied. "Your fame has spread far and wide. You are known as the Teller of Tales."

The old man could not help but smile as he felt a flush of pride. "Some have called me that," he admitted.

"I am not of your people, but I have heard many of their stories. I have heard of the Children of the Lion, and it is said you know more about them than anyone else."

"This is true."

"Could you tell me a story about the Children?" asked the swordsman.

The Teller of Tales considered the fading light of afternoon. Night was approaching, but he sensed that with this man beside him he had little to fear. His smile broadened as he nodded and said, "I could do this."

The swordsman clapped him on the back. "Excellent!" He turned to the youths, who were edging away, and his voice hardened as he said, "You lads there, stay and listen. You can learn a great deal by giving ear to the wisdom of your elders." His tone tolerated no argument, and although the youths glared resentfully at both men, they remained where they were.

An empty keg stood beside the wall of a nearby building. After overturning it, the swordsman gestured toward the Teller of Tales. "Please sit down."

Lifting his robe a little, the old man did so with a nod of thanks. The swordsman pointed to the paving stones, commanded the youths to sit, then sank down himself at *the old man's feet and smiled up at him, petting the dog at his side. "We are listening."*

The Teller of Tales drew a deep breath as he mentally sorted through all the stories that reposed inside his head. Sensing the sort of man the sword-bearer was, he settled on a tale that would likely entertain him.

"This is a tale of the days of our noble King David," *he began, "not long after he was proclaimed by the elders the king of all Israel. I warn you, it is a tale of tragedy but also one of triumph."*

"Say on, my friend," *declared the swordsman. "Say on."*

"Very well." The Teller of Tales leaned forward slightly, anticipating the story himself even though he had told it countless times before. "At this time, David lived in the city of Hebron, and there he met with his advisers, including the armorer Urnan and his son Eri, who were of the great family sometimes called the Children of the Lion. . . ."

CHAPTER
ONE

Urnan looked around the massive table at the other men who had shared the evening meal with him. They were all important men, gathered here in King David's house in Hebron, and he felt honored to be in their presence.

Across the table from Urnan was Ittai, the Philistine mercenary who commanded David's personal guard. Next to Ittai was Hushai, an Archite and one of the elders of Israel. Hushai had once been a follower of the old prophet Samuel and was now a supporter of the man whom Samuel, following God's commands, had anointed the king of Israel. From time to time Hushai glanced warily at Ittai as if he was uncomfortable sitting next to a Philistine, but the mercenary was known as a trusted and loyal aide to the king.

Seated next to Urnan was Zadok, a young priest and assistant to Abiathar, David's spiritual adviser. Abiathar himself sat on the other side of Zadok, and opposite him was Shisha, who served as David's scribe. The Egyptian would make a record of this meeting, as he did all important gatherings.

At the head of the table sat David—son of Jesse, once a shepherd, then a mighty warrior, now the leader of all the tribes of Israel. Following the death of Ishbosheth, the last surviving son of Saul, the former king, David's grip on the reins of power had grown so strong that now no one disputed his right to rule. A tall, broadshouldered, handsome man approaching his fortieth year, David was every inch a king. It was foreknowledge of the great leader he would become that had led Samuel to anoint him Saul's successor, the future king over God's people, when David was a mere shepherd boy.

Now David drained the last of the wine from his cup, placed it on the table, and looked at the men seated around him. "We are agreed, then. We will march to Jerusalem three days hence. By then our scouts will have had ample time to study the city's fortifications."

"And those fortifications are likely to be strong," Ittai observed in his harsh Philistine accent.

David nodded. "I would expect nothing less from the Jebusites. They have held their city for hundreds of years against all who came to conquer it, even Joshua." A smile touched his face. "But they have not faced us, eh, my friends?"

Urnan was tempted to warn the king not to be overconfident, but he stilled his tongue. The mood in the room was exuberant, as it always was when warriors anticipated a lusty battle and a decisive victory. Urnan did not want to ruin it. Besides, David might well be right. He had already succeeded in doing something that no man had ever done before: He had united all the tribes of Israel into one cohesive nation. Even the reign of the great Saul had been beset by divisive influences—not the least of which had been David himself, although he had always loved and respected Saul. The rivalry between them had been of Saul's own making.

With such an accomplishment behind him, David

might well achieve something else that was unheard of: the conquest of Jerusalem, which he planned to make his capital.

Urnan became aware that David was speaking to him and looked up guiltily. ". . . word from your grandson, Urnan?" David was saying.

"No, Your Majesty," Urnan replied with a shake of his head. "You are more likely to hear from Sunu than I, I would wager. After all, he and his companions are on a military mission for you."

"For all of Israel," David correctly gently. "It is up to them to find a way into Jerusalem."

"The hand of God is on them," said Abiathar. "The Lord shall guide them, and they shall discover a means whereby the Jebusites will be defeated."

David nodded. "Let it be so, Abiathar. Let it be so."

Sunu lifted his head and, blinking away the sweat trickling into his eyes, peered at the walls of the great city in the distance. The brassy sun beat down on the hill called Ophel, where Sunu and his companions lay in hiding. To the east, across a small valley, was the hill on which the city of Jerusalem was built.

The Jebusites who lived there were not allied with any of the tribes of Israel. Their neutrality—and the city's location at the juncture of half-a dozen major trade routes—had allowed them to flourish and prosper. Sunu knew that these two factors made Jerusalem the perfect site for the new nation's capital.

All that remained was to take it away from the Jebusites.

Sunu's hand tightened on his lance. He was an intelligent young man and understood the politics behind David's decision to capture Jerusalem, but such considerations meant little to him. Politics did nothing to fire the blood. Sunu lived for the thrill of battle, the glory of seeing his enemies fall beneath his lance or sword. The mere thought of combat made his pulse race and the blood pound in his head.

Yet, seasoned warrior that he was, he also understood that discretion was often the wisest course. This was one such moment.

Sunu's troop of scouts had ridden from Hebron to Jerusalem on horseback but had left their mounts well back from the city's walls, guarded by one man, before climbing to the summit of Ophel to survey the landscape. Had they approached any closer on their horses, the dust kicked up by the animals' hooves might have given away their presence, and David had made it clear this was to be a secret mission. When the Israelite army arrived a few days hence, Sunu and the other scouts would have gathered sufficient information with which to build a strategy for the capture of Jerusalem.

At least that was the plan. Observing the city now, with its watchtowers at each corner, Sunu was not sure he and his companions could get close enough to learn anything without being seen.

Despite his youth, Sunu was as tall as any of the other scouts and heavily muscled from long hours of practice with sword, lance, and battle-ax. His thick black hair fell to his shoulders. He wore a tunic that came almost to his knees and a thick leather belt from which hung a pounded brass sheath for his sword.

One of the other scouts, a man named Lassan, shook his head and said quietly, "That fortress will not be easy to take."

"We will do it," Sunu said firmly. "God has told David to make this city the capital of Israel. We will not be defeated."

"It would help if God made the walls of Jerusalem tumble down, as he did those of Jericho when Joshua marched his men around it for six days in accordance with God's commands," grumbled Lassan.

"Perhaps he will," Sunu mused. "Or perhaps we will find a way *through* the walls."

Lassan gave him a skeptical look. Sunu could not have explained where such an unlikely idea had come from, but he knew instinctively that it was a good one. The Jebusites' confidence in the strength of their famous stone walls was well known. As they were primarily merchants and traders, not fighters, they relied almost entirely on the impregnability of those walls for their safety. They would never expect an attack from within them.

As he studied the city now, however, Sunu could see no way of gaining entrance. The gates were well guarded, and the walls appeared too difficult to scale and too high to shoot arrows over. And Jebusite archers positioned atop the walls could easily pour down a hail of arrows on any army foolish enough to approach within bowshot.

Sunu shook his head. Brooding would solve nothing. He said to the others, "When night falls, we can explore the walls and look for anything that might help David."

Borum, the oldest of the group and its nominal leader, nodded. "We must be careful, though. The Jebusites suspect nothing now, but if they know that David covets their city, they will have time to prepare to repel our army."

The other men murmured their agreement. Like them, Sunu understood the need for discretion, but it chafed at him anyway. Caution was for others. As far as he was concerned, daring usually won the day.

The afternoon passed slowly. Sunu noticed little activity outside the walls of Jerusalem. He knew that for the most part the inhabitants were not tillers of the soil, although groves of olive trees thrived on the hills around the city; the Jebusites purchased most of their food from farmers who brought their goods in carts and wagons. Sunu suspected that the Jebusites stored a goodly supply of rations, however, in the event of a siege.

The sun finally dipped below the horizon, and the heat of the day began to ease. The waiting was almost over. Sunu was grateful; he and his comrades would soon be on the move again.

As soon as full darkness had fallen, the Israelite scouts moved down the western slope of Ophel and through the valley. Torches had been lit at intervals along the city walls, but the light they cast did not reach far. Sunu and his companions stayed well outside the circle of illumination.

As the scouts made a full circuit of the city, Sunu searched intently for any breaks or flaws in the stone walls until they reached the point where they had started, near the spring of Gihon. The pool lay at the bottom of a deep depression hard against the eastern wall; there were no torches nearby, and in the darkness the opening in the ground looked like a black hole that might lead straight to Gehenna.

Suddenly Sunu felt thirsty, and an audacious idea came to him. Putting his hand on Borum's arm, he whispered, "I would drink of Jerusalem's water, if nothing else."

"Are you mad?" hissed Borum. "Sunu, stop—"

The command came too late, and at any rate Sunu paid no attention to it. With his hand on his sword hilt, he stole toward the spring as lightly and silently as a cat. None of the others came after him or tried to stop him.

As he drew closer to the depression, he discerned in the starlight the steps that had been carved into its sides. Peering down into the depths of the pool, he saw the stars reflected in the still surface of the water and, after a moment, moved carefully down the broad, shallow steps.

When he reached the bottom step, he stretched himself full length upon it, then scooped up a handful of water and tasted it. It was cool and sweet, especially after a day spent waiting in the sun with only warm water—tasting slightly of the goatskin that held it—to drink. Sunu plunged his head into the pool, washing the dust from his face and hair and swallowing more water in great gulps.

A faint sound came to his ears, a clicking noise, distorted somewhat by the water. A moment later, as he lay tense and motionless, he heard something else. It sounded for all the world like voices.

The sounds were coming through the water, Sunu

realized. He lifted his head from the pool, water streaming from his hair and drenching his tunic. Several moments of intense listening told him he was right—he could hear nothing with his head above the water. After taking a deep breath, he plunged his head in again.

There! He could hear the sounds once more, and he was certain they were coming from *inside* the city. That could mean only one thing: There was a passageway of some kind connecting this spring to the interior of Jerusalem.

Sunu's heart was pounding now. His companions were no doubt worried about him, but they would have to wait a few minutes longer. He took his sword and sheath from his belt and laid them on the stone step, then slipped into the water. Not knowing how long the passage was, he took several deep breaths before he went under. The pool was not as deep as he was tall, so he crouched as his hands found the wall and searched along it.

A moment later he found the opening. Quickly he explored its dimensions and determined that it was large enough for a man to pass through. After filling his lungs with air again, he worked himself into the entrance and pushed himself along the passage with his hands and feet.

The waterway was only a few feet long. His head broke the surface again and found air. Faint light fell from somewhere above, and when he looked up, he could barely make out another round opening, outlined by dim illumination. He could not see the stars, so he guessed there was a covering of some sort over this end of the tunnel.

But the distorted voices he had heard earlier were clear now and much louder. Two women were talking somewhere above him, and he could understand enough of their words to know that they were Jebusites. He was inside the walls of the city!

This was just what David needed, Sunu thought excitedly. He drew in a deep breath and made his way back through the passage to the pool outside the wall.

He pulled himself from the spring, snatched up his
sword and sheath, and hurried up the steps.

Borum, Lassan, and the others were waiting impatiently for him. "We thought we might have to leave
you," Borum said stiffly. "We feared you had either
drowned or been captured by the Jebusites."

"Neither." Sunu could barely contain his excitement. "I have found a way into the city!"

In the faint starlight the young man could see the
grin that spread across his commander's face.

"Praise God!" Borum whispered as he clapped a
hand on Sunu's shoulder. "You must tell us about it. But
for now, let us be away from here to await the arrival of
David and the army of the Lord!"

The scouts withdrew quickly from the city, heading
for the spot where they had left their horses. Once
mounted, they would retreat to a site well away from
Jerusalem and stay hidden until the Israelite army appeared. As they approached the horses, however, Sunu
heard voices in the darkness, angry voices.

Borum had heard them as well and signaled for his
men to halt.

"Lying Israelite dog!" growled a man's voice. "Why
would one of you pigs of the hills be out here with this
many horses, if not to cause trouble? Did the one called
David send you? Where are your companions?"

The harsh accent marked the questioner as a Philistine. Sunu and the other men exchanged glances. Obviously someone had stumbled across the man they had
left to watch the horses, which were hidden behind a
screen of olive trees. But what was a Philistine doing
here—and more importantly, was he alone?

"I demand answers," the Philistine went on angrily,
"and my masters demand answers. The Jebusites do not
want you pigs skulking around their city."

So that was the explanation, Sunu thought. The
Philistine was a mercenary working for the Jebusites.
Then more men spoke up, and Sunu's other question
was answered: The Philistine was not alone. It sounded
as if he had an entire patrol with him.

"Kill the dog," urged another man. "Anything he tells you will be a lie, Cralor."

"Perhaps," said the first Philistine, evidently the leader of the patrol. "But sufficient torture might perhaps produce a speck of truth."

The hapless Israelite, whose name was Elihu, spoke up bravely. "I will tell you nothing, no matter what you do to me. I fear no Philistines, especially not those who are lapdogs of the Jebusites."

Sunu knew that Elihu was trying to goad the Philistines into killing him quickly rather than torturing him. Better to be struck down with a single blow of a sword than to suffer a lingering death at the hands of a skilled torturer. Besides, if they killed him quickly, the mercenaries could not force any information from him.

It was a brave sacrifice Elihu was prepared to make. But it proved unnecessary. Sunu, Borum, Lassan, and the others acted as one, drawing their swords from their sheaths.

"As quietly as possible, my friends," Borum called softly, "kill them all!"

One of the mercenaries suddenly turned and cried out, "Someone is there!"

The Israelites rushed through the grove, their attack so swift and so ferocious that even with some warning the Philistines were unprepared.

Sunu was at the forefront of the charge. The dark shape of a mercenary loomed up in front of him, starlight reflecting dully off his brass chest armor. Sword in both hands, Sunu aimed a low blow that bit into the mercenary's shins and made him bend over, gasping in pain but trying to bring his own sword into play. Sunu's blade swept up and down, almost too fast for the eye to follow, and met the back of the man's neck with a dull *chunk!* The mercenary, nearly decapitated by the blow, sprawled on the ground at the young man's feet, his head flopping grotesquely.

Sunu whirled, slashing out at another of the Philistines, and heard a whispering sound by his right ear as the thrust of a lance barely missed him. Stepping for-

ward while the lancer was off balance, he drove his
blade into the man's belly, ripped it from side to side in
a disemboweling stroke, then tore it free as the man slid
slowly to the ground.

All around him was chaos. A mercenary's lance
tore clear through the body of an Israelite. Lassan
swung an overhand blow with his sword that bit deeply
into the shoulder of a Philistine. Nearby, Borum grap-
pled with another man. Each had his free hand locked
around the wrist of the other's sword hand, and, grunting and heaving, they strained against each other in a
deadly standoff. Elihu leaped on another of the Philistines from behind, looping one arm around his neck and
choking off his air while with his other hand he drove a
dagger again and again into the man's side.

Yet another Philistine came at Sunu, whirling his
sword overhead. Sunu ducked under the whistling blade
and brought his own sword up between the man's legs.
The Philistine's loins were protected so securely that the
blow was turned aside, but Sunu's thrust still ripped a
great gash in the man's thigh. Blood fountained from it
as the Philistine collapsed. Sunu finished him with a
swift stroke.

As he stepped back, sword dripping, Sunu looked
around for a fresh opponent. None of the Philistines
were still on their feet, however; they all lay sprawled on
the ground, dead or mortally wounded. As Sunu
watched, Lassan silenced the moans of two of them by
cutting their throats.

Borum said fiercely, "Eight dead Philistines, and
only one of us gone to sit at the feet of Yahweh. This is a
good night's work, brothers."

"Will we leave them here?" asked Sunu.

Borum shook his head. "We should take the bodies
with us and find a good ravine some distance from here
in which to toss them. We do not want the Jebusites to
find them. Better for them to simply disappear than to
alert the Jebusites that there was trouble so near
to their city."

Seeing the wisdom of Borum's plan, Sunu nodded.

"They'll likely think these men deserted, seeking a better-paying master."

"Aye." Borum sheathed his sword and grinned fiercely. "They will be a surprised lot, a few days hence, when they look out from their walls and see the army of David encamped before them."

"And they will be even more surprised when we take the city from within." Sunu was already looking forward to that day, because when the king asked for volunteers for the mission that would deliver the city into their hands, he intended to be the first to offer his sword—and his life, if need be—for David and the nation of Israel.

CHAPTER
TWO

"Do not trouble yourself, Eri," Urnan said to his son. They were in the house in Hebron where the family had been living since David had been declared the king of all Israel. "Jerioth and I will care for Leah."

Eri nodded as he buckled on his sword. "I know," he said stolidly.

Urnan tried not to show his disappointment. For a long time now he had been waiting for Eri to show genuine paternal interest in Leah, the daughter he had begotten with his first wife, Sarah. But Eri had never warmed to Leah; Urnan and his wife, Jerioth, had raised the child as their own since the death of Sarah. The entire affair had been a tragedy from the start, Urnan had thought many times: Sarah's insanity following the brutal murder of her parents, when she withdrew into a childlike state; the obsessive rage that had gripped her when her wits finally returned and she discovered that her husband had taken a second wife,

Baalan, and was the father of a strapping young son, Sunu; her betrayal of Eri to his enemies; and finally her death as a disease-ravaged prostitute.

It was Urnan and Jerioth who had found the infant Leah at the side of her dying mother and then fled the town of Gilgal with her before the Philistines ravaged it. Eri, later presented with the daughter he had never seen, closed his heart to her because she reminded him too much of Sarah. But, much to her good fortune, Leah had a doting grandfather and his wife to care for her. Urnan and Jerioth could not have loved the child more had she truly been their own.

Now Eri was preparing to march to Jerusalem with David's army. Although he was a master weapons maker like Urnan, he was also more of a warrior than Urnan had ever been. As young men Eri and Saul had bedeviled the Philistines in a series of daring raids. Later Eri had been a close friend to Saul's son Jonathan, and the two of them had dealt much misery to the Philistines.

That was all behind him now. Eri was a staunch supporter of King David, as were his father, Urnan, and his son, Sunu. Three generations of Children of the Lion served the king. But each generation, Urnan mused, spent more time on the battlefield than the one before. He was not sure that was a good thing.

Jerioth came into the room, Leah trailing behind her as usual. Urnan looked fondly at his wife. Despite her matronly proportions and the streaks of gray in her dark hair, Jerioth was still a very beautiful woman. She reached down and took the hand of the little girl, who wore an unusually solemn expression.

"Your daughter wishes to bid you farewell, Eri," said Jerioth.

Eri nodded, looking equally solemn. He turned to Leah and held out his hands. "Come to me, child."

Leah walked across the room, took her father's hands, and looked up at him. "Good-bye, Father."

For a long moment Eri stared down at her. Urnan wondered what he was seeing there. Was he seeing

Sarah as she had once been—the beautiful young woman with whom he had fallen in love—or Sarah as the spiteful, hate-filled creature she later became? Either way, thought Urnan, it was unfair. Leah was not Sarah, and she should not be punished for the weakness and the sins of her mother.

Suddenly Eri bent over and scooped Leah into his brawny arms. The child might as well have been weightless for all the ease with which her father picked her up. As he cuddled her against his broad chest, her arms stole slowly around his neck.

"Be good," Eri whispered to her. "Obey Grandfather Urnan and Jerioth. I will be with you again as soon as I can."

"Will you be careful, Father?" asked Leah.

"Of course I will," Eri said with a laugh. "I am always careful."

Jerioth came to Urnan and slipped a hand in his as they watched father and daughter bidding each other farewell. Urnan smiled. This was the affection he had hoped to see between the two.

The child pressed her cheek against Eri's for a moment as she hugged him again. Then she drew back in his arms and stared intently into his eyes. Eri, seeming slightly discomfited by her gaze, said, "What is it, little one?"

"You *do* love me," Leah said.

"Of course I do. You are my daughter."

"Yes, but now I *know.*"

Jerioth's hand tightened almost painfully around Urnan's. He looked at her and saw the worried frown creasing her brow. Unsure what was wrong, he was about to ask, but Eri turned toward them just then, and Jerioth's expression smoothed into a smile.

Leah held out her hands toward Urnan, and he stepped forward and took her from Eri. Cradling her in his left arm, he reached out with his right and clasped Eri's wrist.

"Go with God," he said fervently.

"And may Yahweh watch over you while I am

gone," Eri replied. After hugging Jerioth he picked up his lance. "We march in less than an hour. When I return, Jerusalem shall be ours."

"God willing," Urnan said.

"The city has been promised to David. He will find a way to take it." Eri smiled confidently, patted Leah on the shoulder, then turned and walked out of the house.

"Take our love to Sunu," Urnan called after him, and Eri turned to nod and wave. Then he was gone, joining the other men who were gathering for the march to Jerusalem, some twenty miles to the north.

"God grant you a safe and speedy return, my son," Urnan said in a whisper.

"Do not worry, Grandfather Urnan," said Leah. "My father will be all right. I *know.*"

Urnan looked at her, then glanced at his wife. She was staring at the child and frowning again, as if she had just heard something that alarmed her.

With David and his advisers and commanders riding at its head, the army left Hebron. Urnan, Jerioth, and Leah joined the rest of the city to watch and cheer as the soldiers marched forth, and when they saw Eri, riding tall at David's side, their hearts swelled with pride.

Once the soldiers were gone, the citizens went about their business again. Some returned to their homes, some went to the market, and others journeyed to the fields and vineyards outside the city to work. Urnan and Jerioth went with Leah back to the house they shared with Baalan, Eri's wife, and Mara, Sunu's wife. Mara had joined the crowd watching the army leave Hebron, but Baalan had not. Earlier, she had bidden Eri farewell in private.

"I think Baalan wishes Eri had not gone with David," Jerioth said to Urnan when they were alone. "He grows too old for war."

"Too old?" Urnan snorted. "He has seen but forty years in this world. I am a score of years older, and there are still times when I must fight."

"You did not go with David this time," Jerioth pointed out.

Urnan shrugged and sat on a stool. "It was not necessary. Our king already has a master armorer with him: my son."

"True." Jerioth came closer and laid a hand on his shoulder. "But I am glad you are here and not going into battle, just as Baalan would be glad if Eri had stayed behind. No woman likes to watch her man riding off to what may be his death."

"Eri will be fine," Urnan said gruffly.

"I pray it is so."

Something about his wife's tone made Urnan look up sharply. "What is wrong?" he asked. "Have you had a vision?"

Quickly Jerioth shook her head. "Visions do not come as easily or as frequently to me as they once did." She sighed heavily. "Sometimes the powers of a necromancer fade with time. I would not mind if mine disappeared completely. They have seldom brought me anything but grief."

Urnan stood up and took his wife in his arms. He knew she meant what she said. In the past she had been known as the Witch of Endor; her fame—or infamy—as a necromancer had spread throughout the land of Israel. It was Jerioth who, at Saul's request, had raised the spirit of the prophet Samuel, but Saul had not been pleased with what Samuel had to tell him. Jerioth was fortunate that Saul had not ordered her death as the bearer of bad tidings, which, as king, he could easily have done. Willingly, then, had she put her days as a mystic behind her. Now she was content to be simply Urnan's mate.

He pressed her against him and stroked her hair, sensing—with no magical power other than his love for her—how disturbed she was about something. He did not think it had anything to do with Eri's riding off to help David lay siege to Jerusalem.

"What is it?" he asked quietly. "What is it that concerns you?"

"I should have known that you would see how I was worried," Jerioth said with a faint smile. "It is the girl. Leah."

"What about her?"

"Did you see the way she looked at Eri?"

"She was . . . very intent," Urnan admitted.

"I have seen that look before. She was . . . searching. Searching his mind, his heart, his soul. She was looking into his thoughts and hearing them as if he spoke the words aloud."

It was Urnan's turn to frown. "You mean—"

"I mean that the child has powers of her own, similar to mine but perhaps even . . . even stronger."

Urnan shook his head and said gently, "You must be mistaken. I know you love Leah like a grandchild, or even like your own child, but she is not of your blood. The powers you speak of could not have been passed down to her from you."

Jerioth slipped out of his embrace and began to pace back and forth across the room. "I never claimed that they did," she said. "Others have practiced sorcery besides those of my lineage. You yourself have told me of your friend Prince Kemose of Egypt, who could bend the wills of others in manners of his own choosing. And there were your ancestors, the Children of the Lion, who had similar powers."

Urnan nodded slowly. She was right, of course. Without Kemose's magical skills, he and the Egyptian prince would never have escaped from the copper mine in the island of Kittem, where they were both slaves of the Philistines. And Jerioth was right about the Children of the Lion as well. Along with the mark of the lion's paw on their hips—the mark of Cain, some called it—some of the descendants of Belsunu of Ur had indeed demonstrated another inherited trait: sorcerous powers exactly like those she had described.

The only magic Urnan had ever possessed was the knowledge of how to work iron into weapons. That had always been enough. Nor had he ever discerned the faintest flair for sorcery in either his son or his grandson, though both bore the lion's paw. Leah did not bear the wine-colored birthmark, of course, since only male members of the family did, but she could certainly have inherited some of her ancestors' other traits.

Urnan put his fingers to his temples and rubbed them wearily. "I do not want to think about this now. I have enough with which to concern myself. My son and grandson will soon be fighting the Jebusites at the side of our king. My thoughts should be with them."

"As you will," said Jerioth. "But I will watch Leah and see if she demonstrates any other powers."

"And if she does?"

"Then I will try to teach her how best to use them." Jerioth had a faraway look in her eyes. "Who better to do that than I? After all, I *am* the Witch of Endor."

"Indeed you are, my dear," Urnan said fondly. "Indeed you are."

Leah was bored. She wished her father had not gone off to fight the Jebusites. He had been gone for only a few days, but already it seemed much longer to the little girl. She would be glad when Eri came home.

True, for a long time he had not demonstrated much love for her, but lately he had begun, though haltingly, to acknowledge it. Leah knew that because she had heard it in his head. It was good to know finally that her father truly loved her.

In the meantime she had Grandfather Urnan and Jerioth. Sometimes her father's wife, Baalan, played with her, too, although the woman just as often treated her coolly. Leah supposed that was because she reminded Baalan too much of Sarah. Baalan had been a slave whose job, long before she became Eri's wife, was to care for Sarah, and she doubtless knew that she might never have married Eri had Sarah not gone mad.

If those were unusually mature thoughts for a child of seven years, Leah did not know it. All she knew was that she was beginning to understand the world more and more—and particularly the people around her, since she had learned how to look into their eyes and "hear" their thoughts.

Today Leah had gone to the market with Jerioth. Dutifully she held Jerioth's hand as they made their way through the maze of shops and carts full of produce and other goods. The market was buzzing with noise and activity: vendors hawking their wares, merchants arguing with each other, customers haggling with merchants over prices, donkeys braying, pigs snuffling, a cock crowing raucously although it was long past sunrise. Competing for the attention of the senses were the smells, some sweet and tempting, some pungent, some unutterably foul. Everything—sights, sounds, odors—blended into a rich tapestry that held the little girl's rapt attention.

For a while, anyway.

Now Leah was tired of listening to Jerioth argue with a vendor over the price of fruit. She slipped her hand out of the older woman's grasp, but Jerioth did not appear to notice. Although Leah did not intend to wander off, she was eager to look around a bit.

A dog was trotting down one of the many alleyways that branched off from the central market. The animal had something in his mouth—a bone with some strips of meat hanging from it, Leah discerned. Where the dog had gotten the bone, she did not know, but from his furtive behavior she guessed he had stolen it. Her curiosity piqued, she started walking down the alley after the animal.

As if sensing that someone was coming after him, the dog sped up and disappeared around a corner. Leah quickened her own pace, her little legs working strenuously as she broke into a trot. She gave no further thought to Jerioth, so consumed was she by the desire for adventure. She turned the corner, saw a flash of brown as the dog vanished into another alley, and hurried to catch up.

Jerioth studied a basket of dates the merchant was trying to sell her. The fruit looked none too fresh, and

Jerioth said idly, "What do you think, Leah? Should we buy them?"

There was no answer.

Jerioth looked around. "Leah? Where have you gotten off to? Leah? *Leah!*"

Age had not dimmed the keenness of Jerioth's eyes. Quickly she scanned the market square but saw no sign of the little girl. As panic threatened to overwhelm her, she tried frantically to remember how long it had been since she had seen the child. She had been holding Leah's hand, but somehow she had slipped away. Anger at her own carelessness mixed with her growing fear. What she had done was inexcusable. Now she could only pray that she found the child before any harm befell her.

The dates forgotten, Jerioth hurried away, ignoring the cajoling of the merchant behind her. She made her way around the market, asking every vendor and customer who would listen to her if they had seen a little girl wandering off. No one could help her. People came to the market to do business, and there was room for little else in their minds.

After long minutes of searching, Jerioth stopped and took a deep breath, trying to calm herself. Hebron was not a large city, and most of the people who lived here were decent and civilized. Wherever she was, Leah was probably not in any danger. Given time, Jerioth was sure she could find the girl.

But with Urnan's help she would probably find Leah sooner. Though loath to admit to her husband that she had lost the little girl, Jerioth knew she had to tell him. His forge was nearby.

As her steps turned in that direction, Jerioth wished her own sorcerous powers had not diminished so over the years. She concentrated, trying to bring a vision to her mind, a vision that would tell her where Leah was.

Nothing.

The Witch of Endor, she thought bitterly as she hurried on. What good was being a sorcerer when a child, a mere child, was hidden from her inner sight?

Leah was beginning to think she would never catch up to the dog. He was always one turn ahead of her as he fled with his prize. Every time she went around a corner, she caught a glimpse of him loping into yet another alley.

Suddenly a frenzy of barking and growling erupted ahead of her as she rounded another corner. She slowed her pace, but not quickly enough. Before she knew what was happening, she found herself in the midst of a snarling pack of dogs snapping viciously at the one with the bone.

The mongrels were scrawny, half-starved by the look of them, and they fell on the newcomer, trying to take the bone from him. Faced with overwhelming odds, the cur did the only thing he could: He dropped the bone and rolled onto his back, seeming to plead for mercy. But the other dogs were having none of that. They tore into him with their teeth, eliciting howls of pain.

"Stop that!" cried Leah.

A couple of the dogs kept up the attack, but others swung their heads toward the little girl, muzzles dripping saliva and blood, fangs bared in angry snarls. Fear shot through Leah. She looked around urgently, but there was no one in sight. Her instinct was to turn and run, but something kept her rooted to the spot.

As she watched, a hazy red mist formed around the dogs and floated through the air toward her, billowing like a cloud of hate and menace. The dogs started toward her.

As if in a trance, she lifted her hands and held them out toward the growling, slavering animals. "Stop!" she commanded.

The mist subtly changed color then, shading toward violet. And the dogs stopped.

"You don't have to be afraid of me," Leah intoned,

her voice gaining strength. "I won't hurt you, and you don't have to hurt me. We can be friends."

The mist was thinning now as it changed color again, this time to a deep blue. The dogs stood watching her with a confused, wary look, as if they were being restrained from attacking her by some invisible force.

The dog who had blundered into the fray rolled over and shakily got to his feet. He padded toward Leah, his brown fur dotted with blood, then stretched his snout tentatively and licked her hand. She rubbed his head and said, "Good dog."

The other animals whined as if they, too, wanted attention. Leah smiled and chirped, "You are *all* good dogs."

Except for a faint tinge of deep purple, the mist had dissipated, and Leah was struck by the thought that probably no one else could see it.

No one but her new friends.

"There she is!" gasped Urnan. "There, down that alley!"

He pointed, and Jerioth followed his finger. She saw Leah sitting on the filthy paving stones, surrounded by a pack of wild mongrels. Jerioth put a hand to her mouth and whispered, "Oh, dear Lord . . ."

"They'll tear her limb from limb," Urnan muttered, reaching for the sword at his belt. He would have to wade into the pack with his blade and hope that he could scatter them before they harmed Leah.

Jerioth's hand on his arm stopped him. "No, wait," she said. "Look! They are not hurting her. They seem to be . . . protecting her."

It was true. The dogs had formed a circle around the child, and she was petting each in turn. They were some of the roughest-looking creatures Urnan had ever seen, but at this moment they were as gentle as lambs. One of them, a scruffy brown mongrel, was licking her face.

"Grandfather Urnan!" Leah exclaimed happily. "Jerioth! See my new friends!"

Urnan and Jerioth started down the alleyway toward her. Some of the dogs growled at their approach, and Leah admonished them. "There's no need for that. They won't hurt you," she said clearly, as if the dogs could understand every word. She cocked her head for a moment, then nodded. "Yes, I'm sure."

The pack parted, and Urnan scooped her up and held her tightly. "Are you all right?"

"I'm fine, Grandfather Urnan. Why would I not be?"

"Urnan," Jerioth began, "I am so sorry—"

"There is no need," Urnan told her with a relieved smile. "The child is unharmed. We will talk of this another time. For now, let us go home."

The dogs moved out of the way and sat on their haunches to watch as Urnan, Jerioth, and Leah started toward the mouth of the alley. But the brown dog who had lured Leah away from the market trotted along behind. Urnan noticed him and tried to shoo him away.

"No," Leah said solemnly. "He is coming with us."

"But Leah—" said Urnan.

"He is my friend."

There was no arguing with that. Urnan sighed. He was so relieved and grateful Leah was all right that he could not bring himself to deny her anything she wished. If she wanted to keep the dog, so be it. The only thing that made him uneasy now was the way she had seemed to be *talking* to the dogs when he and Jerioth found her. Even more alarming, the dogs had appeared to understand her—and was it possible *they* had somehow been talking to *her?*

That was mad, and Urnan knew it. People and animals could not talk to each other. But Jerioth had already warned him about the inexplicable powers Leah seemed to be developing. Who could say what was possible and what was not?

Besides, Leah was a Child of the Lion. A special destiny—the destiny of those who were different in some way from the rest of humanity—had traditionally followed that tribe, although not always favorably.

Urnan knew from the stories handed down from his ancestors that it was unwise to discount the hand of fate.

But for now, he thought as his arms tightened around Leah, he had his granddaughter back, and that was all that mattered.

CHAPTER
THREE

Kaptar stood waiting patiently outside the royal bedchamber in the palace. There was no point in getting angry, he knew. Sheshonk I—King of Egypt, Lord of the Two Lands—would see his chief armorer and Master of the Horse when he was ready and not a moment sooner. Still, Kaptar could not suppress a slight irritation. Sheshonk, son of Princess Tania and the Libyan lord Musen, was Kaptar's half-brother—and some twenty years younger at that—and Kaptar chafed as any grown man would whose actions were governed by a mere stripling, a boy.

But Sheshonk *was* the ruler of this land, and Kaptar reminded himself of the promise he had made to his late uncle, Prince Kemose. Kaptar had pledged to serve the king and to assist him in one day reuniting Upper and Lower Egypt so that Sheshonk—or one of his heirs—would be Lord of the Two Lands in more than name only.

That would be a glorious day, Kaptar reflected, for it would represent a triumph for Egypt, a vindication of pure Egyptian blood over mongrel Libyan. Of course few would know the full extent of that triumph, for only Kaptar, of all men now living, was aware of the truth concerning Sheshonk's parentage: The late Lord Musen was *not* the boy's real father. Princess Tania, Kaptar's beautiful, noble mother, had taken to her bed a common man, a soldier, but one of pure Egyptian bloodlines. *He* was Sheshonk's true father. Tania never revealed this to the despised Musen, and she also refused to bear any more children. After suffering her taunts and insults for several months, the Libyan murdered her, dismembered her body, and fed her to the crocodiles in the Nile. For that hideous crime Kaptar had sworn to one day take his revenge on Musen.

Natural death took Musen before Kaptar could, but if fate had cheated him of his chance for vengeance, it had rewarded him in other ways. The joy of his life was his wife, Nefernehi, the Beautiful One of the South, daughter of the high priest of Waset, who before his death had arranged the marriage of Kaptar and Nefernehi to strengthen the ties between Upper and Lower Egypt. Despite its political origins, the union proved a solid one.

Nefernehi was on Kaptar's mind even more than usual these days because of the mission his half-brother had asked him to undertake. Accepting would mean being away from her for months, perhaps even years, and Kaptar was not sure he could tolerate such a long separation.

He recalled his own father, the wanderer called Urnan. Urnan had come to Egypt after he and Kemose had escaped from slavery on the island of Kittem. Here he had met and married Princess Tania, Kemose's cousin. But it had not been seemly for a foreigner to be married to a noblewoman of the Black Land, and eventually Urnan had been forced to leave Egypt for his wife's safety as well as his own. He had left Tania behind, as well as the child she was carrying—Kaptar.

Surely, Kaptar often thought, Urnan had hoped someday to be reunited with his Egyptian family. But that day had never come, and Kaptar knew it was unlikely that Urnan was still alive. When he had left Egypt, his destination had been his adopted homeland of Canaan, the land of the Hebrews. That land had been rocked by strife for the preceding two decades: first a war against the Peleset—known by the Hebrews as the Philistines—who lived along the coastal plain; then internal dissension and civil war as different factions fought for control of the land. Kaptar knew this because he was privy to reports the king received periodically from the outlying areas of what was still considered Egypt's empire, which included the land of the Israelites.

Now Sheshonk wanted more than sketchy details about the ongoing troubles in Canaan. He planned to bring the land under more direct control of the empire, and for that he needed a fuller picture.

That was the task he hoped to assign to Kaptar.

The huge, gilt-framed doors of the royal bedchamber swung open, breaking into Kaptar's brooding reverie. A girl came out, perhaps twelve years old, wrapped in a transparent robe that did nothing to conceal her budding breasts and the lissome lines of her figure. For an instant she turned eyes much older than her years toward Kaptar, then looked away and hurried on. Kaptar recognized her as one of Sheshonk's concubines.

He felt a fresh surge of irritation. He resented being kept waiting while Sheshonk rolled around in bed, satisfying his lusts with the girl. But that was only one of the indignities one suffered in the service of the king, he supposed. Like everyone else in the Black Land, he acted at Sheshonk's whim.

A few moments later a servant appeared in the doorway and summoned Kaptar into the bedchamber. Sheshonk stood beside a tall window, looking out at the city of On. He was wearing only a girdle of white cloth and looked anything but regal. When he turned to meet Kaptar, an ingenuous smile enlivened his face, and the affection Kaptar felt for his young half-brother won out over his earlier impatience and irritation.

"Ah, there you are, Kaptar!" said Sheshonk. "How fares it with you?"

"Well, my lord," Kaptar replied.

"You have thought over the proposal I made to you?"

Kaptar nodded. "Indeed I have. As always, I wish to please you and serve Egypt, but I humbly request a bit more time to ponder the situation."

A frown replaced Sheshonk's smile. "What is wrong? It is but a simple request."

"Simple perhaps for some, but for a man with a wife whom he loves very much . . ."

"Ah! The lovely Nefernehi!" Sheshonk shook his head. "You do not wish to be parted from the Beautiful One of the South, and I cannot blame you for that, brother. But the welfare of our nation sometimes demands sacrifices of us all."

What was the last sacrifice you *made, brother?* Kaptar wanted to ask, but he swallowed the question before it could leave his lips. "You are right, of course," he said, "and I wish to serve my nation and my king. I will do as you command."

Sheshonk began to pace back and forth. "I do not want to command you, Kaptar. You and I are brothers and friends as well as ruler and subject. I need your help, but only if you can offer it willingly. Although there is no one in the kingdom I trust as much as I do you, surely there must be someone who can travel to the land of the Canaanites and bring back word of the situation there. If it pleases you, brother, I will offer this mission to another." He paused and stroked his chin. "Saddar, perhaps?"

Kaptar grimaced. Saddar was a minor Libyan noble, plodding and none too intelligent but probably trustworthy. But he *was* a Libyan, and Kaptar hated the thought that by his own inaction he might be promoting one of the invaders from the west to a position of greater importance. Sheshonk was no doubt counting on that reaction.

Stiffening his back and squaring his shoulders, Kaptar said, "That will not be necessary, my lord. I will undertake the mission to the land of the Canaanites."

"Excellent!" Sheshonk reached up to clap Kaptar on the shoulder. "I knew you would not fail me. Perhaps while you are there, you will find your father, if he still lives. When he left Egypt, he went to dwell among the Hebrews, did he not?"

"He did," Kaptar replied. Of course Urnan had not really left Egypt—he had been forced out—but it would accomplish nothing now to bring up old wounds. An idea suddenly occurred to him. "With your permission, my lord, I will take my wife with me on this journey. That way we will not have to be separated after all." It was not a good solution to his dilemma, Kaptar thought, but it appeared to be the only tolerable one.

The suggestion seemed to take Sheshonk by surprise. He frowned and fretted for a moment, then shook his head decisively. "I could not allow that. It would be much too dangerous for her."

Kaptar felt his heart sinking. "I mean no disrespect, but why should it be so? This is not a military mission I am undertaking. It is more in the nature of a diplomatic journey, is it not? It should not be too perilous."

"We cannot know that," said Sheshonk. "The Peleset are a notoriously unstable people. They may once again be engaged in a war against the Hebrews. We do not know what transpires there, which is why you are making the journey."

Kaptar could not argue with his brother's logic. Only his desperate desire not to be separated from Nefernehi for so long had led him to make the proposal. He murmured, "You are right, my king."

"Besides," Sheshonk said with a laugh, "the only reason I am sending you far away is so that I will have a chance to steal Nefernehi from you!"

Kaptar felt a flash of anger. But Sheshonk was still laughing at what he evidently considered an uncom-

monly good jest. Forcing a smile, Kaptar bowed slightly
and said, "Then I shall endeavor to return as soon as
possible to the loving arms of my wife."

Sheshonk waved a finger at him. "Not too soon!"
he gibed. "Give me a fair chance to win the affections of
the Beautiful One of the South, brother!"

That would never happen, Kaptar told himself, but
he wished he could be that confident. As the Lord of the
Two Lands, Sheshonk could do as he pleased . . . but
he was quick-witted enough to know what a valuable
ally Kaptar was. Surely he would do nothing to jeopar-
dize that relationship.

Surely . . .

Nefernehi ran the comb through her long, lustrous
hair, which hung down her back in a fan as black as
midnight. Kaptar leaned against the cushions in the bed
and watched her, taking in every tiny detail, searing the
vision of her on his brain. He would be apart from her
for a long time, and he wanted to be able to summon up
her image whenever he wished.

They were in their bedchamber in another part of
the royal compound. Night had fallen. Already they had
made love, and then Nefernehi had left the bed and
repaired to the stool in front of her dressing table while
he rested. In the yellow glow of the oil lamp, she was as
beautiful as he had ever seen her. No, he decided, she
was more beautiful tonight than she had ever been.

She placed the comb on the table and stood up,
then turned and came slowly toward him. The faint
smile on her face told him she was well aware of the
effect she was having on him. His eyes traveled over her
lovely features, down the smooth curve of her neck to
the proud jut of her breasts, firm globes of flesh
crowned with dark nipples. His gaze slid along the flat
plane of her stomach, past the pearl of her navel, over
the slight rondure of her abdomen, to the triangle of
fine-spun hair at the juncture of her thighs. The triangle
was as dark and luxurious as the hair on her head, and it
drew him with a potent force that would not be denied.

Nefernehi lowered herself on the edge of the bed and reached out to place her hands on either side of his face. She held him still while she leaned over and brought her mouth to his, kissing him with sensual tenderness. For a long moment they communed thus before Nefernehi moved her hands and lips along his body, the heat of her touch shaking him to the very core of his being. He forgot about the mission that would soon take him from his homeland to the far reaches of the Egyptian empire. He forgot about his promise to his uncle and his duties to the king, forgot about his desire to search for his father in the land of the Hebrews. He forgot everything except what was happening at this moment, in this place, and in that he reveled, feeling the sensations in every nerve ending, his heart overflowing with love.

Then he reached for her and began to return some of the pleasure she had given him. Soon, as he pressed himself to her and she opened herself to him, both cried out in ecstasy. The night stretched out, the stars seeming to wheel more slowly through the sky, as man and woman strove to make this treasured time last as long as possible.

But everything has an ending, and eventually they lay sated in the bed, the lamp long since burned out, and held each other in the darkness.

"The sun will not shine again until you return, my love," Nefernehi whispered.

"Nor will it follow me on my journey," Kaptar told her, his tone equally hushed and solemn. "It will be as if we are both slumbering, to awaken only when we are together again."

"Yes," she breathed. "That is how it will be. . . ."

He stroked her warm, smooth flank and debated whether or not to tell her about the jest Sheshonk had made. Kaptar had not found it amusing, despite the smile he had forced in the king's presence, and he knew that Nefernehi would not be pleased, either.

But, almost as if she had read his mind, she whispered, "I will be true to you."

He lifted his head from the cushion in surprise. "I know," he said. "I never thought otherwise."

"I do not want you to worry. You have enough with which to concern yourself, just staying safe on this dangerous journey."

"Perhaps it will not be so bad," Kaptar mused. "The last report we had from the Canaanites said that there was peace in the land."

"An uneasy peace."

He shrugged slightly in acknowledgment of her point. "I will be traveling as the official representative of Sheshonk I, Lord of the Two Lands. None will dare to harm me or those accompanying me."

"I pray it will be so."

Kaptar tightened his embrace. "I will be true to you," he pledged, "and I will return safely."

A quiet sob escaped her lips, wrenching at Kaptar's heart. "But I do not know when I will see you again."

"No," he said, "but you *will* see me again. We *will* be together. This I vow with all my heart."

She pressed her face against his chest, and he felt the warm sting of her tears. He thought only to lie there and comfort her, but her hands abruptly began to search his body again with an urgency she had not displayed before. To his surprise he found himself responding. He had thought himself totally sated by their lovemaking. Now it was rapidly becoming obvious that he had been wrong.

"If we must be parted," she said as she moved over him, "I want as much of you with me as possible. I want to remember the way you filled me with your passion."

He could not deny her, even if he had wanted to—which he did not. The rest of the night passed, filled with soft cries that did not die away until the coming dawn shone red and golden in the east.

CHAPTER FOUR

Jerusalem! The name echoed through Eri's brain as he sat on his horse and looked up at the walled city on the hilltop.

"There it is, my old friend," David said beside him. "Soon it will be ours, and it will shine in the sun as the capital of the nation of Israel."

"A shining city for the shining king," said Eri.

David vehemently shook his head, looking slightly embarrassed. "Others have called me so, but I do not take that name for myself. I am but a servant of God and His people."

This was not false modesty speaking, Eri knew; David's humility was one of his strengths as a leader. He had never placed himself above the other Israelites—God had done that.

The two men had reined in at the head of the column of soldiers. Now David tugged his horse's head to the left and rode in that direction. Eri followed him.

When Ittai, the Philistine mercenary, joined them, David commanded, "Take the men up the hill and set up camp there, so that the Jebusites can see us plainly."

"Do you not plan to take them by surprise?" asked Ittai.

David waved a hand at the cloud of dust that followed the marching men. "How could we surprise anyone save a blind man, and then only if he was deaf as well?" He laughed. "No, I mind not that the Jebusites can see us. I *want* them to get a good look."

Eri grinned in appreciation of David's strategy. Since there was no way to approach the city without being noticed, David had decided that it would be best to appear in full daylight, in full force. The Jebusites could not help but worry when they saw a huge army encamped little more than a bowshot away. Eri had forged many a weapon in his time, but he knew that sometimes fear cut deeper than the sharpest iron sword.

By midafternoon the soldiers' tents had been erected on the hilltop. Then and only then did David ride to the summit of Ophel and show himself to anyone watching from inside the city. From this vantage point— slightly higher than the hill on which the city sat—the Israelites had a commanding view of Jerusalem.

Eri swung down from his mount and joined David. After observing the city's inhabitants for a few moments, he grunted, "They do not seem overly concerned. Everyone is going on about their business, as far as I can see."

"Perhaps," David admitted, "but they are going about their business with one eye on our camp, I can assure you that."

Ittai and Hushai came up to join them. "When do you intend to attack?" asked Hushai.

"Who said I intend to attack?" David replied. "I'll not waste a single man against the walls of Jerusalem if I can avoid it."

"But how else can we take the city?" Ittai demanded harshly. "We must attack and breach the walls."

David shook his head. "I will make no decisions until I have talked to my scouts. Are they here?"

"Not yet," said Ittai. "But we expect them soon. Like the Jebusites, they must know by now that we are here."

David asked Eri, "Your son is among the men in the mounted patrol, is he not?"

"Sunu is one of them," Eri answered proudly. "If there is a way to take the city, he and his friends will have found it." He hoped he was right. If he was not, a great many good men might die before Jerusalem fell.

By later that afternoon the Jebusites had apparently decided that some response to the presence of the Israelite army was necessary. Men climbed to the top of the city walls and shouted taunts across the little valley. "Go away while you still can!" they called. "Jerusalem is so strong that it can be defended with none but the blind and the lame! Your army will be defeated, as all the armies in the past have been!"

It was true that others had tried to capture the city before. Trade routes from Gaza, Joppa, Shechem, Jericho, and Bethlehem all came together here. Whoever controlled Jerusalem—for centuries that had been the Jebusites—also had a strong measure of control over the caravans that plied the hills and deserts.

But that was all going to change, Sunu thought as he made his way through the Israelite encampment that evening. David would see to it.

Sunu and the other scouts had seen the dust of the marching army from their hiding place to the east of the city, where they had spent the two days since their bloody encounter with the mercenary patrol. So swift-moving was the Israelite force, however, that it was well in place atop Ophel by the time Sunu, Borum, Lassan, and their companions reached the camp. Sunu had expected to report to the king immediately, but when they went to his tent, the priest Abiathar had turned them away, saying that David was communing with the Lord and asking them to return later.

Sunu decided to look for his father and found him alone in his tent, chewing on a loaf of hard bread and washing it down with wine from a goatskin. He stood up hastily, grinned, and threw his arms around his son. "Sunu!" he exclaimed. "Are you well?"

"Well indeed, Father," he replied. "Our mission was a success."

"Have you told David?" Eri asked quickly. When Sunu shook his head, Eri went on, "Keep your own counsel, then. The king must hear what you have to tell him first. Have you been to his tent?"

"The old priest sent us away, bidding us return for a meal later tonight." Sunu rubbed his belly, which had begun to rumble. "I am not certain I can wait."

Eri laughed and waved a hand at the blankets spread on the ground. "Sit down. I have bread and wine, but likely not enough to satisfy your appetite before you sup with the king."

Sunu accepted the invitation. He sank down cross-legged, took a sip from the wineskin Eri offered him, then tore a piece of bread off the loaf and gave the rest back to his father. "This will be plenty."

In the glow of the torch outside the tent, Eri and Sunu looked more like brothers than father and son. Both men were tall, broad-shouldered, and brawny from long hours of work at the forge and furnace. They were both fighting men in the prime of life, though Sunu was just entering that period and Eri was moving toward its end.

"How fares our family in Hebron?" asked Sunu as he gnawed on the hard bread.

"Well," replied Eri. "Mara misses you, I am certain, but she and Baalan and Jerioth occupy each other's time."

"And Grandfather?"

"Urnan is as he always is," Eri grunted. "He works at the forge more than a man of his years should, but he says that work keeps him young."

"What of Leah?" Sunu smiled at the thought of his cheerful, active little half-sister.

"She, too, is well, I suppose."

"Suppose?" Sunu repeated. "Father, she is your daughter, as I am your son."

Eri's broad shoulders rose and fell in a shrug. "You sound like your grandfather," he said. "Urnan believes that Leah and I should be closer. He is right . . . but it is not always easy." With a shake of the head Eri made it clear that he no longer wished to discuss the subject. Instead he asked, "Did you and your companions encounter any trouble while you were scouting the city? You can tell me that much without revealing what you discovered."

Sunu nodded solemnly. "There was fighting. The man we left to watch our horses while we scouted on foot was discovered by a group of Philistine mercenaries patrolling the area around the city for the Jebusites. We came upon them just as they were about to torture our companion for information."

Eri frowned. "You killed all of them, I hope?"

"Every one. And we lost only one man. Then we took the bodies and threw them in a ravine a long distance from here, so that the Jebusites would not know what happened to their mercenaries."

"That was wise."

"Of course, we did not know that King David and the army would arrive so openly."

"David wants the Jebusites to see our forces and fear them," Eri explained. "His hope is that somehow we can take the city without having to attack the walls and losing many men."

"There may be a way," Sunu said cryptically. "But could he not simply lay siege to Jerusalem?"

"No. We could not carry enough food and supplies for a long siege, nor could caravans bring food from Hebron without causing hardships on the families our men left behind." Eri took a sip of wine and went on, "The Jebusites think they are invulnerable in their citadel. It would be good to teach them that they are wrong."

Sunu smiled at his father. "If God is willing, the Jebusites are going to have a very rude awakening."

David looked around at the men gathered outside his tent. All his closest advisers and commanders were there, along with several of the men from the scouting party, including Sunu, who sat next to his father. The group circled a blazing fire on the summit of Ophel, one of many that dotted the entire hill on which the Israelites were camped. As if in answer, more fires than usual burned inside the city.

David nodded to the scouts and said, "Tell me what you have discovered, my friends."

"There is a way into the city," said Borum. "Our young companion Sunu discovered it."

David's intense gaze turned toward Sunu, who was unprepared for the sudden attention. He had assumed that Borum would report the patrol's discovery without specifying that it was he who had found the tunnel leading into the city from the spring of Gihon. But Sunu was young enough to feel a glow of pride in that achievement.

"Tell us, Sunu," David said quietly.

"There is a spring next to the wall," he began. "It is called Gihon."

David nodded. "I know of it. It supplies the Jebusites with good water." His face lit up with understanding. "But where is their well, and how does the water get to it?"

Sunu blinked in surprise. Just like that, David's keen brain had grasped the direction in which Sunu's account was heading. Even without the scouts' discovery, David would probably have figured out on his own the connection between the spring and the city. Sunu grinned in admiration.

"The waters of the spring go through a tunnel in the wall and form a pool underground," he went on. "I believe the women fill their buckets there."

"You have seen this pool yourself?" asked David.

Sunu nodded. "I swam through the gutter from the

spring. It is not very long and is wide enough for a man."

A buzz of excited conversation broke out around the fire. Ittai said, "If a small force of men were to penetrate the city in this manner, they could open the gates to the rest of us."

"Yes," agreed David, "and then the battle would be over, because the Jebusites are not hardy fighters. Many would surrender rather than be put to the sword."

"But we will kill them anyway!" Ittai growled.

"No!" David said sharply. "Those who do not bear arms against us will not be put to death."

Hushai stood to protest. "In times of old, Samuel ordered that all our enemies be slain, yea, the women and babes as well as the warriors, even the sheep of the field. When Saul put himself above the word of God's prophet and refused to do this, he incurred the prophet's wrath. That mistake was one of the things that led to his downfall."

"I recall," David said curtly. "I was one of Saul's followers then. But Samuel is dead, and the Lord has given me no such command, either directly or through another prophet. The Jebusites are merchants, businessmen. Once they have been conquered, they will quickly see the wisdom of working with us rather than against us." His stern demeanor softened. "They are more interested in profits than prophets, if you will. So, pass the word to all the men. Slay only those who make it necessary to do so."

The men around the fire nodded in agreement.

"Now," David continued, "we reach the question of who will lead the force that goes through the wall of Jerusalem. This man must be strong and skilled in the art of war, who cares less for his own safety than for the success of his mission. I know there are many such among you, but I would ask for a man to go of his own free will. I will not order him to what may be his death. But if any man is willing—and if he survives—I swear this day that he shall be the captain of all my armies."

Eri and Sunu exchanged a quick glance, and Eri

leaned forward, opening his mouth to speak. It would be an honor to lead such a mission for David, even if it meant death.

But before he could say anything, a voice from the outer ring of men said harshly, "I will lead." The man who had spoken stood up and strode forward until he was directly in front of the king.

David asked coolly, "Why does Joab, son of Zeruiah, approach me?"

Again Eri and Sunu looked at each other. They were not the only ones surprised by this development; all around the fire there was much consternation. Joab, David's nephew and the former commander of his army, was generally regarded with disfavor these days. In one of the many tragedies that grew out of the rivalry between David and Saul's son Ish-bosheth for the throne of a united Israel, one of the most wrenching had been the death of Joab's brother Asahel at the hands of Abner, Ish-bosheth's general. Abner later left Ish-bosheth's service and offered to form an alliance with David. Consumed by the desire for vengeance, Joab had lured Abner to a rendezvous outside the gates of Hebron, where he treacherously stabbed him to death.

Faced with a crisis that could have ruined his efforts to unite Israel, David had had no choice but to remove Joab from command of the army and call down a curse on him and his family. Since then, Joab had served as a common soldier.

Now, here was an opportunity to redeem himself and earn back the exalted position he had once held, and in such a manner that it would cause no embarrassment, political or otherwise, to David.

"The king asked for a man of strength and courage, a man willing to lay down his life for Israel," Joab declared. "I am Joab, son of Zeruiah, and I say before all of you and before the Lord God, *I* am that man."

For a long moment David stood motionless, saying nothing. Then he placed his hand on Joab's shoulder. "I accept your offer, son of Zeruiah," he said in a voice loud enough for all to hear. "You will lead ten men into the city and open for us the gates of Jerusalem."

Joab nodded. "And will I be allowed to choose those men?"

"You will."

The words were barely out of the king's mouth before Eri was on his feet. "You have only to choose nine men, Joab," he said, "for I am one of the ten."

"And I as well," said Sunu, springing to his feet beside his father.

Joab turned and regarded them with hooded eyes. Then he nodded curtly and said, "Let it be so."

"And I will also be with you," David said.

Above the murmurs of surprise among the men, the priest, Abiathar, raised his voice in protest. "You must not, David. You are too important to Israel."

"Your place is at the helm of your army, my lord," Ittai added. "If you were to fall, my men would follow no other."

"*We* will do this task, David," said Joab. "Eri, Sunu, and I, and the other men I choose. *We* will open the gates of Jerusalem."

David pondered a moment, then sighed. "You have spoken wisely. A leader must know when to follow the will of his people, when to heed his own. I will accompany you to the well, but no further." He put a hand on Joab's shoulder once more and with the other hand squeezed Eri's arm. "When the time comes, you will go with God, my friends. Because the fate of the nation of Israel may well go with you."

CHAPTER FIVE

For another day and most of a night, David allowed the Jebusites to sit behind their walls and wonder when the Israelites would strike. The waiting would make them nervous—and possibly confused and disorganized—when the actual attack came, he believed.

But if waiting was difficult for the Jebusites, it was doubly so for the men who would infiltrate the city through the spring of Gihon, Sunu thought several times during the seemingly endless day. His hand ached for the feel of a sword.

"The time will come soon enough," Eri counseled his restless son that afternoon.

"Not soon enough for me," Sunu declared hotly as he paced back and forth in the shade of a tent. "I long to slay the enemies of Israel."

"There is more to life than ending it for others," Eri said dryly. "Think of your wife."

Sunu shook his head. "I do not want to do that. I

have been away from Mara for so long that to dwell on her image would only make me feel worse."

"You may be right," Eri said with a shrug. "Ah, well, go back to thinking about slaying Jebusites, I suppose."

Sunu took his advice, and the time did pass, though slowly. Night fell, the moon rose, and the stars wheeled through the sky as the hours crept by. Finally, long after midnight, David summoned Joab and the ten men he had chosen.

They gathered at the lower edge of the camp, well away from the fires so that any guards watching from the walls of the city would not see them. All were clad only in cloth girdles and sandals, for battle armor would weigh the men down as they made their way through the tunnel. Each man carried a single sword. David took the weapons and bound them together with a piece of twine. He also had a coil of rope slung over his shoulder.

"Lead us to the spring, Sunu," he commanded, and Sunu was honored to obey.

Walking as quietly as possible, the group crossed the valley and approached the hill on which Jerusalem sat. With the unerring instincts of a born warrior, Sunu led the men straight to the spring in the thick, cloaking darkness. When they reached it, each man slipped quietly into the water. Silence and stealth were of the essence now.

When all had lowered themselves into the pool, Sunu put a hand on the king's arm and led him to the opening of the tunnel. David took a deep breath, plunged underwater, and vanished into the tunnel, carrying the bundle of swords and playing out another length of twine behind him. Sunu handed the cord to his father, who took up position on the other side of the opening.

Joab went next, then Sunu. Eri would keep the other men in the pool for the time being, since the underground chamber on the other side was small and would hold no more than three of them. Two tugs on the cord would be the signal to begin sending the rest of the men through, one at a time.

Sunu felt his way along the pitch-black tunnel, experiencing a slight tingle of panic at the thought of the thick stone walls so close around him. But the sensation passed quickly, and within moments his head broke the surface of the other pool at the bottom of the well. David and Joab awaited him.

"Joab will climb to the top of the well," David whispered as he pointed to the opening above their heads. "You and I, Sunu, will lift him."

David and Joab had planned their strategy the night before. Joab would have to rely on his great strength to make the climb, for he would have to inch his way up the shaft by pressing his back against one side of it and his feet against the other. When he reached the top, he would attach one end of the rope David had brought to a post or a rock and drop the other end back down the well. The rope would make the climb much easier for the other men.

The pool was not deep. David handed the rope to Joab, who slung it over his shoulder. David and Sunu knelt side by side, Joab stepped up onto their shoulders, and, balancing him carefully, they straightened. Joab took his foot from Sunu's shoulder and planted it against the stone wall of the shaft, then worked his back into place before lifting his other foot. For an instant he slipped on the slimy rock, and Sunu feared he would drop into the pool with a huge splash. But Joab splayed his hands against the wall and caught himself. With a grunt of effort he began to edge upward.

His progress was maddeningly slow. David and Sunu could see him only as a black shape against the faint light filtering from above. But gradually Joab rose higher and higher, and then, so suddenly that Sunu gasped in surprise, he was gone. Sunu knew he had reached the top and rolled over what was probably a low stone wall around the well.

Several moments passed before the rope fell between the king and his warrior, slithering like a snake into the water. David grasped it and tugged hard. "Good!" he said. "Joab has made it fast." He handed the bundle of swords to Sunu, who slung them around his neck. "You are sure you can make the climb with the extra weight?" David asked him.

"I am sure, my king." Sunu took the rope with both hands and pulled himself up until he could reach out with his feet and position them on the shaft wall. After that the ascent went more quickly as he climbed hand over hand, bracing himself with his feet, the bundle of swords slapping against his back.

Down below, he knew, David would be signaling for Eri to send the rest of the men through the tunnel from the spring. They would follow up the rope one by one until the entire force was inside the city and ready to strike. But they would wait until Ittai and his mercenaries began an attack on the smaller, western gate of the city, which would come when David returned to the camp and gave the order. The attack was designed to draw the Jebusite forces to the western wall, at which point Joab and his handpicked men would strike at the main gate on the eastern side. Once that gate was open, the main body of the Israelite army would pour through it and into the city.

Sunu reached the top of the well and pulled himself over the low wall that circled it. Joab was beside him immediately, taking the swords and untying them.

Sunu glanced around. They were in a shed of some kind that had been built over the well. It was deserted now, of course, and Sunu prayed it would remain so for a while. He took a sword from Joab and moved to stand guard beside the doorway.

Soon the other members of the group joined Joab and Sunu in the shed. Eri was the last one out of the well, and he gave the others a grin as he whispered, "David has gone to give the order for Ittai's attack."

Now there was more waiting. David had to return to the encampment on Ophel, from where he would direct Ittai and his mercenary troops to launch their attack on the west gate. While that was being done, the

rest of the army would move into position on the eastern side.

The night was cool, but Sunu's hand was sweating
on the hilt of his sword. He wiped it off on his girdle and
gripped the weapon again. *Soon,* he thought, forcing
himself to remain calm. *Very soon* . . .

Suddenly a great clamor arose on the western side
of the city. Shouts and calls and the thunder of running
feet could be heard by the men who waited in the shed.
Obeying Joab's gestured commands, Sunu and the others flattened themselves against the walls. The entire
plan would be ruined if they were discovered and
trapped here by the Jebusites.

Finally the uproar in the street immediately outside
the shed died away, although now the unmistakable
sounds of battle could be heard to the west. Doubtless
some of Ittai's men were dying there, Sunu thought.
Brave men, all; Sunu and his companions could be no
less.

Joab went to the doorway and looked out. "Come,"
he growled over his shoulder. "The way is clear."

Like restless spirits abroad in the night, the men
slipped out of the shed and ran toward the eastern gate.
Sunu was glad that Joab seemed to know where he was
going, because to Sunu the twisting streets looked much
alike. He tried to glance up at the stars to orient himself
and make sure they were going in the right direction,
but even that was difficult.

Then they rounded a corner and saw the eastern
gate looming before them in the light of torches, some
thirty paces away, and all doubt vanished. Half a dozen
guards holding lances stood beside the gate. At the
sound of the Israelites' sandals slapping the paving
stones, the guards swung around in surprise, and one of
them cried out an alarm.

"The Israelites are inside the walls! The Israelites
are—"

That was as far as he got. One of Sunu's companions had drawn back his sword arm and cast the weapon
forward like a spear, and his aim had been true and

deadly. The blade was buried in the throat of the Jebusite guard. He staggered backward and fell, pawing feebly at the sword.

The others were among the guards by then. One man was gutted by a Jebusite lance, but his opponent went down with a spray of blood from the throat as Joab's sweeping sword thrust found its target. At Joab's side Eri knocked a lance aside with the flat of his blade, then chopped at the guard, taking his right arm off at the shoulder. Shrieking in agony, the man fell.

Sunu was in the thick of the fighting, slashing right and left. Drops of blood, stark black in the dim light, spattered his hands and arms as he wielded his sword. The other Israelites were equally efficient with their blades, and within moments all six Jebusite guards had been cut down.

"Open the gate!" called Joab.

Sunu and Eri sprang to the thick lengths of rope that lashed the gate closed. There was no time to untie them, so they hacked at them with their swords.

The bold strike inside the walls had not gone unnoticed. Men came running from nearby buildings to stop the Israelites from opening the gate, but they were not soldiers, and Joab and his men disposed of them easily. Eri and Sunu were forced to turn away from their task, however, and defend themselves. The gate was still closed.

"Close ranks!" Joab shouted as he wrenched his blade free from the body of the Jebusite he had just killed. "Close ranks around Eri and Sunu! Get that gate open!"

Knowing that their fellows would watch their backs, Eri and Sunu turned to their work again. Some of the rope had given way. Another few minutes and he and his father would be able to swing the massive gate open, Sunu thought.

The whistle of arrows abruptly filled the night air, and two Israelites cried out as they staggered back. Arrow shafts seemed to have sprouted from their bodies. They fell, joining the litter of dead bodies in the street.

The Israelites closed ranks again as Jebusite reinforcements pounded toward them. Now there were only eight of them, however, and with Sunu and Eri occupied with the fastenings on the gate, only Joab and five men were left to fight off the Jebusite counterattack. They met the charge valiantly, but within moments only Joab and two others were still fighting, and it seemed inevitable that they, too, would be cut down.

An arrow whipped past Sunu's head and thudded into the timbers of the gate. His sword seemed to have grown heavier in his hands as he continued to slash at the stubborn rope, but, ignoring the bloody havoc behind him, he chopped away at the last one until it parted under his sword.

"Now!" cried Eri. "We must open the gate!"

Normally a gate of that size required four or five men to open it. Now there were only two to perform the task: Eri and Sunu. Joab and the other two men were still fighting desperately for their lives against the Jebusites. Dropping their swords, Eri and Sunu grasped the gate and pulled on it. It budged only a fraction. Father and son strained against its weight, grunting in effort.

The gate moved a little more.

Joab's two companions went down, one with a Jebusite lance in his belly, the other decapitated by the swing of a Jebusite sword. Joab stumbled backward as his opponents pressed him. His torso was slick with blood from a multitude of cuts, and his arms were stained crimson to the elbows. Still he kept fighting.

Eri and Sunu groaned as they threw all their remaining strength against the gate. It moved again, so that the opening was now two handspans wide, and a huge shout went up on the other side. Eri let go of the gate and grabbed Sunu's arm. "Get back!" he cried as he pulled his son out of the way. "Joab! Look out behind you!"

Joab cast a glance over his shoulder and dived out of harm's way as the full force of the Israelite army hit the gate. He sprawled on the ground next to Eri and

Sunu as the massive gate was slammed open by more than a dozen men. The huge timbers crushed several Jebusites unlucky enough to be in their path. But they were no more unfortunate than their fellows, who were caught in a screaming flood tide of iron-edged death as hundreds of Israelite soldiers poured through the opening and into the city of Jerusalem.

As David had predicted, resistance in the city quickly waned. The Jebusite defenders were clearly outnumbered, and their main advantage had been the strength of their walls. Now that those walls had been breached by David's cleverness and the daring of eleven stalwart men, the Jebusites were all but defeated.

Beside the wall next to the gate, Eri picked himself up, then extended a hand to his son and Joab in turn. The fighting had swept past them, and although the clash of swords and the cries of dying men filled the air, it was strangely peaceful by the gate. *The peacefulness of death,* Sunu thought, for scores of bodies, Israelite and Jebusite alike, littered the ground. The three companions were the only survivors of the small band that had penetrated the city from the spring of Gihon.

"Praise God David did not come with us," Joab said hoarsely as he looked at the carnage around them. "He surely would have been killed."

"We live," Eri pointed out. "Who is to say what Yahweh would have wrought? It is enough that our hearts beat and we have won the battle."

"Aye," Joab agreed with a weary smile. "Though it may take us quite a while to wash all the blood off, eh?"

Sunu looked down at himself. He was as grisly a sight as his father and Joab. Noticing a deep gash on his leg and a sword cut on his left side, he wondered when he had suffered the wounds, for he had no memory of them. Other minor cuts and scrapes were scattered over his body, but fortunately none of them appeared to be serious. He sighed deeply. God must have been watching over him—and over Eri and Joab as well. The three of them had lived to see the sun rise on another glorious day, and Sunu was grateful for that.

Although he had always believed that communing with God was an activity better left to the priests, Sunu closed his eyes now and sent a brief prayer of thanksgiving toward the stars overhead.

Not long before dawn, David entered the city. Silence reigned over Jerusalem now. The fighting was over; the city was firmly in the hands of the Israelites. As David had ordered, any man among the Jebusites who surrendered was spared and not put to death.

The king found Joab, Eri, and Sunu cleaning their swords not far from the eastern gate. Ignoring the bloodstains on their bodies, he embraced each of them. "My friends!" he said. "My great good friends! You and you alone, along with your valiant companions who gave their lives, have won the day for Israel!"

"God has won the day," Joab said quietly.

David nodded. "Those are wise words, son of Zeruiah. But God worked His will through you three and through those who fell. Today you are the most honored of men in the kingdom. And I will keep my promise to you, Joab. Once more you are the captain of my armies, my strong right arm."

Joab bowed. "Thank you, my lord."

David turned to Eri and Sunu. "And what rewards do my armorer and his son wish? Anything in my power to give you is yours."

"I want only to continue serving God and my king," said Eri.

"Another good horse," said Sunu.

David laughed. "You are a practical man, Sunu. You shall have your horse."

"And, of course, I wish to continue serving you as well, my king," Sunu added quickly.

"You shall have that opportunity," David promised. "We shall all have the opportunity to serve God as we make Jerusalem our capital. Today, my friends . . ." David turned his face toward the rising sun. "Today our nation has put the pains of its birthing behind it. Today Israel has come of age."

CHAPTER
SIX

As the bracing, salt-tanged wind of the open sea blew in Kaptar's face, he decided he had never experienced anything more thrilling. He had traveled often on the slow-moving barges that plied the waters of the Nile, but never before had he felt the deck of a ship fairly shiver under his feet as the sails caught the wind and sent the vessel racing smoothly across the surface.

Gazing at the Great Sea from the shore was one thing; sailing so far out that the land was no longer visible was quite another. Kaptar had always thought of himself as a courageous man; yet a faint tingle of fear went down his spine whenever he realized anew that his life depended on this fragile wooden construction. But none of the Egyptian sailors seemed worried, so Kaptar convinced himself not to worry, either.

The ship had set sail early that morning from a small port at the mouth of the Nile delta. Its course was northeast, toward the coastal plain southwest of Canaan. The voyage was expected to last five or six days, and then Kaptar and the small troop of guards accompanying him would go ashore. The easiest leg of the journey would be behind them then. The rest of the trip would be overland, and it would take several weeks, possibly more than a month, to reach Canaan. Kaptar had spent long hours studying the maps prepared by the royal mapmaker in On, and he knew he would have to travel inland a good distance to skirt the land of the warlike Peleset before turning north toward the country of the Israelites.

Thinking of the city reminded him of Nefernehi, and he felt a sharp pang of longing. He was standing at the bow of the ship, his hands tightly clasped at his back. Only a few days away from the Beautiful One of the South, and already he missed her almost more than he could bear. How was he going to survive being parted from her for months on end?

Kaptar closed his eyes for a moment and told himself not to dwell on these things. He would survive because he had to. The time would pass, and eventually he and Nefernehi would be together again—he felt the certainty of that in every fiber of his being.

A hand fell on his shoulder. Phatome, the captain of the ship, was grinning at him. "Do your feet long to feel the land beneath them again, my friend?"

Kaptar returned the man's smile and shook his head. "No, I am beginning to understand the lure the sea has for some men. I would not make it my home, as you do, but the voyage has been pleasant so far."

"We will sail for two more days, then put in to shore," said Phatome. "This will bring you to the land of the Amalekites. You and your men should be able to buy donkeys there for the rest of your trip."

"After today I think I would prefer the deck of a ship to the back of a donkey."

Phatome threw back his head and laughed. He said, "Long have I known the truth of that, Kaptar. But you are Master of the Horse. You should be accustomed to riding."

"A man can always learn new things. I believe I could learn to like this sailing."

Phatome laughed again and went on about his business. Kaptar turned his gaze back to the sea. But instead of the gently rolling waves he saw the face of Nefernehi.

"May the gods watch over you, my darling," he murmured, "until I return."

She was called the Beautiful One of the South, and there was no doubt she deserved the name. Nefernehi was the loveliest woman Sheshonk I, Pharaoh of Egypt, Lord of the Two Lands, had ever seen.

But she was also the wife of his brother, Kaptar.

Sheshonk lounged on soft cushions beside the low table, on which was piled a bounty of meats, fresh fruit, and sweets. Other dignitaries of the city of On were in attendance at this feast, but Sheshonk had eyes only for Nefernehi. He had had his servants place her at the other end of the table so that he could look directly at her. She smiled at him often, she was polite—but how could she not be? He was the lord of the land. But she did not look at him in the same way she looked at Kaptar.

That knowledge burned inside Sheshonk. Kaptar was far away and would be gone for a long time. Nefernehi would doubtless be lonely. He smiled to himself. In the fullness of time, everything would be as he wished it to be. How could it be otherwise? Was he not the pharaoh? Was he not the closest thing to a god on earth?

And what a god wanted could not be denied him . . . no matter what.

Kaptar did not know the name of the village where Phatome brought the ship into port and could not recall if it had been marked on the maps he had studied. The settlement was a cluster of small, one-room huts around a harbor barely deserving of the name.

The Peleset had once been known as the Sea People, but hundreds of years earlier they had made their home along this coast, which was almost completely devoid of natural harbors. One had to sail considerably farther north, to Phoenicia with its great cities of Sidon and Tyre, to find worthwhile ports. Kaptar supposed that was why they had turned their eyes eastward, toward Canaan. Their seafaring days were over, and if their empire was to expand, it would have to be overland.

But the nameless Amalekite village suited his purposes. Once the Egyptian ship had docked in the tiny indentation in the coastline, Kaptar and his companions unloaded the supplies they had brought with them and bade farewell to Phatome.

"May Amon watch over you," Phatome called as the crew cast off.

Kaptar watched the ship sail away with mixed feelings of regret and excitement. As long as he was aboard the vessel, he had felt its strong ties with Egypt. Never before had he been this far from his homeland. Even when he had journeyed to Upper Egypt, to Waset and beyond, he had remained within the borders of the land of his birth. Now, for the first time, he was on a foreign shore, treading on ground that, while claimed by Egypt, was not truly a part of it.

This was the land of the Amalekites, some of whom had turned out to witness the arrival of the ship and greet the travelers who disembarked. They were simple people in plain robes, and they stared in awe at Kaptar's more ornate clothing. Smiling genially, he addressed a man who was standing at the front of the crowd. "Are you the elder of this village?"

"I am," replied the man, in an accent that sounded as harsh and barbaric to Kaptar as Kaptar's accent must have sounded to him. "Who are you, and why do you come among us?"

"I am Kaptar, Prince of Egypt, servant and subject of Sheshonk I, Pharaoh and Lord of the Two Lands. I come in peace, an emissary of my lord Sheshonk, on a voyage of discovery and exploration. I seek the land of the Israelites."

"They live far from here." The village elder was not going to volunteer much information—or much help, Kaptar sensed.

"I know this." Kaptar bowed slightly. "I hope that my companions and I may trade with you for horses or donkeys, which will make our journey easier."

The elder shook his head. "We have no horses. We can sell you . . . three donkeys."

"Six would be better." Kaptar had eight guards with him, and if they could obtain six donkeys, three men would have to travel on foot—four, if one of the donkeys served as a pack animal. But the guards could take turns riding, and the group would still travel faster than if they had no donkeys at all, Kaptar speculated. And perhaps they could pick up more animals later, in another village.

"Four donkeys are all we can allow you to take," grunted the elder.

Kaptar looked around at the villagers gathered by the shore. They were a suspicious lot. Some of the men wore daggers, while others carried pikes of some sort. Kaptar did not want trouble with them.

"You do us an honor," he said to the elder. "We will purchase the four donkeys and be very grateful to you."

A bargain was soon struck. The village elder became less suspicious when he saw the pouch of gold coins Kaptar was carrying. Four donkeys were brought out, and Kaptar ordered his men to load the supplies on one of them. He claimed another for himself while the guards drew lots to determine in which order they would ride the last two.

Kaptar hoped the elder might invite them to share a meal once their business was done, but no such offer was forthcoming. The Egyptians left the village, heading east toward the village of Raphia. The elder in the small port settlement had confirmed that Raphia was where Kaptar's maps said it should be.

Hardly an auspicious beginning, Kaptar thought as he and his men walked and rode away from the village. But it could have been much worse, he supposed. He would try to purchase more donkeys in Raphia before setting out on the longer leg of the journey that would ultimately take the travelers to the city of Beer-sheba, in the southern reaches of Judah. From there they would travel north.

In Beer-sheba Kaptar would begin his search for his father. He would ask everyone he encountered if they knew anything of a man called Urnan, a smith and armorer. Kaptar held out only a small hope of finding Urnan or even of learning what had happened to him when he returned from Egypt to the land of the Israelites.

But even a small hope, Kaptar decided, was better than none.

As Kaptar had anticipated, they were able to obtain more donkeys in Raphia, so that each man could ride. As they set out across the arid, sparsely populated wilderness between Raphia and Beer-sheba, they resembled a trade caravan, Kaptar thought. But they were not riding camels, and instead of the burnooses of the desert people, they proudly wore the headdresses and girdles of their native land.

From time to time they encountered shepherds tending to their flocks or traders heading for some distant city. Less frequently they came upon small villages surrounded by tilled fields. This was not particularly good soil for farming, Kaptar judged, certainly nothing like the rich black loam irrigated by the waters of the Nile, but the Amalekites stubbornly managed to scratch out a living. Although the Egyptians were welcomed in these villages, the inhabitants warily kept them at a distance. A people who had spent generations being conquered by one despot after another would naturally develop such a cautious demeanor, Kaptar supposed. He went out of his way to be pleasant and to ask them about affairs in Israel.

The Hebrews had united themselves behind a king called David, Kaptar learned. David had captured Jerusalem, the city of the Jebusites, and made it his capital. Kaptar's hosts expressed the concern that sooner or later the Israelites would turn their eyes southward and seek to conquer the land of the Amalekites. Knowing intimately how the minds of kings worked, Kaptar thought that scenario likely, but he kept that opinion to himself.

The Egyptians pushed on toward Beer-sheba, and Kaptar had trouble remembering how many days had passed since they had left the ship. Traveling like this made the days blend together in an indistinct blur. He guessed that a little over a week had gone by.

Late one morning they were riding through a small valley with a stream to their right, a steep hillside to the left. Kaptar was about to call a halt for the midday meal when he saw a man suddenly stand up behind a clump of brush in front of him.

The man held a bow and a nocked arrow. Before Kaptar could shout a warning, the archer let fly.

The arrow was not aimed at Kaptar, although he was in the lead, but whipped past his head and buried itself in the chest of the man immediately behind him. The guard cried out, clawed at the arrow, and toppled loosely from the donkey's back.

The other guards reached for their swords, but it was too late for resistance to be anything but futile. More archers stepped out of hiding in the rugged landscape all around them, and the air was filled with the sound of flying arrows and the grisly thud of those arrows striking human flesh.

Kaptar tried to turn his donkey around, but the animal balked with typical stubbornness. Frustrated, he slid from the donkey's back. He saw that all eight of his companions were on the ground, too, but he was the only one on his feet. The others lay sprawled, some already dead, others only wounded. Kaptar yanked his sword from its sheath as the attackers dropped their

bows and rushed forward, drawing their own swords to
finish off the wounded guards.

With a hoarse cry of rage Kaptar leaped to challenge them. He had no idea why he had been spared,
but he recognized the men who were now busily killing
the last of his companions. They wore the pointed hel-
mets and short, armored kilts of the Peleset—the Sea
People, ancient enemies of Egypt, known by the
Hebrews as Philistines.

Kaptar plunged among them, slashing left and right
with his own blade. He knew he could expect no mercy
from them, but he was determined to sell his life at as
high a price as possible.

But the soldiers merely parried his thrusts and
dodged away, as if they wanted to avoid hurting him.
Kaptar's keen mind seized on that fact, and he knew
they must have been given orders to take him alive. For
what purpose he could not fathom, but he did not intend to give them that satisfaction. He would put up
such a struggle that they would be forced to kill him.
Savagely he swiped his blade across a man's throat and
had the pleasure of seeing him fall backward, blood gur-
gling from his mouth.

Kaptar wondered what the Philistines were doing
here, out of their domain on the coastal plain, far from
their sphere of influence. Perhaps this was a scouting
expedition into the land of the Amalekites, sent to
assess whatever defenses that wandering tribe might
have in place. Perhaps the Peleset planned to invade
this territory.

But there was no time to ponder such questions.
Kaptar had enemies to kill and a life to sell dearly.

And then he thought of Nefernehi.

Her lovely features seemed to leap before him in
his mind's eye, and the vision gave him pause. If he was
killed, what would happen to her? Who would care for
the Beautiful One of the South? Kaptar was sure there
would be no shortage of suitors. Yet he was her husband, and he had promised to return to her. In a moment of fear and rage and madness, he had almost

thrown his life away . . . but it was not his to discard so easily. It was pledged to another.

The hesitation was his undoing. The butt of a lance struck the back of his head, staggering him, and then the flat of a sword caught him on the shoulder, numbing his arm. He dropped his own sword. Hands grabbed him, and he felt himself being borne to the ground. Something else smashed into the side of his head, and darkness clouded his vision, overwhelming him as he tried to whisper the name of his beloved Nefernehi.

Kaptar awoke in a tent, unsure for a moment where he was or even if he was still alive. After a moment he was certain he had *not* crossed over to the far side of death; surely if he were dead he would not hurt so much or be so sick.

He was lying facedown on hard ground. He rolled to his side and retched, although his belly was empty and the spasms did nothing more than cause him more pain. Someone outside must have heard his distress, because the tent flap was thrust aside and a man strode in.

A sandaled foot dug into Kaptar's shoulder and rolled him onto his back. A burly Philistine loomed over him and rested the point of a spear at his throat. "So, you are awake, Egyptian cur," he snarled.

"Wh-who . . . ?" Kaptar croaked.

"I am Atmos, captain in the army of General Galar of Ashdod, commander of the Army of the Five Cities. You are my prisoner. I demand to know who you are and what you are doing here, so far from your decadent country."

Kaptar's vision had cleared somewhat, and he could make out the trappings of rank on the man's armor. He said, "I . . . I am Prince Kaptar, an emissary on a diplomatic mission for . . . for Sheshonk I, Pharaoh of Egypt, Lord of the Two—"

Atmos pressed the point of the spear harder against Kaptar's throat. "I care nothing for that," he said harshly. "I took you for some sort of nobleman. That is why I told my men not to kill you with the rest.

General Galar will be happy to see you." He laughed. "He loves making slaves out of foreign dogs almost as much as he loves killing the pigs of the hills, the Hebrews."

"S-slaves . . . ?" Kaptar repeated, conscious of the spearpoint pricking his neck.

"Slaves. That is why I and my men are here in the land of the Amalekites. Philistia has need of slaves, now that the men of the Five Cities will soon be going to war again."

"War? Against—"

"Against those who dare to call themselves Israelites." Atmos took the spearpoint from Kaptar's throat and grounded the butt of the shaft beside his right foot. "We will smash the pigs of the hills, and they will think twice before they ever again try to form themselves into one nation. The lords of the Five Cities will not stand for such a threat to our east."

Kaptar closed his eyes. He understood now. "I am to be pressed into service in your army?" he asked. How horrible it would be to take up arms against the adopted countrymen of his own father.

Atmos laughed again, and without warning he kicked Kaptar in the side. As Kaptar curled up against the pain, Atmos said, "We have no need of dogs such as you to fight our battles, Egyptian. But any labor you do will free a fine fighting man of Philistia to smite the Hebrews. I would not venture to guess where you will wind up. Building a road, perhaps, or digging a pit. It is no business of mine. I am charged only with bringing you and your fellow captives back to Philistia. Others will dispose of you." The Philistine tapped the butt of the spear against the side of Kaptar's head. "On your feet now, and go in with the others. I care not for what you were in your homeland. Now you are no better than the lowly Amalekite shepherds who are also our prisoners."

Kaptar was prodded to his feet. He staggered out of the tent, flinching violently when the brilliant afternoon sunlight struck his eyes. For a moment he could see nothing.

But he did not need to see to understand precisely how grim his situation was. He faced a life of slavery, a brutal existence that would no doubt be short, and then a death that would be no less brutal.

CHAPTER SEVEN

For all its vaunted reputation, Jerusalem was little
more than a large village when David captured it. But
the king immediately set out to remedy that situation.
Israel was becoming a mighty nation that needed an
appropriately impressive capital. He would build Jerusalem into a magnificent city, David vowed, a city that
would come to symbolize his reign over a strong and
united Israel.

His first step was to have the walls extended so that
they encompassed not only the city itself but also the
hilltop on which the Israelite army had camped. The hill
would no longer be called Ophel, David decreed, but
would in the future be known by its other name—Zion.
It was there that he would erect a palace that would
serve not only as his home but as the center of Israel's
government. Perhaps he would build a temple, too, he
thought often as he stood on the hilltop and saw in his

mind's eye the glories of the city that would be. As the weeks passed, David's vision slowly took physical shape.

Jerusalem's population was exploding now. The Israelite soldiers' families had come from Hebron to make their homes here, and among them were Urnan, Jerioth, Leah, Baalan, and Mara.

Urnan was put in charge of expanding the already existing blacksmith shop in Jerusalem so that it could handle the needs of the growing city and the army of David. To Eri fell the task of using the existing facilities to repair and replace weapons damaged or lost during the fighting. Sunu was placed in command of another mounted patrol force whose range encompassed a large area around Jerusalem.

One day, about a month after the capture of the city, Eri was summoned to the king's temporary quarters. He and David were discussing the work at the forge when Zadok, the priest, appeared at the door. "There is a delegation here to see you, my king," he announced.

David looked up at him curiously. "A delegation from where and whom?" he asked.

"They have been sent by King Hiram of Tyre."

David and Eri exchanged glances. Tyre was the most powerful of the Phoenician city-states to the north as well as the closest one to Israel. The Phoenicians were generally not a bellicose people; their interests tended more toward commerce and the pursuit of wealth. But it was possible they might regard Israel's recent military successes as a threat.

"What say you?" David asked his friend and adviser.

Eri shrugged. "You cannot ignore them. It would be best to see what they have to say."

"I agree." David turned to Zadok. "Send in the delegation from King Hiram."

Half a dozen Phoenician diplomats trooped into the room, faces wreathed in friendly smiles as if war were the farthest thing from their minds. Eri relaxed, as did David, but both men were still cautious. Evil intentions could lurk as easily behind a smile as a frown.

But it quickly became obvious that the warmth was genuine. After the formal exchange of greetings, the leader of the Phoenician group declared, "Our king, Hiram, wishes to make a treaty with you, David. Hiram has heard that you are building a city here worthy to be Israel's capital, and he wishes for Israel's king to have a worthy palace. We will supply timber from our mountains and artisans and woodworkers to build this palace for you. We will give you and your people access to our port, which as you know is the best on the Great Sea. We would be friends to the people of Israel and have them be our friends as well."

"Is that all you want in return?" David asked shrewdly. "Friendship?"

"Our country is a rugged, mountainous one, save for the narrow strip of land along the coast," the Phoenician said smoothly. "We have nothing like your *shephelah,* good farmland where food can be grown. If you are agreed, there can be much trade between your nation and ours."

David nodded slowly. "To the greater good of both nations."

"Such is Hiram's most devout wish."

"So it shall be," David said firmly.

Eri was glad. The proposed treaty would be of great benefit to Israel, which lacked a good seaport. And political ties with Tyre would further isolate the Philistines and reduce their influence in the region. Eventually, Eri knew, it was David's wish to drive his former masters back into the sea so that Israel could claim all the land east of the Great Sea.

Such ambitious goals would have to wait for another day, however. For now, the treaty with Tyre was sufficient. It would bring a palace and increased trade to Israel. Eri was well satisfied with this development, and he could tell that David was, too.

News of the negotiations with the Phoenicians spread rapidly through the city, and when Eri returned to his home that evening, he found Urnan, Jerioth, and Baalan already discussing the matter. Mara was nowhere to be seen, and Eri supposed she was in her room, sulking because Sunu had been gone for several days with his mounted patrol. *Ah, to be that young again and so inflamed with passion,* Eri thought wryly.

Leah was playing in a corner with the dog the family had brought from Hebron. When Eri entered the room, she stood up and ran to him, throwing her arms around his leg and calling, "Father!"

Awkwardly Eri reached down, disengaged her grip, and lifted her in his arms. At the urging of his father and Jerioth and Baalan, he was trying to pay more attention to Leah these days, although it was still not easy for him.

Urnan was seated on a bench beside the table. Eri joined him, perching Leah on his knee as he sat down. "You have been to the king's house today," Urnan said eagerly. "Are the rumors we have heard true? Will there be a treaty between Israel and King Hiram of Tyre?"

"It is true," said Eri. "Hiram wishes only peace and prosperity between the two nations."

"Good!" Jerioth said fervently. "Israel is surrounded by enemies. We will need friends if we are to survive."

Eri laughed. "If Sunu were here, he would say that friends are unimportant as long as we can conquer all our enemies."

"Our son believes too much in the sword, perhaps," said Baalan.

"How could he believe otherwise?" asked Urnan. "He is a Child of the Lion. And he has seen so much strife already."

Leah was becoming restless with the talk of the adults. She squirmed on Eri's knee and turned to look at him. "What is the Leb . . . Lebanon?"

Eri frowned at her. "That is what the people of Tyre call the mountains to the east of their seaport. Cedar trees grow there, and the timber from those cedars will be used to build King David's palace. Where did you hear about the Lebanon?"

"You spoke about it just now," Leah replied.

Eri shook his head. "No, I did not. I was about to—" He broke off and looked from Urnan to Jerioth to Baalan, his frown deepening.

Leah shrugged her little shoulders and said carelessly, "Oh. I thought you spoke of it."

"Well, now you know what it is." Eri lifted her down from his knee. "Go along and play. It is time for more grown-up talk."

"It is *always* time for grown-up talk," Leah complained, but she toddled back to the corner where the dog lay and was soon absorbed once again in playing with it.

Eri faced the others and said quietly, "The words were in my head, but I had not spoken them. Yet she heard them. She *heard* them."

Jerioth reached out and placed her hand on his. "Do not trouble yourself over it, Eri. It is out of our hands now. Truly, it always has been."

"Not trouble myself over the fact that my child is a . . . a witch!" Eri hissed the word between clenched teeth.

Jerioth drew herself up, making a visible effort not to appear offended. "I was once known as a witch," she said quietly. "Am I not a good wife to your father?"

Eri's reply was quick. "Of course you are. But Leah is only a child. She cannot begin to understand what . . . what she can do."

"That is why Jerioth is teaching her," said Urnan. "I worry, too, Eri, about the child's powers, but there is nothing we can do about it. You have heard the old stories. The Children of the Lion have always been a force for good. Leah will learn to use her gift wisely."

"The Children of the Lion have always been followed by troubles and tragedy," Eri snapped. "Who is to say that Leah's *gift* is not more of the same?"

Baalan moved over to sit beside her husband and embrace him. "Please, Eri," she said. "Leah may not be my daughter, but I have grown to love her as if she were my own. Even though I see Sarah in her—"

"Sarah," Eri repeated bitterly. "How do we know that this power Leah has is not because of Sarah's madness?"

"We know not what caused it," Urnan said evenly, "but we know Leah. We know she is a good child. You must put this out of your mind for now, Eri. You have much to do. David is depending on you to make weapons. All of Israel is depending on you."

Eri took a deep breath, then let it out slowly. "You are right, all of you. And she is my child, whatever magical powers she may possess. I will love her, no matter what."

He stood up and went across the room to kneel beside Leah and pet the dog, too. Beaming, the child laughed and chatted with her father about her new pet as, at the table, Urnan, Jerioth, and Baalan observed in smiling wonder the power of love.

Love was treacherous, thought David as he looked at the angry, twisted features of his first wife, his first love—Michal, daughter of Saul. Lately, whenever tender feelings crept into his heart, they soon turned around on themselves and became petty and spiteful. *Ah, Michal, how I loved you once, and how you loved me.*

Michal glared at him. "You might as well have taken your sword and cut off my brother's head yourself."

It was an old argument. Many months had passed since Baanah and Rechab, two brothers, had come to Hebron seeking an audience with David. When they were brought before the king, they had opened the sack they were carrying and dumped its grisly contents on the floor.

The head of Ish-bosheth—son of Saul, brother of Michal, claimant to the throne of Israel—had stared up at David through the glassy eyes of death.

Even now David grimaced as he recalled that awful moment. Baanah and Rechab had sought to curry favor

with him by murdering his only rival for the throne and
had brought Ish-bosheth's head with them as proof of
their deed. But their ambition had brought them only
their own deaths: David had them executed for their
crime.

But even that swift punishment had not placated
Michal. Years before, Saul had given Michal, his youn-
gest and most beautiful daughter, to David as a reward
for killing one hundred Philistines. The love between
the two blossomed to the point that Michal had risked
her own life to save David during one of Saul's bouts of
madness, but over the years a wall had sprung up between husband and wife. For a time, while Ish-bosheth
ruled east of the Jordan River and civil war racked the
land, Michal had lived with her brother and was given
by him in marriage to another man. With Ish-bosheth's
death and the uniting of Israel, David had ordered that
she be brought back and restored as his favored wife,
first among several.

But he could not as easily command that the love
she had once felt for him be restored.

Unwilling to face her anger any longer, David
turned and went to the window. They were in Michal's
bedchamber in the new palace, the palace built for him
by King Hiram's artisans and woodworkers, a glorious
monument to God and all Israel. But hardly a monument to love, David mused bitterly as he stared out at
the night.

"Why do you even come to me?" Michal demanded. "Why do you not go to Maacah or Ahinoam or
one of your other royal whores?"

David's hands clenched into fists. He knew Michal
was jealous of his other wives and jealous as well of the
children they had borne him while she herself remained
childless. But it was his right as king to have as many
wives as he wished, and he loved all his children, especially the son and daughter borne by the lovely Maacah,
daughter of the king of Geshur, a small city-state to the
northeast of Israel. Tamar and Absalom were his two
favorite children, along with Amnon, his son by Ahi-

noam. He would not stand by and hear their mothers slandered.

Turning to Michal, he said firmly, "You will not speak of your sisters in this manner."

"They are your wives," snapped Michal. "They are not my sisters." She lifted her chin defiantly. "I will speak of them in any manner I wish."

David seethed in frustration. The love he had once felt for Michal—and the desire he still felt, for she was undoubtedly one of the most beautiful women in the kingdom—kept him from taking any action against her. He could not bring himself to banish her, although that might be exactly what she wished him to do. He turned away from her again, but this time he left the room, her derisive laughter ringing in his ears as he stalked away.

Despite his troubles with Michal, David told himself, he ought to be happy. Jerusalem was growing rapidly, the army was strong and vigilant, the palace was all any king could desire. But still he felt a great dissatisfaction. Shaking his head as he strode down the corridor, he wondered if God was trying to tell him something, if there was a task the Lord had set out for him that he had somehow failed to see. He would have to pray about the matter and seek the advice of Abiathar.

Then he saw another wise man: Urnan the smith was waiting in an anteroom to see him. Grinning broadly, David clasped Urnan's wrist and asked, "What brings you here, old friend?"

"The new forges and shops are complete," Urnan reported. "Eri and I can now fashion as many swords and spearpoints as Joab requires for the army."

David rubbed his hands together in satisfaction. "Excellent! I knew I could depend on you, Urnan. You have served me as faithfully as you served Saul before me." The mention of Saul reminded David of Michal, and his momentary burst of enthusiasm quickly waned. With a sigh he added, "Would that a bond between people could be forged as strongly as one of your swords, my friend."

"I'm afraid I know little of such matters," said

Urnan. "My ancestors and I bear the lion's paw print, the mark of Cain. Always have we been doomed to wander, with no true home, no ties that bind us but the knowledge of how to work iron into weapons. The allegiance I and my son and grandson feel to Israel is perhaps the strongest any Children of the Lion have felt since old Belsunu left Ur in ancient times."

"I speak not of politics or nations," David said wearily, rubbing his forehead. "I speak of the bond between man and woman."

"Ah." Urnan looked uncomfortable. "Then I regret that I may be of no use to you at all, my lord, for when it comes to affairs of the heart . . ." He shrugged helplessly. "The Children of the Lion are as mystified as anyone."

That evening Sunu and his mounted patrol rode back into Jerusalem after several days away on a scouting mission. Although Sunu was tired, there was a spring in his step as he walked to his house after caring for his mount. He would soon be reunited with Mara, and he could think of little else.

Eri was seated alone at the table when Sunu came into the house. A single oil lamp illuminated the chamber. Eri stood and greeted his son, first clasping his wrist, then throwing his arms around the young man and slapping him on the back.

"Are you well?" asked Eri as he looked at his son.

"I am very well, Father," Sunu said. "Where is everyone?"

Eri smiled. "Baalan and Jerioth have already retired for the night. Leah went to sleep hours ago. Urnan has gone to the palace to speak to the king, but I will wait down here for his return." His gaze moved toward the ceiling. "Mara awaits you on the roof."

"How . . . how did you know?" Sunu realized what his family was doing. They all wanted to give him privacy for his reunion with his wife.

"Word passed quickly that the patrol had returned," Eri explained. "Baalan and Jerioth prepared a meal for you while you were tending to your horse and reporting to Joab. Mara has the food on the roof."

Sunu grinned. "It is good to be home, Father." He turned toward the door, intending to go outside and climb the stairs that led to the roof, to the meal awaiting him . . . and to Mara.

Eri stopped him with a hand on the arm. "Did your patrol encounter any trouble?"

Sunu shook his head. "None. There is peace in the kingdom, at least for now."

With a sigh of relief Eri said, "God grant that it remain so."

"I cannot bring myself to wish that. My blade grows thirsty for the blood of Israel's enemies."

Eri squeezed Sunu's arm and peered searchingly into his eyes. It was clear he had no idea how to react to his son's increasingly aggressive nature.

Sunu hurried out of the house and up the stairs. As Eri had promised, Mara was waiting on the roof, arms outstretched to greet him. She looked beautiful in the moonlight. The silver glow shone on her raven hair, striking highlights that rivaled the stars themselves for brilliance. She came into his embrace, and he felt the soft warmth of her body under the simple robe she wore. His lips plunged down to meet hers in a long, passionate kiss.

The meal could wait, Sunu decided. At this moment Mara was food and drink to him. She was all he needed.

Which was not to say that the repast prepared by Baalan and Jerioth was insufficient in any way, Sunu reflected later. In fact, the food was exceptionally delicious, and he felt wonderfully sated when, after they had eaten, he leaned back on the cushions Mara had brought to the roof.

She lay beside him, her head resting on his shoulder. They had dressed again after their lovemaking, but Mara's robe was pulled up over her thigh where she had thrown her leg across Sunu's. He stroked the warm, smooth flesh, luxuriating in the silky feel of her skin. Once again he felt extraordinarily lucky to have won the love of this proud and beautiful granddaughter of Saul. When they had first met, under much less pleasant circumstances, he would not have thought it possible.

"I am glad you are home, Sunu," she murmured. "I worry so much about you when you are gone."

"There is nothing to worry about," he assured her. "My patrol and I can outrun any enemy, and even if we cannot, we can outfight them."

Mara stiffened in his embrace. "But you should not have to fight. You are a smith, like your father and grandfather. Just because you fashion the weapons does not mean that you have to wield them."

"A smith I may be," said Sunu, puzzled by her vehemence and the turn the conversation was taking, "but my heart cries out to smite the enemies of Israel and the Lord. I cannot imagine laboring in the heat of a blacksmith's forge for the rest of my days and being content with that."

"What about your family? What must they content themselves with?"

He hugged her and laughed. "You are my family, and you are happy, are you not?"

"I am happy when you are here with me. But I am not the . . . the only member of your family."

"My father and grandfather understand—"

"I speak not of Eri and Urnan." Mara sat up and pulled away from him. "Nor of their wives or of your sister Leah. I speak of another."

Sunu frowned, more confused than ever. "Another? I do not understand."

"This is the one of whom I speak." Mara took his hand and brought it to her belly, resting his palm there. He felt nothing, only the usual flat plane of her stomach.

Then understanding descended like a lightning bolt, and, awestruck, he looked up into the face of his wife.

"A child?" he whispered.

Mara nodded.

Sunu sank back against the cushions, overwhelmed by this revelation. A child. He was going to be a father. Within Mara's womb, a son or daughter—a new Child of the Lion—was growing.

"You see now why I am concerned," Mara said quietly.

Sunu managed to nod. This changed everything.

And yet it changed nothing. Israel still had to be defended from its enemies, and that defense began with its scouts—like Sunu. He could not turn his back on his nation just because his wife was with child.

But this was not the moment to ponder such matters, he sensed. He sat up and drew Mara into his arms. He would think about the decisions facing him later.

Right now all he wanted to do was hold his wife and glory in the knowledge that they were going to bring a new life into the world.

CHAPTER EIGHT

Kaptar stumbled but quickly caught himself, knowing that if he fell, Atmos or one of the other Philistine overseers would beat him mercilessly until he got to his feet. His body was already covered with painful red welts and bruises where his captors had whipped and kicked him.

For long days Kaptar and two dozen or so Amalekite prisoners had been marched north and west toward the land of the Philistines. By now Kaptar had grown accustomed to calling them by that name rather than by the Egyptian term, "Peleset," because that was how his companions referred to them. Of course, when the soldiers could not hear, the Amalekites usually appended such epithets as "dogs" or "bastards" or "lovers of donkeys" as well.

"Keep moving there, you miserable sheep herders," one of the guards ordered, punctuating his command with a crack of his whip. The slaves staggered on.

They were given little food or water, just enough to keep them alive but not enough to make them troublesome to their captors. Once they reached their destination, they would be better cared for, Kaptar assumed. Otherwise they would be wasted as slaves, for none of them would be strong enough to do any work.

When the forced march began, Kaptar had not been sure he himself had the strength for it. Several times along the way he had seriously considered admitting defeat, falling down, and lying there until the Philistines beat him to death.

But Atmos would not allow that to happen. He was proud of his Egyptian captive and eager to display him for General Galar's approval. Atmos would make certain that Kaptar reached the land of the Philistines alive.

Kaptar did not know who this General Galar was, but from snippets of conversation he overheard as the Philistines talked among themselves, he gathered that Galar was a military hero, a soldier who through sheer ruthlessness had risen through the ranks to assume command of the Army of the Five Cities. No one enjoyed killing the Hebrews more than General Galar, Atmos declared more than once, and the statement was greeted with laughing approval by the other Philistine officers. For many years and in many conflicts, Atmos said, Galar had clashed with the pigs of the hills, and always he had been victorious. The war that loomed ahead would be no different.

Night finally came, after another seemingly endless day, and Kaptar was glad to collapse on the dirt and stretch out his aching body. His mind retreated into a hazy netherworld that was neither sleep nor wakefulness, and his senses did not return to him until a pair of Philistine soldiers brought around the evening's meager rations.

"I am told this Hebrew David still professes to be a vassal of Achish," one of the soldiers said to the other.

"No one is foolish enough to believe that, not even Achish of Gath himself," snorted the second man.

"Mark my words, the Hebrew intends to attack us as soon as he grows strong enough. That is why General Galar is gathering the army. We must strike first at the pigs of the hills, before they can strike at us."

"I hope I am one of those who march on Jerusalem," said the first soldier. "I long to let my sword drink deep of Hebrew blood."

The second man laughed harshly. "Kill one of these slaves if you must. One fewer Amalekite matters little. Just do not take the life of the Egyptian. Atmos wants him alive when we reach Ashkelon."

"Aye."

So Ashkelon was their destination, Kaptar thought, careful not to give any sign that he had been eavesdropping. Before leaving Egypt he had studied maps of the area and knew that Ashkelon was perhaps the largest and most important of the five cities that made up Philistia. It was a port, although not particularly suited for that function, and most of the nation's commerce passed through it. General Galar himself was from Ashdod, Kaptar knew from other conversations he had overheard, but apparently he was gathering his army in Ashkelon for an attack against Israel.

Kaptar's purpose on this mission had been to gather information about the political situation, he thought wryly as he forced himself to sit up. He was certainly doing that, though not in the manner he had intended. He took his allotted sip of foul-tasting water from the goatskin that the prisoners were passing around, then ate the hunk of stale bread and the piece of moldy cheese he had been given. That would be all the food he received until morning, when once again there would be a sip of water and a bite of bread, but no cheese.

When he had finished his skimpy meal, Kaptar curled up on the hard ground and tried to sleep. Although the days were blazing hot, the nights were cold, and he knew he would be shivering with the chill before morning.

None of it mattered, he told himself. Not the

marching that left every muscle in a man's body aching. Not the hunger and deprivation. Not the beatings and taunts handed out in equal measure by the brutal Philistines. He could endure all of it, because nothing mattered more than staying alive. He had to survive.

He had to live so that one day he could be with Nefernehi again.

She walked down the long, high-ceilinged corridor in the palace, her head held proudly erect, her lovely features composed and calm. But fear shone in her eyes, and her heart beat wildly, like that of an animal captured in a snare.

Nefernehi had been summoned into the presence of Sheshonk I, Pharaoh of Egypt, Lord of the Two Lands.

This was the moment she had awaited with dread, a dread that had begun growing shortly after Kaptar left on his mission to the land of the Israelites. She had noticed the way Sheshonk looked at her; she would have had to be blind not to see the lust in his eyes. It did not matter that he was not long past adolescence; he clearly had the appetites and desires of a grown man.

And the object of those appetites and desires was Nefernehi.

Over the past weeks she had avoided him as much as possible, but he had insisted that she attend the feasts he hosted, and she could not refuse a royal command. Fortunately there were always many other people in attendance at those gatherings, so all he could do was gaze at her with hooded eyes that burned with lust.

Nefernehi wondered if all of On was talking about the pharaoh's obsession with her. Isolated as she was within the palace walls, she heard little gossip. It had been taken for granted that she would stay in the palace while Kaptar was gone, since she was of royal blood, but she wished now she had protested the arrangement. She knew she could do nothing about it now. Sheshonk would never allow her to move out of her quarters, which were so conveniently near his.

He had been patient, though . . . at least she suspected that was the way *he* would view his behavior.
Tonight was the first time he had sent for her like this—
the first time she would be alone with him.

The two female servants who had come to deliver
the summons walked on either side of Nefernehi, their
eyes downcast. Surely they knew what Sheshonk had in
mind, but neither had voiced a warning to her. It didn't
matter; she knew without being told. The presence of
two male guards walking behind the women was more
than enough proof—they were there to keep her from
fleeing before she was ushered into the pharaoh's presence.

The little group reached a pair of tall, ornate brass
doors. One of the female servants opened them and
stepped back. There was no need to announce her,
Nefernehi realized. Sheshonk would be expecting no
other visitors tonight.

She looked searchingly at the women, but neither
of them would meet her gaze. A glance over her shoulder told her that the two guards were standing stolidly
nearby, their faces expressionless. There was no hope,
Nefernehi realized. Her heart seemed to plummet
through her body. No hope at all.

She forced herself to take a deep breath, then
stepped inside the bedchamber of Sheshonk I.

It was a large, airy room with windows on two sides
to catch the night breezes. Ornate columns supported
the ceiling, a large woven rug covered much of the floor,
and exquisitely carved ivory statues stood in two corners
of the room: one a nude man, the other a nude woman.
The low bed was piled with soft cushions, and tallow
lamps burned on either side of it. Nefernehi had never
been in the room before, and she was struck by its opulence. Of course the pharaoh, the god-king, the ruler of
all Egypt, deserved no less.

Sheshonk lounged on the bed, smiling at her as the
brass doors clanged shut behind her. The royal headdress covered his shaven skull and fell to his shoulders.
His eyebrows had been plucked, and his chest, arms,

and legs were also smooth, hairless. A wide collar of thin beaten gold adorned his neck. His lean hips were wrapped in a simple girdle of plain white cloth.

As for Nefernehi, her own raven-dark hair was the only headdress she affected. She wore a dark blue gown tied around the waist with a golden cord. Though the gown swooped low over her bosom, both her breasts were covered. She could feel Sheshonk's eyes studying her and suddenly burned with shame, as if she stood naked before him.

That would come soon enough, she realized bleakly.

"The Beautiful One of the South," murmured Sheshonk as he stood and slowly came toward her. "No one ever more richly deserved her name. You are beautiful, Nefernehi. You are the loveliest woman in the kingdom."

"Thank you, my lord," she said, trying to keep her voice steady.

He circled her, brushing his fingertips across the bare flesh of her upper arm. "You must be very lonely with my brother gone."

"Kaptar is doing your bidding, my lord, and I am proud of him. Every day I pray to the gods for his safe return."

Sheshonk came around in front of her again. "But surely you miss being . . . held by a man," he murmured suggestively.

Nefernehi pursed her lips to keep from laughing at his woefully awkward and transparent courting. And yet, what else could she expect from him? He had his choice of any of dozens of royal courtesans, merely by lifting his hand and commanding it. He had never had to woo or even seduce a woman—why should he have bothered to learn how?

"My lord, I am a bit weary. With your leave, I would like to return to my quarters." She risked nothing by this attempt to deflect his desire, Nefernehi knew. The worst he could do was refuse her request.

That was exactly what he did. He frowned and

shook his head. "No, no. I had you brought here tonight because I know that you must be sad and lonely. I wish to comfort you, Nefernehi. That is the least I can do for my brother's wife."

He reached up, spread her gown apart, pushed it off her shoulders. As the garment fell from her breasts, Nefernehi's breath caught in her throat. She was accustomed to nudity—what Egyptian was not?—but there was something different about this. Many men had seen her body, but Sheshonk seemed somehow to look inside her, and she did not like the sensation. She liked it even less when he cupped her breasts and rubbed his thumbs over her nipples.

Her breasts seemed larger and heavier than normal, but that was probably because his hands were small. With a firm caress that was almost painful, he kneaded the globes of flesh. Nefernehi endured it as stoically as possible. When she glanced down, she saw his aroused manhood pressing against the girdle around his hips. Perhaps he would spend himself before he could do anything else to her, she thought. She would welcome that.

But Sheshonk pushed the gown over her hips and down her thighs, leaving her naked as the garment fell around her ankles. "I would have you," he said huskily, taking her hand and leading her toward the bed.

Nefernehi's heart was crying out for her to pull away from him and run out of the room. But she could not. He was the pharaoh, and she was a loyal subject, a loyal Egyptian. She could not refuse any request of the god-king.

Kaptar. His name echoed in her head. If only Kaptar were here . . . But he was not. He was far, far away and could not help her.

Sheshonk turned to her, dropped his girdle, and pulled her into his arms. Lifting himself on his toes, for she was several inches taller, he kissed her.

The very ludicrousness of the situation was suddenly too much for Nefernehi to bear. The humiliation and the degradation she could endure, but the thought of this . . . this mere child naked in her arms, kissing her and strutting his manhood like a proud rooster—a bantam rooster—was simply too much.

She laughed.

Sheshonk slipped out of her arms, his face flushing in confusion as Nefernehi threw back her head and laughed, long and hard. "What are you doing?" he snapped. "What is wrong with you?"

"Nothing . . ." she gasped between peals of laughter. "I . . . I cannot . . . You are a *boy,* nothing but a boy! This is mad! I cannot do it!"

Like the closing of a gate, rage swept across Sheshonk's face, and Nefernehi knew she had made a terrible mistake. Better, perhaps, to have suffered his attentions in silence and gone on her way. He was not an evil king, but the combination of wounded pride and adolescent lust was a dangerous one. Nefernehi's fit of laughter subsided as she stumbled back a couple of paces from the young man's cold glare.

"A boy," he repeated, his voice little more than a whisper. "You say I am nothing but a boy and that you will not come to my bed. You forget who I am! I am the pharaoh! My word is law! I can have you killed!"

"But you cannot force me to desire you."

For a moment she thought he was going to strike her. Instead he said, "Not even in the face of death?"

"No, not even in the face of death would I desire you." She knew she was casting lots with her own life by saying this, but she could no longer do anything else. The confrontation had gone too far to surrender now.

A malicious spark burned in his eyes. "But what about Kaptar?"

Nefernehi frowned. "Kaptar is . . . far away. You said so yourself."

"True. He is far away . . . *now.* But he will be back, and when he returns, I can have *him* killed. I can have a greeting of swords and spears waiting for him."

"But he is your brother!" Nefernehi gasped. "You could not—"

"I could!" He grasped her shoulders roughly. "And I will, if I do not have you."

"You are the king." A shudder ran through her. "You can do as you wish."

"Then I would have you desire me," said Sheshonk, peering into her eyes, "or I will have Kaptar and every other member of your family killed. You must want me, Beautiful One of the South, as much as I want you."

The threat was as cold and merciless as the eyes of an asp. And every bit as real, Nefernehi realized. Sheshonk would not hesitate to go through with his horrible vow. She had no choice in the matter.

Her heart thudding madly, she put her hands on Sheshonk's chest and leaned closer, kissing him with as much a show of passion as she could muster. He embraced her, his hands sliding over the curves of her hips and pulling her closer to him. Locked in each other's arms, they fell onto the bed.

Nefernehi closed her eyes and opened herself to him. She tried not to gasp in revulsion as he pierced her. "Beautiful One," he murmured. "If you cannot truly desire me, Nefernehi, then for your sake—and the sake of your husband—make me believe you do anyway, at least for a time."

That she could do, she told herself grimly as she began to move her hips back and forth to meet his quickening thrusts. She could live that lie.

But she prayed that Kaptar would never discover what had happened here tonight. She knew him, knew that he would never forgive Sheshonk. A wedge would be driven between the two of them that might bring tragedy not only to the brothers and the woman they both desired—but to all of Egypt as well.

CHAPTER NINE

Ashkelon was impressive, even to one who had grown up in the great city of On. It was certainly the largest settlement Kaptar had seen since leaving Egypt. Under other circumstances he might almost have found the city attractive.

But being pushed and prodded along as a slave in chains made everything look different, he discovered. This important Philistine city on the Great Sea was just one more stop on a nightmarish journey—the final stop, at that.

All the captives save for Kaptar were to be marched to the docks. When they reached the outskirts of the city, Atmos plucked Kaptar from the line of trudging figures and roughly led him to a large house near an open field where several chariots were standing. Philistine soldiers were marching and drilling in the field. Atmos hauled Kaptar into the house and then thrust a sandaled foot between his ankles. Kaptar tripped and lost his balance, and Atmos shoved him down onto the earthen floor.

"Prostrate yourself, dog," Atmos growled, "before the might of General Galar."

Remaining on hands and knees, Kaptar tried to catch his breath. A cultured voice said from somewhere above him, "What is this you have brought me, Atmos?"

"An Egyptian, my lord," Atmos replied proudly. "We captured him in the land of the Amalekites. He was traveling with a handful of guards, whom we slew. But I thought you might want to see this one. He is a noble of some sort."

"Let me get a better look at him," General Galar commanded.

Atmos kicked Kaptar in the side. "On your feet, Egyptian!"

Kaptar's wrists were still lashed together, his ankles bound by iron shackles, but awkwardly he pulled himself upright.

He found himself facing a tall, imposing, vital man of some sixty years, whose keen dark eyes were studying him intently. The hostility between Egyptians and Philistines went back hundreds of years, and Galar's expression was cold and cruel as he examined the captive.

"Who are you, and how did you come to be in the land of the Amalekites?" he demanded.

Kaptar's head lifted. He refused to appear weak or beaten before this man. "I am Kaptar, prince of Egypt, personal emissary from Pharaoh Sheshonk I, Lord of the Two Lands."

Galar laughed harshly. "Lord of the Two Lands," he repeated disdainfully. "Lord over a nation of inbred weaklings! That is what you really mean, is it not, *Prince* Kaptar?"

Kaptar's mouth tightened into a grim line. He made no response to Galar's taunt.

"You did not explain why you were in the land of the Amalekites," Galar went on. "Why would your pharaoh send you there?"

Kaptar said nothing.

Galar shrugged. "Go ahead and be stubborn. I do not fear anything that Egypt might do. Your pharaoh's plans are no concern of mine, because he is no threat to the Five Cities." He sent his gaze up and down the Egyptian's body. Kaptar had been lean to begin with, and now, after the arduous march, he was all hard muscle, bone, and sinew. Galar grunted to his subordinate, "Send him down to the docks with the others. We shall see if an Egyptian nobleman makes as good a slave as an Amalekite shepherd."

Atmos nodded eagerly. "It shall be done, my lord." He grabbed Kaptar's shoulder and gave him a hard shove. "Move along, Egyptian!"

Kaptar stumbled out of the house, glad to be away from Galar's intense scrutiny. Despite the heat of the day, being in the man's presence had sent cold prickles down Kaptar's spine. He did not know if such a thing as true evil existed—but if it did, one of its vassals was surely the man called Galar.

"You'll make a fine slave," Atmos said as he prodded Kaptar along the crowded streets of Ashkelon toward the docks. Dogs followed them, nipping at Kaptar's ankles. Philistine women jeered at him, and children threw rotten fruit that splattered on his back and shoulders. Ignoring these indignities, he turned his head to look at Atmos.

"How do you know?" he asked. "What makes you think I will be a good slave?"

Atmos snorted. "Because if you do not, you will quickly die. Either way, you will know that none can oppose the power of the Philistines."

Sturdy wooden piers had been built out into the water along the shore of the Great Sea. With no natural harbors nearby, the Philistines had had to construct a stone jetty to protect the docks. The artificial harbor thus created was fairly small, but a great many ships came and went, some from Phoenicia to the north, others from the island of Kittem, others from even farther away. Trading was brisk, and the main job of the slaves who toiled on the docks was to load and unload the ships. Kaptar was put to work alongside them.

The slave quarters to which they were later herded were in a low stone building not far from the docks. Inside, it was divided into pens that reminded Kaptar of the royal stables in On. Dozens of men were crowded into each pen. There was little ventilation, and sanitary facilities consisted of a hole scratched into the dirt in each enclosure. The stench was almost overpowering, but after a few days Kaptar barely noticed it when he and the other slaves were brought in at nightfall. Thoroughly exhausted from long hours laboring on the docks, he wanted only to rest, even amid such squalor.

Kaptar had made no friends among the Amalekites during the trek from their land. He had kept to himself then and continued to do so now, not because he considered himself above them—his father, Urnan, had been a common man, after all—but because it was the only way he could cope with his enforced captivity. He could not admit, even to himself, that he was as much a slave as the lowliest Amalekite shepherd.

Men from far-flung lands shared the slave pens with Kaptar—Canaanites, Mesopotamians, Greeks, Kushites. How they had all wound up in the land of the Philistines was a puzzle, but their destiny was the same, no matter where they had come from. The Philistines intended to use them until they dropped, then discard their broken bodies and start over with new slaves. All the while, General Galar and his men prepared for their war against the Israelites.

Kaptar often wondered if his father might still be alive. If he was, had he made his home among the Hebrews again, as in days of old? Or had the hereditary wanderlust of the Children of the Lion moved him to travel elsewhere, perhaps to lands Kaptar had never heard of? Was it possible he had even gone back to Ur, from whence the family had sprung many, many generations earlier, before Abraham had led his people out of Egypt and unto the Promised Land?

Toiling on the docks day after day, Kaptar realized

bleakly that his chances of finding Urnan or any information about him were becoming more and more remote. And if Urnan *were* alive, he might be killed when the Philistines invaded Israel. Kaptar wished there was some way he could escape from the Philistines, not for his own sake but to warn the Hebrews of the Philistine threat. But that seemed yet another futile hope, for the Philistines were too alert, and they ruled with an iron hand. They left nothing to chance.

The other slaves had noticed Kaptar's aloofness, and he saw their resentful glances. But he had more important things on which to concentrate: patience and survival. His time would come. Sooner or later it would come.

He was thinking about that one day as he trudged along the dock, a barrel of Phoenician dye balanced on his shoulder. The dye had come from a ship from Sidon that had docked that morning, and all day the slaves had been unloading the cargo and carrying it to a stone warehouse nearby. Although the barrel on Kaptar's shoulder was heavy, he was managing fairly well with it.

Suddenly something was thrust between his feet, and he tumbled forward, the barrel toppling from his shoulder. It crashed to the pier and burst open, spraying rich purple dye all over Kaptar and the planks beneath him. Some of it spattered his eyes and stung, and he heard raucous laughter as he tried desperately to paw the irritant out.

"What is wrong, Egyptian?" asked one of the laughing voices. "Is your noble blood so thin you lack the strength to perform a simple task?"

When Kaptar's vision finally cleared, he looked up to see several slaves clustered around him. The one who had spoken was a tall, burly Mesopotamian with a prominent nose that looked as if it had been broken several times. The men with him were somewhat smaller but cut from the same cloth, and all of them jeered as Kaptar pushed himself back onto his feet. He was certain that one of them—probably the Mesopotamian—was responsible for tripping him.

The accident had not gone unnoticed. Two Philistine overseers were hurrying along the dock toward the group, brandishing whips as they came. "What is the meaning of this?" one of them demanded angrily when he saw the broken barrel and the spilled dye. His eyes fastened on Kaptar, who was splattered with purple. "Did you do this, slave?"

Kaptar pulled off the loincloth that was his only garment and used it to wipe the dye from his face. There was no point in denying his part in the affair, for it was obvious from the visual evidence that he had been carrying the barrel.

"Someone tripped me," he said coldly. "It was not my fault."

Snarling, the overseer cracked his whip like a snake around Kaptar's thighs. Kaptar clenched his jaw to keep from crying out as the whip was jerked back, leaving a fresh red welt behind it.

"Who tripped you?" demanded the overseer. "Name the man."

Kaptar looked at the Mesopotamian, seeing a flicker of unease in the man's eyes. He was certain the Mesopotamian was to blame for what had happened, but he would not give the Philistines the satisfaction of saying as much. Turning his gaze back to the overseer, he said, "I know not. I never saw the man."

The Philistine shook his whip angrily. "You'll bear the lashes alone unless you speak! Tell us the man!"

"I know not," Kaptar said stubbornly.

The overseer drew back his arm to use the whip, but his companion stopped him. "There may be some truth to what the Egyptian says," he suggested, leering. "Why not whip all of this group, just to make certain we punish the right one?"

The first overseer nodded slowly, a cruel gleam in his eyes. "That is a good idea, my friend." He made a motion to several guards who stood nearby, holding spears. "Take them all to the whipping posts."

Kaptar saw the fear in the other men's faces as they were herded off the dock and into an open lot where four sturdy posts had been sunk into the ground. Slaves were often tied to those posts and flogged when they did something to displease their Philistine masters—or simply to give the overseers some entertainment whenever they desired. Kaptar had escaped such a lashing so far, but it seemed his luck had run out. He wondered if some of the other men would crack under the strain and admit that it had been the Mesopotamian who had tripped Kaptar. But all remained silent, even when the whips sang through the air and left long, bloody stripes on their backs.

Kaptar and the Mesopotamian were left until last, apparently so they could watch the other men being flogged. Finally they were tied side by side to two posts. As the overseers backed off and raised their whips—which by now were sodden with blood—the Mesopotamian glared at Kaptar and said out of the corner of his mouth, "You will pay for this, you Egyptian dog!"

Kaptar made no reply. None of it had been his fault, but it would do no good to point that out to the Mesopotamian. All he could do now was endure.

The leather whip slashed across his back. Involuntarily Kaptar lurched forward against the post as if he were trying to find some way to escape the lash. But there was nowhere to go. Tears sprang to his eyes, but he did not cry out as the whip struck again.

And again and again . . .

He was only half conscious when he was taken back to the slave quarters and dumped into a pen. The part of Kaptar's brain that was still functioning was proud of the fact that he had not made a sound throughout the entire flogging. Neither had the Mesopotamian beside him, even though both of their backs had been slashed into ribbons of bloody flesh.

Kaptar had moved beyond pain now. He was numb, unfeeling. He lay facedown in the slave pen, his cheek pressed against the dank dirt floor, knowing he dared not roll over onto his back. The easiest thing to do now was to slip into senselessness, so that was what he did.

Sometime during the night he awoke in agony, and this time he could not stop himself from uttering a short cry. Suddenly something cool and moist was placed gently on his back, relieving for a moment the piercing, fiery pain. Although it soon returned, the respite gave Kaptar strength, and he was immensely grateful for it.

"Rest," whispered an unfamiliar voice. "I stole a bit of water and this cloth. I will clean your back."

Kaptar turned his head a little and squinted into the darkness, but he could not make out the face of the man helping him. "Wh-who . . . ?" he gasped through cracked lips.

"A friend," came the whisper close to his ear. "Lie still, and be quiet."

Normally there were more than a score of men in the pen with him each night, and his benefactor could have been any one of them. A tiny shudder went through Kaptar as he felt the damp cloth soothe away some of the pain in his back. He hoped his newfound friend was not one of those twisted ones who used a man as a woman. In his current condition Kaptar would not be able to fight off an advance of that nature.

He lost consciousness again—or perhaps merely fell asleep—while the stranger was ministering to him. When he awoke the next morning, he knew immediately that he had not been molested during the night. Evidently the stranger had had only Kaptar's welfare in mind.

Kaptar pushed himself into a sitting position, wincing as the movement pulled at the scabs that had already formed on his back. He knew better than to hope that he would be excused from his work today just because he had been flogged the day before. After the slaves had been given their meager breakfast, he trooped out with the others, biting his lip against the pain that shot through him with every step.

None of the other men who had been flogged had been in the same pen with him that night, which was a good thing, else one of them might have tried to kill him in the darkness. He had to work on the docks with them, however, and he saw the Mesopotamian before the morning was over. The big, broken-nosed man looked as if he was in as much pain as Kaptar, and Kaptar could not miss the murderous hatred in every glance. He had made an enemy for life, all because *he* had been the victim of a cruel joke. It was madness.

But *life* was madness, Kaptar thought. He had never fully realized that until he had undertaken this journey and wound up a slave in the hands of the Philistines. Life was a mad joke, and there was no such thing as justice, no point to the capricious twists and turns of fate that put all of humanity through its paces. Truly, what purpose was served by all the pain and humiliation he had suffered?

No purpose, thought Kaptar. No plan. Only life, with all its cruelty and insanity. Only life . . .

And he was going to do everything in his power to hold on to it anyway.

CHAPTER
TEN

Sunu reined in his horse at the top of a ridge, scarcely believing what his eyes were telling him. He looked out over the Valley of Rephaim, also called the Valley of the Giants, southwest of Jerusalem. Far across the valley, where the hills rose once more, were the Vale of Elah and several other passes.

And through those passes was coming the largest army Sunu had ever seen.

The proud chariots came first, followed by rank after rank of marching men. The distance was too great for Sunu to discern any details of armor or weapons, but he did not need those details to identify this army. Only one of Israel's enemies could put such a large force in the field of battle.

The Philistines. It had to be them.

Sunu tried to estimate how many soldiers were pouring into the Valley of Rephaim, but he soon gave that up as an impossible task. The irrational urge to attack them suddenly struck him, but he forced the idea out of his head. He would serve Israel much more effectively by riding back to Jerusalem as fast as he could and telling the king this news.

His features grim, Sunu wheeled his mount, dug his heels into its flanks, and prompted it forward into a gallop. He was alone today on this scouting mission. These days he seldom rode with an entire patrol, for life around Jerusalem had been peaceful since David had captured the city.

That was all about to change, Sunu thought grimly. He leaned forward over the neck of the horse, urging it on to greater speed.

When he reached Jerusalem, he went directly to the great palace atop the hill of Zion and was ushered into the presence of David, who sat in a luxuriously appointed room playing his harp. As he approached, Sunu heard the king singing and was struck anew by the power and beauty of his voice. Even Sunu, a young warrior who had no time for things he considered frivolous, was deeply moved.

As he bowed before David, the king set aside the harp and said, "You are out of breath, Sunu. Why have you come here in such a hurry?"

"The Philistines, my lord," Sunu replied. "Their army is even now in the Valley of the Giants, and they come toward Jerusalem."

David rose quickly, grasped Sunu's arm, and peered intently at him. "You saw this with your own eyes?"

Sunu nodded. "Yes, my lord." The king's grip on his arm was almost painful, but he did not flinch.

After a moment David released him and began to pace back and forth across the room. To one of the servants standing nearby he snapped, "Send Joab to me at once." As the man scurried away, David added to Sunu, "You should only have to tell what you saw one time, so we will wait for Joab."

It did not take long for the commander of the Israelite army to answer the king's urgent summons. As

Joab strode into the room, a fierce expression on his bearded face, he asked, "Is there trouble in the kingdom?"

"You are as perceptive as always, my friend," said David. "Sunu, tell us what you saw."

Quickly Sunu explained his discovery. Joab's already grim expression hardened. "The Philistines may plan to lay siege to the city. We must not allow them to reach Jerusalem."

"I agree," said David. "It will take them some time to cross the Valley of Rephaim. We will meet them there. Have the men ready to march as soon as possible."

"It shall be done," Joab promised. He turned and hurried out of the room. There was no need for further talk.

David put a hand on Sunu's shoulder. "Well done, my faithful scout. You have done your duty. You may return to your home."

"I will return to my home," replied Sunu, "but only to fetch my spear and say farewell to my wife."

Mara would not be pleased to hear of this, Sunu thought, especially with their child on the way. She had already told her husband several times that it was time to put aside the ways of war and prepare for fatherhood. But Sunu could not turn his back on his country in its time of need. He would fight for Israel, even to his dying breath.

David's grasp tightened on Sunu's shoulder. Smiling, he said, "I expected no less from you, my young friend. We go this day to smite the Philistines, eh?"

Sunu nodded, his own smile tight. Somehow he feared the Philistines less than he did telling Mara that he was once more going off to war.

"How can you do this?" she demanded. "Do you think your child has no need of a father? What will we do when the Philistines kill you?"

Sunu wished Mara would lower her shrill, angry voice. It was bad enough that she should heap so much guilt on his head, but to do it when his father and grand-father could hear her in the next room was a shame to him. As he picked up his spear, he said quietly, "My child needs a father *now*. I would not have my son or daughter live under the yoke of the Philistines and suf-fer as my grandfather and his family did during those dark days before Saul and David freed us. *That* is what my child needs most from a father: the promise of a life lived in freedom."

"Bold words for such a young man, little more than a boy himself," Mara snapped. Yet Sunu could see her face softening. The speech, as uncomfortable as he had felt making it, had reached her, and she knew he spoke the truth. She came a step closer and rested a hand on his broad chest, and when she spoke again, it was with a tone of worried resignation. "You must not let the Phi-listines kill you."

Sunu grinned. "Their arrows and spears and swords shall not touch me. This I pledge to you."

"It is a promise beyond your power to keep."

"I shall do my best," he said firmly. "And I cer-tainly shall not be alone. My father and grandfather are marching with the army as well."

Mara raised her eyebrows in surprise. "It does not surprise me that Eri is going. He is still as much warrior as smith. But Urnan is too old for such things."

"You may tell him so if you wish. I prefer not to." Sunu chuckled, then went on more solemnly, "Israel is his homeland now and has been for many years, since his return from Egypt. And he owes many debts of blood to the Philistines."

Sunu thought of his grandmother, long since dead, raped and murdered by a troop of Philistine soldiers in the days when the brutal conquerors had held sway over all the land of Canaan. Urnan and Eri both had suffered greatly at the hands of the Philistines. Now, at last, ven-geance might be theirs.

Mara came into Sunu's embrace and rested her head upon his shoulder. "If you must go, then go with

God," she whispered. "I shall pray every day for the Lord to watch over you."

Sunu stroked her dark curls. "And I shall pray for you and for our little one growing inside you. Soon we will all be together again."

If that is the will of God, he added silently to himself.

With Galar and the army gone to attack the Israelites, Ashkelon was much quieter and less crowded. The slaves had been herded from their pens and forced to watch as the army marched from the city with much pomp and splendor. Kaptar was almost sorry to see them go, though he was grateful that for an afternoon, at least, he did not have to labor on the docks. But he had hoped to escape from Ashkelon before this, so that he could travel to Canaan and warn the Israelites. Now it was too late.

The wounds on his back had healed. In the weeks since his ordeal, Kaptar had often wondered who his mysterious benefactor had been, but he had never discovered the answer.

He was beginning to hope that the Mesopotamian had forgotten his oath of vengeance. Kaptar saw the burly man often on the docks, but the Mesopotamian never even acknowledged Kaptar's existence after the day they were both flogged. Perhaps, Kaptar mused, the man and his friends did not want to get into even deeper trouble.

After the army left Ashkelon, the work on the docks settled down into the same never-ending drudgery. Kaptar's muscles had been strengthened by the hard work to the point that he could handle the same tasks as the other men. Or most of them, anyway—one muscular giant could carry two barrels of dye at once, or four bolts of cloth, or almost anything the overseers commanded him to carry. More than once Kaptar had stood in awe, watching the bearded man's feats of strength, until an overseer prodded him back to his own work.

Late one afternoon Kaptar was carrying a large jar of oil from a ship toward the warehouse in which similar jars were stored. The day's work would soon be over, and that blessed cessation could not come soon enough as far as he was concerned. Weariness suffused both body and mind. He wanted only to sit down and rest and eat his meager supper.

Suddenly Kaptar became aware that someone was calling his name. He looked up and saw a small man, an Amalekite slave, standing at the rear corner of the warehouse. The man lifted a hand and beckoned to him.

Kaptar frowned and looked around. The nearest overseer, some distance away, was paying no attention to him. The Amalekite gestured urgently to Kaptar, who wondered if one of the other slaves was hurt and needed assistance. He put the jar of oil down by the entrance of the warehouse and hurried around the corner, moving along the stone wall of the building to join the Amalekite.

"What is it?" Kaptar asked. "What do you want of me?"

The man suddenly ducked away, vanishing around the corner, and Kaptar felt a surge of alarm. Before he could do more than take a single step backward, several men rushed around the corner and grabbed him. He tried to lash out, but they were holding his arms too tightly. Although he struggled mightily, they managed to drag him into the narrow alley behind the warehouse.

Kaptar considered shouting to the overseers for help, but if he knew that if he did, he might only bring more trouble on his head. The Philistines would likely whip everyone involved in this altercation, including him.

Kaptar was not surprised when he saw the Mesopotamian standing in the alley, his brawny arms crossed and a look of smug satisfaction on his face. "I told you that I would settle my account with you, Egyptian," he said as Kaptar was hauled before him. "That day has come."

Kaptar jerked his head angrily toward the men

holding him. "You require the help of these lackeys to bring about your vengeance," he spat.

One of the men struck him in the back of the head with a clenched fist. "We are no man's lackeys! We were all whipped, Egyptian, because of you! All of us shall smite you in turn."

They intended to beat him to death, Kaptar realized coldly. If each of the men took a turn while he was held helpless in the grip of the others, they would surely pound the life out of him. He might have to shout for help after all, no matter how much his pride told him not to.

Before he could open his mouth, the Mesopotamian stepped forward and smashed a blow across it. Kaptar sagged back in the grip of the other slaves and tasted blood in his mouth. He spat it out as best he could. The Mesopotamian drew back his fist for another blow.

"Let him go."

The low, rumbling voice was as cold as the grave. Fist still cocked, the Mesopotamian paused and looked past Kaptar and the other slaves.

The huge, bearded man from the docks stood there, massive body clad only in a loincloth like the others, hands clenched into fists, craggy features set in a glowering stare.

"This is no concern of yours, Nestor," growled the Mesopotamian. "Leave us. Go back to your tasks."

"I will not," said the huge slave called Nestor. "Release the Egyptian . . . *now!*"

If the Mesopotamian was frightened, he gave no sign of it. He merely smiled and said, "There are five of us. Poor odds for a battle."

"True," said Nestor with a slow nod. "But perhaps not too unfair for you."

A look of pure hatred flashed across the face of the Mesopotamian. "Smite the fool!" he snapped at his friends. "Leave the Egyptian to me!"

The gripping hands fell away from Kaptar's arms as the other slaves turned and attacked Nestor. At the same instant, the Mesopotamian stepped forward and swung another blow at Kaptar's head. Kaptar was free now, however, and as he ducked, the Mesopotamian's fist sailed harmlessly over his head. With a quick step Kaptar brought himself closer to the Mesopotamian and sank a fist in his stomach. Hot, sour breath puffed in his face.

All the rage that had festered inside him during his enslavement came boiling up. Before the Mesopotamian could recover his balance, Kaptar grabbed him around the waist and lunged forward, plucking him from the ground. With a bellow of anger he drove the man into the warehouse wall. The Mesopotamian's head slammed into the stone and bounced off, and he went limp in Kaptar's grasp. Kaptar released him and stepped back. As the Mesopotamian sprawled senselessly in the dirt, Kaptar wondered if he had killed him but then saw that the man was still breathing.

At the sound of fists thudding against flesh Kaptar turned to see how Nestor was faring with the other four men. There was nothing to worry about on that front, Kaptar realized. Two of the Mesopotamian's cronies were already unconscious at Nestor's feet. The huge slave had his left hand wrapped around the throat of a third man, and he dropped the fourth with one swing of his malletlike right fist. Like a dog shaking a rat, he shook his last opponent and then flung him aside carelessly. The man slammed into a wall, then slid slowly down the stone surface to join his unconscious companions in the dust.

"I warned them it might not be fair," Nestor rumbled as he surveyed the bodies.

Kaptar laid a hand on Nestor's upper arm, which seemed as thick and solid as the trunk of a young tree. "You have my thanks, friend," he said, "but come quickly. We must return to our tasks before the overseers realize we are neglecting them."

"What about these dogs?" Nestor waved a huge hand at the slumbering men.

"Let the overseers discover them. It has nothing to do with us."

A grin of understanding spread over Nestor's face. After a quick glance around the corner of the warehouse to make certain no one was watching too closely, the two men hurried back to their tasks.

The overseers realized what had happened only when the Mesopotamian and his friends came stumbling out from behind the warehouse a little later. The whips sang their bloody song that evening as the men were punished for neglecting their work. By that time Kaptar and Nestor were back in the slave pens with the others, their day's tasks finished.

The two men sat together with their backs against a wall, eating their skimpy rations. A thought had occurred to Kaptar, and he gave voice to it now. "You have been in this pen before. I remember seeing you. You were the one who came to my aid the night after I was whipped by the overseers. Your voice sounds much different when you whisper."

"That is true," Nestor admitted, his eyes shifting away as if he were uncomfortable. Kaptar had noticed that he seldom looked directly at him.

"Why did you do it?" Kaptar asked. "Why did you help me before, and again today?"

"It is my duty," Nestor replied after a long moment of silence. "In my homeland I was given the task of guarding the members of our royal family. I can do no less here."

Kaptar frowned in puzzlement. He was a member of the royal family in Egypt, but Nestor was no Egyptian. Kaptar could not identify what race the big man belonged to, but he was certain he did not come from the Black Land of the Nile.

"How can this be?" he asked. "Where are you from, Nestor?"

The huge slave swallowed the last of his bread and again hesitated before finally replying, "I come from a land far away. Very far away."

"Across the Great Sea?" Kaptar pressed, in his interest forgetting how tired he was.

"*Beyond* the Great Sea."

Kaptar's eyes widened. "But . . . there are no lands beyond the Great Sea."

"Once there were," Nestor said softly. "Perhaps . . . perhaps there still are." His voice strengthened, though it remained quiet. "There is an even greater sea beyond what you call the Great Sea, and in it is an island that is a great nation. That is my homeland. Its name is sacred, and I dare not speak it."

It was difficult for Kaptar to believe what his new friend was telling him, but he tried to understand. "And you think I am part of the royal family from this island nation of yours?"

"You bear the mark," Nestor said. "I saw it the day the Mesopotamian tripped you and made you drop the barrel of dye. I knew then that I must pledge my service, my very life, to you."

"The mark?" Kaptar repeated. "The only mark I possess is—"

"The lion's paw." Nestor's voice was hushed, almost reverent. "The ones who rule my homeland bear that mark, and they also possess the secret of iron."

Kaptar's heart began to pound. He had heard all the stories of his family's beginnings, but they went back only as far as old Belsunu of Ur. But Belsunu and *his* ancestors must have come from *somewhere*. An island nation in the Greater Sea beyond the Great Sea? Kaptar could not say with complete certainty that it was impossible.

"How did you come to be here in the land of the Philistines?" he asked eagerly.

"I was on a ship, sailing from my homeland to another nation with which my people traded. The ones who lived there were dark, like the people you call Kushites, and they were very warlike, but they traded with us anyway because we had iron. The young prince of the royal family whom I served was on the ship as well. He was called Ammaron and was more than my charge—we were also friends.

"But we never reached our destination. As we sailed across the sea, a strange thing occurred. The sky turned green, and the air was filled with the prickling of a storm on a summer day, even though there were no clouds in the heavens. The wind died, and yet we kept moving, as if pulled on by some mysterious force. The men all wailed with fear, save for Ammaron and myself. We stood with our swords drawn, ready to meet any foe that might attack us.

"But there were no foes we could touch, only the green sky and the pricking air and the force that drew us on, and then suddenly the sea rose up and smote our ship, smashing it. I went into the water and thought I would drown, but I felt something like hands holding me up. I saw visions then . . . strange visions that frighten me still . . . new worlds, new people, great vessels that moved through the air like birds—" Nestor broke off and shuddered. "I do not like to speak of it, even to this day."

"What happened?" asked Kaptar, almost breathless with anticipation.

"A great wind came. A true wind this time, not like the strange force that had drawn us on earlier. I found myself clinging to some wreckage from our ship. Eventually the wind brought me to a shore. I knew not where I might be, but I was glad to see land again. The people who lived there took me in, a bit of flotsam cast up from the sea, and nursed me back to health. I stayed with them for a time. Then they gave me a boat, and I sailed on alone. I wandered for a long time, and then I fell into the hands of these men you call Philistines, who enslaved me." Nestor shook his head. "Never again did I see Prince Ammaron or my homeland or any of my own people . . . until now."

"I am not sure I come from your people, Nestor," said Kaptar. "I do not see how it is possible. My father is of a line descended from a man of Ur, and my mother was an Egyptian princess."

"You bear the mark," Nestor said stubbornly.

"Yes, this is true. We are called the Children of the Lion. But as for the true wellsprings of my line, I cannot say."

Nestor shook his head. "I care not for mysteries. It is enough for me to know that you bear the mark of the lion's paw, and to know that I am pledged to serve you."

"No." Kaptar held out his hand. "It is enough that you are pledged to be my friend, and I yours."

Nestor hesitated, then clasped Kaptar's wrist, and there, in the growing darkness of the slave pens of Ashkelon, a bond was forged between the two men that might never be broken, save by death.

CHAPTER
ELEVEN

David looked intently at the old priest Abiathar, who had been his spiritual adviser for many years. Just outside the walls of Jerusalem, the Israelite army had assembled, waiting to march forth and meet the Philistines in the Valley of the Giants. But before he gave them the command to do so, David urgently needed to do one more thing. He said solemnly to Abiathar, "Ask the Lord if I should go out and smite the Philistines and if they will be delivered into my hands."

Abiathar knelt, closed his eyes, and clasped his hands before him. For a long moment the old man was silent. Then he looked up at David and said, "The Lord has said unto you, go out, for the enemy will surely be delivered into your hands."

The answer was exactly what David wanted to hear. Smiling grimly, he buckled on his sword, drew on his battle helmet, and strode forth to give the order to his army.

A great shout went up when the men saw him. David drew his sword and stood before them, his powerful voice carrying to all the ranks as he declared, "We march today to the Valley of Rephaim to repel the craven attack of the Philistines! They shall flee back to their cities on the coast and never again dare to invade the land of the Israelites!"

More lusty cheering answered David's call. Among the soldiers, the three generations of the Children of the Lion stood together. Sunu lifted his spear and shook it fiercely as he joined in the shouting. Eri stood quietly, his arms crossed on his breast, but in his eyes burned the same eagerness for battle. Only on the weathered face of Urnan were any misgivings visible. But as much as he had grown to dislike war, he knew that the threat from the Philistines could not be ignored. If Israel was to remain free, the invaders had to be repelled.

At noon, with the sun overhead, the army left Jerusalem. By the middle of the afternoon it had reached the Valley of Rephaim. David's swift response to the news that the Philistines were approaching ensured that the enemy advanced no farther than the middle of the valley. When the Israelite army appeared, the Philistines halted in their steps.

David, Joab, and Eri dismounted and moved to the forefront of the army, where they could get a good look at the Philistines.

"They have goodly numbers of men," Eri observed.

"Then goodly numbers of them shall die," Joab responded before the king could speak.

"There are none better at seeing the simple answer than you, my friend and commander," David said to Joab. "But the simple answer is not always the best one. If we attack them directly, many of the Philistines will die. That is true. But many of our men will die, too."

"Then what shall we do?" asked Joab. "Should we stand here and glare at one another, hoping the Philistines will think better of their adventure and return to their cities?"

Slowly David shook his head. He knew the Philistines as well as any man in Israel. "They will not do that. But neither will they attack us while we hold the higher ground."

"Then we should attack them," Joab argued.

David looked at Eri. "What say you, my friend?"

Eri thought for a moment, then said carefully, "The time will come when we must fight them. We all know this. But it cannot hurt to wait for a while and make the Philistines wonder what we are doing."

"This is the same path my thoughts have taken," said David. "We will wait and let the Philistines watch us. Then—when the time is right—we shall strike and drive them back to the sea!"

"And who is to say when the time is right?" asked Joab, his tone bordering on arrogance.

"God will say," David replied firmly. "God will give us a sign that it is time to go forth and smite the Philistines."

Sunu was consumed with impatience. He longed to feel the heady thrill of battle, to experience the fiery surge that shot through his blood every time he dispatched another Philistine. Although he would never disobey a command from his king, waiting was the one command he had the most difficulty obeying. He wished mightily that David would give the order to attack.

But the order did not come during the long afternoon, and as the sun sank below the horizon and darkness settled over the land, Sunu knew it would not come today. Rarely did the Israelites or the Philistines fight at night.

Tents were pitched for the king and his commanders. Sunu and two of his friends, young warriors named Azhad and Malachet, were on guard duty near David's tent. It was unlikely the Philistines would leave their own encampment tonight, but it was imperative that the king be protected at all times. Sunu's gaze was fixed on the distant fires of the enemy camp, where he could see dark shapes moving about.

David had been in his tent all evening with Joab,

Eri, Urnan, Abiathar, Zadok, and his other advisers. Sunu had heard their voices, sometimes raised in disagreement, but he could not make out what they were saying. No doubt Joab was trying to persuade David to attack the Philistines immediately, and his father and grandfather were counseling caution, Sunu guessed. Eri and Urnan were sometimes *too* cautious to suit Sunu, but, he told himself with a sigh, they were old. They no longer relished killing their enemies as they once had. That was their loss.

The tent flap was thrust back, and David emerged, followed by the other men. "We shall speak of this again in the morning," he said wearily.

Joab muttered, "Let us pray that the Philistines do not fall upon us with the rising of the sun."

"We shall be watchful. If they move, we shall know it."

Sunu hoped David was right. What the king needed to do, he thought, was to send out scouts to keep a closer watch on the Philistines. He and Azhad and Malachet would be perfect for that job.

Sunu knew he would have to wait for the right moment to suggest that to the king, however. It was not his place to decide tactics, especially to someone with a reputation as a brilliant military leader. But when all the advisers were gone, Sunu decided the king would not mind a carefully worded suggestion.

The opportunity to give it to him did not arise. David moved to the edge of the camp and peered out at the Philistine fires in the distance. Sunu followed at a respectful distance—it was his duty to guard the king, after all—and was close enough to hear the sigh that escaped David's lips.

"Oh, that someone would give me a drink of water from the well of Bethlehem, which I knew as a child!"

Sunu's muscles tensed. He knew the place of which David spoke, for he was well acquainted with the village of Bethlehem, which lay beyond the Valley of the Giants —and beyond the camp of the Philistines. A man would have to be mad to attempt crossing the lines of the enemy—twice!—simply to bring back a drink of water for the king.

And yet . . . Sunu felt his heart pound with excitement. What the king wished for, the king commanded.

Hearing the faint scuff of a sandaled foot behind him, he turned and saw Azhad and Malachet. "Heard you what the king said?" he whispered to his friends.

Azhad nodded. "We heard. Do we dare?"

"I say we do!" declared Sunu. "How say you, Malachet?"

With an emphatic nod, Malachet made known his decision. He was a grim-faced youth who seldom smiled, unlike Azhad, who was always laughing and flirting with the young women of Jerusalem. The two were good friends despite their differences, and Sunu had grown close to both of them.

David, who had heard nothing of their whispered discussion, turned and went back to his tent, too distracted to pay attention to the huddled group of guards. When he was inside the tent, Sunu said to Malachet, "Fetch more guards to watch over the king, and then we shall do what we can to fulfill his wish."

Malachet nodded and hurried away. Within moments he was back with three more young men, all full of questions about what Sunu and his friends planned to do.

"We cannot tell you," replied Sunu. He had decided that silence was the wisest course not only because he didn't want to be talked out of undertaking this mission but also because it was possible they would not succeed.

With the new guards in place, Sunu and his friends slipped down the hill toward the floor of the valley. Sunu thought briefly about his father and grandfather back in the Israelite camp. Eri and Urnan would not understand what he was doing and would certainly not approve, but it had always been thus. Young men went forth with daring while older men fussed and fretted.

And to the young men went the glory. Sunu's pace

quickened with anticipation at that thought, and he and Azhad and Malachet moved on quickly but silently toward the camp of the Philistines.

Like many of his men, David slept but little that night. His thoughts were occupied with the Army of the Five Cities waiting out on the plain. Sooner or later there would be a battle, and although David had God's assurance that the Israelites would prove victorious, he hoped that the sign he had spoken of the night before would materialize, and soon. He would feel more confident if he were certain he was attacking at God's own appointed time.

Not long after sunrise David thrust aside the tent flap and stepped out into the cool, early morning sunshine. Hands on his hips, he moved to the edge of the slope and surveyed the Philistine camp.

A disturbance from the outskirts of his own camp drew his attention. A group of soldiers was coming toward him, three young men at the forefront: Sunu, Azhad, and Malachet. They had stood watch near his tent during the night—or at least he had thought they were. He saw now that perhaps they had not been there after all, for all three bore the marks of battle, and he would surely have awakened had they suffered their wounds in the vicinity of his tent.

Malachet was limping, his left arm bore an ugly-looking gash, and a bloodstained cloth was wrapped tightly around his left thigh. Azhad's grinning face was marred by a livid bruise on his cheek, and his bare chest was scratched in dozens of places, as if he had run through a thornbush. The most battered of the trio was Sunu. The deep gashes on his arms and legs appeared to have been inflicted by swords, and his face was badly bruised. But he wore an even wider smile than Azhad as he lifted a goatskin in his left hand.

The three young men and the soldiers following them stopped in front of David. Extending the goatskin, Sunu said, "For you, my king."

David frowned in puzzlement. "What is it?"

"Water, my lord," said Sunu proudly. "Water from the well of Bethlehem, which you wished last night to drink."

David's blood roared in his ears as the full import of Sunu's words sank in. These three young men—loyal, courageous, valiant young men—had overheard his words the night before and acted on them. Overcome with emotion, he had trouble speaking for a moment. Then he took the goatskin from Sunu and said, "You breached the lines of the Philistines and risked death . . . to bring this water to me?"

Sunu and the others nodded. "Yes, my lord," said Sunu.

David's expression became stern. "You were foolish to risk your lives on such a whim."

The young men's faces fell. But in the next instant David laughed delightedly and went on, "But the Lord smiles at such daring, and I . . . I love you for this." Lifting the goatskin so the gathering crowd could see it, he raised his voice and declared, "This is water from the well of Bethlehem, brought to me by three brave young men who risked their lives to secure it! I will not dishonor their courage by merely drinking the water! Instead, I pour it out as a sacrifice to God, who has given these young men the courage to go among the enemy!"

David dropped to his knees, threw his head back, and called out a prayer of thanksgiving and homage. Then he tipped the goatskin and poured the water out onto the ground in front of him. *This is the moment,* he thought. *This is the sign for which I have been waiting.*

The shouts that issued from the throats of hundreds of soldiers told him he was right. Sunu, Azhad, and Malachet were watching him, transfixed, overwhelmed by the knowledge that the king considered the water they had brought exalted enough to sacrifice to God. But the rest of the men were thrusting their weapons in the air and yelling jubilantly.

David came to his feet, drew his own sword, and held it high over his head. "We are armed with the courage of the Lord!" he cried. "We cannot fail! We go to drive the Philistines from our land!"

As they poured down off the hill and into the Valley of Rephaim, the soldiers of Israel took the Philistines by surprise with the ferocity of their charge. Armed with swords, spears, arrows, and slings, still in the grip of an emotional frenzy, the Israelites clashed with the enemy.

Sunu found himself in the middle of the battle. Weary from lack of sleep and the loss of blood he'd suffered in skirmishes with Philistine sentries during the night, he was nevertheless caught up in the excitement of the attack. With fire in his soul, his exhaustion forgotten, he hacked and slashed at every Philistine who popped up in front of him until his arm felt like lead, his sword seemed as heavy as an anvil, and his muscles would no longer obey his commands. But at least when death found him, he thought, he would have in his hand a blade coated with the blood of his enemies.

His father and grandfather found him instead, appearing on either side to skewer a pair of Philistines who were advancing on him. Eri's hand closed firmly on Sunu's arm and dragged him back. "Come!" he shouted over the tumult. "You have done enough!"

"No!" cried Sunu. "I must slay the Philistines—"

"If the bodies of the ones you have slain were piled at your feet," said Urnan, "you would not be able to see over them, grandson. Come with us."

Reluctantly Sunu allowed them to lead him to the edge of the battlefield. Eri and Urnan cut a path with their swords through the carnage around them, and when they were clear of the melee, they sat Sunu down upon a rock to rest.

From their spot a short distance up the hillside, they could see the battle spread out before them. Philistine soldiers were breaking and running toward the hills on the opposite side of the valley, their forces in complete disarray. Soon a full-scale retreat was under way. Mercilessly the Israelites pursued them, cutting down any stragglers.

"They will run all the way back to their cities by the Great Sea," Eri said proudly as he surveyed the scene. "Never again will they dare to invade our land."

Urnan was more cautious. "I would not be so certain of that. I have seen the Philistines retreat before. They always come back."

Sunu's chest was heaving as he tried to catch his breath, and the sweat that coated his torso stung where it seeped into shallow wounds. He lifted his head and raised his sword, using his free hand to push his matted hair out of his eyes as he stared across the valley at the retreating enemy. "If they come back, we will smite them again!" he declared, savagely shaking his sword.

"Aye." Eri rested a hand on his son's shoulder. "That we will."

By late afternoon the only Philistines remaining in the Valley of Rephaim were dead, their corpses scattered across the plain. Following David's orders, Israelite soldiers made their way through the litter of bodies, collecting *teraphim*, the small, carved wooden idols Philistine soldiers wore on cords around their necks. These were thrown into great piles and then put to the torch. The *teraphim* represented various heathen gods, but if they truly possessed any magic, as the Philistines believed, it did not save them from the fire of the Israelites. Soon thin columns of black smoke rose all over the valley from the piles of burning idols.

Sunu, Eri, and Urnan watched the smoke rising into the sky and knew what it symbolized. More had been won today than a battle between armies. The one true God had conquered the false deities of the Philistines. The military victory might belong to David and the Israelites, but the real victory belonged to the Lord.

CHAPTER TWELVE

Even on the docks Kaptar heard talk of the rout suffered by General Galar and the Army of the Five Cities in the Valley of Rephaim. The slaves who had earlier been captured in Israel were overjoyed to learn that their king had turned back the Philistines' incursion. The other slaves also enjoyed hearing of the soldiers' undignified retreat in the face of the Israelite counterattack. Such news made their captors seem less powerful and bolstered hope in the slaves' hearts that someday they would be free.

Kaptar was no different. His desire for freedom was as urgent as always, and he never stopped thinking about ways to escape from the slave pens of Ashkelon. Now that he and Nestor were fast friends, Kaptar believed his chances had improved. He recalled often the stories of how his father, Urnan, had escaped from Philistine slavery in the copper mines of Kittem with the aid of the big slave Kemose, who had turned out to be an Egyptian prince and high priest.

Nestor was no nobleman, but he possessed more strength, courage, and loyalty than any man Kaptar had ever encountered. Under these cruel circumstances it was a strangely benevolent fate that had thrown the two men together.

During the long, dark nights in the slave pens, when he should have been sleeping, Kaptar lay awake turning over in his mind the things Nestor had told him. The idea of a powerful island nation somewhere beyond the Great Sea, an island nation ruled by people bearing the mark of the lion's paw, intrigued Kaptar greatly, as did the story of the mysterious phenomenon that had wrecked Prince Ammaron's ship and cast Nestor adrift. Someday, Kaptar decided, after he had escaped from the Philistines, discovered the fate of his father in Israel, and returned to Nefernehi in Egypt, he would sail beyond the Great Sea and try to find that island himself. He was sure Nestor would be glad to accompany him. The dream of discovering his family's origins exerted a powerful pull on Kaptar's mind.

But in the meantime there was the matter of survival here in Ashkelon. The threat of revenge from the Mesopotamian and his cronies seemed to have passed following Nestor's rescue of Kaptar behind the warehouse. With Nestor as his friend and companion, no one wanted to bother Kaptar. The work on the docks was still grueling, however, and the Philistine overlords certainly had no fear of Nestor.

Not long after the return of the defeated army to Ashkelon, General Galar appeared on the docks, accompanied by several guards and the chief overseer. The slaves continued working, but Kaptar watched from the corner of his eye as the general strode up and down, studying the men laboring there. Galar had taken the chief overseer's whip and was pointing with its handle to various slaves as he passed them. Kaptar heard him saying, "That one . . . that one . . . and that one over

HANDSOME COLLECTOR'S EDITIONS
LONG AFTER THE ADVENTURE FADES

Stake your claim to this FREE book offer.
Send for your Collector's Edition of SACKETT,
and your FREE Louis L'Amour wall calendar.
Try the Louis L'Amour Collection with no
obligation. See details inside.

DETACH HERE BEFORE MAILING

BUSINESS REPLY MAIL

FIRST CLASS MAIL   PERMIT NO. 2154   HICKSVILLE, NY

POSTAGE WILL BE PAID BY ADDRESSEE

The Louis L'Amour Collection

PO Box 956
Hicksville NY   11802-9829

NO POSTAGE
NECESSARY
IF MAILED
IN THE
UNITED STATES

there, he looks to be a sturdy one . . . that man there
. . . and that one."

Kaptar had no idea what Galar was doing, but he
noticed that all the men the general had selected were
large and muscular, even for dock slaves. So it came as
no surprise when Galar indicated Nestor with the butt
of the whip. "This one, certainly," he grunted to the
chief overseer. "What a brute."

"Yes, he is, my lord," the overseer whined. "But if
you take these men for your army, my work here on the
docks will be made that much more difficult."

Galar waved off the complaint. "You can always
find more slaves. When I return to the land of the ac-
cursed Hebrews, my army will be larger than ever before. The pigs of the hills will fall before us like grain
before the scythe." He pointed once again with the whip
handle. "That man there . . . and that one."

Kaptar's brain was whirling. Galar had obviously
decided that the Army of the Five Cities was not large
enough to conquer King David and the Israelites. He
wanted to expand the ranks of his fighting men by ap-
propriating the largest, strongest slaves he could find.
Forcing men whom the Philistines had enslaved to fight
in their army was a risky proposition, but it had its ap-
peal. Surely many slaves, in return for even a promise of
freedom, would pledge their loyalty to the Philistines
and be fierce fighters; Kaptar could understand that mo-
tivation. And when most of the slaves were killed—as
surely they would be, because the Philistine commanders would no doubt place them in the front ranks
for any battle—their deaths would be considered no
great loss, especially if they took plenty of Israelites with
them when they died. It was a stroke of cunning on
Galar's part.

Yet Kaptar was bitterly disappointed, for he did not
want to be separated from Nestor. Their partnership
represented for him the best hope of escape.

As the chief overseer and Galar's guards prodded
the chosen slaves into a group, Nestor cast a confused
glance over his shoulder at Kaptar. He seemed unsure

of what to do. He had pledged his loyalty to Kaptar, and he might be unwilling to leave the docks and the slave pens as long as Kaptar remained behind. But if he refused to follow orders, he was inviting a severe beating, and he would eventually be forced to go along with the others anyway. Kaptar did not want that happening to his friend. It was better that they should be parted.

And yet, why should they be? he suddenly asked himself. Galar planned to take his army back to Israel, and that was where Kaptar had wanted to go from the first. Why not allow the Philistines themselves to assist him in reaching that goal?

To think of the idea was to act on it. Without hesitation Kaptar stepped forward, saying loudly, "General Galar! I would go with you to fight the Hebrews."

Galar had been standing with his back to the docks, watching his slave recruits being readied to march. When he heard Kaptar's voice, he stiffened and turned to see who had dared to address him thus. The chief overseer growled an oath and took a step toward Kaptar, lifting the whip Galar had returned to him, but the general stopped him with an outstretched hand.

"It seems we have a volunteer," he said, his mouth stretched in a cold, thin smile. "Who spoke?"

Kaptar took another step forward. "I did, my lord." The honorific did not come easily to him, but he forced it from his mouth. Pointing at the group of slaves, he went on, "You are taking these men to join your army and fight the Hebrews, willingly or unwillingly. I say to you now that I would do the same, only I would not have to be forced to do so."

"You look familiar," Galar mused as he strode closer to Kaptar. "Yes, I know you now. The Egyptian prince, the one whose diplomatic mission was so rudely interrupted. What was your name again?"

"Kaptar, my lord."

"Ah, yes, Kaptar." Galar clasped his hands together behind his back. "Then tell me, Kaptar, why would you fight for Philistia against the Hebrews?"

Kaptar smiled humorlessly and indicated the docks

with a wave of his hand. "I would rather fight than labor here forever as a slave."

"You might die in battle."

"But I would die a free man," Kaptar pointed out, "or at least with the promise of freedom."

Galar fixed him with an intense stare. "I have said nothing of a promise of freedom. These men are slaves. They will fight because they are ordered to."

"Yes, but you are a military man with much experience. You know that men fight better and harder when they fight for something they want."

Slowly Galar nodded. "True, true. Perhaps you have divined my true purpose in coming here today." He looked Kaptar up and down. The Egyptian was a muscular, broad-shouldered man, but he knew he was no more impressive a physical specimen than any of the other slaves who worked on the docks. Many, like Nestor, were larger and stronger. "But why should I take you? You must answer that, *Prince* Kaptar, before you can join us."

Once again Kaptar had to think quickly. He was skilled with a bow and arrow, but surely no more so than the archers Galar already had in his army. Nor was his expertise with a sword or spear anything more than adequate. But there was one aspect of war in which he *was* an expert.

His chin lifted a little as he said, "In my homeland, I am known as Master of the Horse. There is no better charioteer in all the Two Lands."

Despite himself, Galar appeared to be interested. "A charioteer, eh? I suppose you would be willing to demonstrate your skill?"

"Of course," Kaptar answered without hesitation.

The chief overseer spoke up. "Surely, General, you do not believe anything this man says. He is a mere slave—"

"I am willing to give him a chance to prove he is more than that," Galar said sharply. He turned back to Kaptar and went on, "I came here today in my own chariot. I would see you drive it."

Kaptar nodded his agreement.

"Come along, then," Galar said. To his subordinates he added, "Take those other slaves back to the camp. Be careful not to let them get their hands on any weapons."

"Yes, General," replied one of the guards.

"Wait a moment," said Kaptar, knowing that he might be asking more favors of fate than that fickle mistress was willing to grant him. But he wanted to keep Nestor with him, so he pointed to the big slave and said, "I would have that man for my archer, once I have been given a chariot."

Galar cocked an eyebrow. "You *are* confident, aren't you?"

"It seldom profits a man not to believe in himself."

The general seemed surprised by Kaptar's boldness, but with a curt motion he indicated that Nestor should be pulled from the group of slaves being marched away. Smiling thinly again, he said to Kaptar, "You shall have the services of this man as your archer . . . providing that your claim of being an expert charioteer is not an empty boast. If that is all it is—you shall both die."

Kaptar's mouth tightened into a grim line. He was risking not only his own life but Nestor's in this gamble. But it was one he was certain he could win.

Galar and several guards led Kaptar and Nestor to the general's chariot. To Kaptar's surprise, another chariot was drawn up beside it, with two Philistines standing inside.

"My best charioteer," Galar said, gesturing toward the man holding the reins of the second chariot. "All you have to do to enter the Army of the Five Cities, my young Egyptian friend, is to defeat that chariot in a fair race."

Kaptar suppressed a groan. He had expected only to demonstrate that he could easily handle a chariot; nothing had been said about a race. But he had no choice if he wanted to save his own life and Nestor's. "Whatever you command, my lord."

"Take your friend with you." Galar indicated Nestor. "You will understand, of course, if I do not give him a bow and arrows."

Kaptar nodded as he stepped up into the chariot. As Nestor climbed aboard behind him, Kaptar felt the floor of the chariot sag a little under the big man's weight. Perhaps he had made a mistake, he thought grimly. The driver and archer in the other chariot surely did not weigh as much as he and Nestor did. The lighter the load, the faster the chariot.

But the pair of horses attached to Galar's chariot were fine-looking animals, Kaptar saw, and if they had enough speed and strength—and heart—they could defeat the other team. Kaptar could only pray they did.

He took the reins from Galar's driver and tested their tautness. The pull of the leather against his finger-tips told him the reins were stiff and would require a hard tug to communicate his wishes to the horses. He would have to remember that.

Galar, standing between the two chariots, said, "The course will be so: down this street to its end, where my army is encamped. Around the camp, making a complete circuit, and then back here, where I will wait. The first chariot to return will win the competition."

Kaptar nodded. "And with the victory comes a place in your army, my lord."

"Agreed . . . if you are victorious. You know the penalty if you are not." Galar looked at the driver of the other chariot. "Gillus, I expect you will not disappoint me."

The man shot a look of contempt at Kaptar and Nestor and said, "I will not, my lord. You can begin sharpening your sword for the necks of these foreign dogs as soon as the race has begun."

"Talk seldom wins the day," said Kaptar quietly.

Galar gave the other driver a curt nod, and without warning the man suddenly whipped his reins against the backs of his horses and called out to them. The animals lunged forward, the chariot's iron-rimmed wheels

squealing against the paving stones of the street as the
vehicle careened away.

Caught by surprise, Kaptar called out to Nestor,
"Hold fast!" and whipped his own team into motion.
Apparently none of the usual rules would apply in this
competition. That did not matter, Kaptar told himself;
he would win because he had to. His life and his future
—and Nestor's—were at stake.

The chariot swayed madly from side to side as it
rolled down the street. Nestor hung on for dear life as
Kaptar lashed the long trailing ends of the reins against
the rumps of his horses and shouted encouragement to
them. He did not know if Nestor had ever been in a
chariot before; the big man had never mentioned such
an experience. But Kaptar had faith in the strength of
Nestor's grip, at least. Once they had won their place in
Galar's army, he could teach Nestor the finer points of
chariot archery.

While they were on the long, straight street that led
to the army encampment, Kaptar could not close the
gap between his vehicle and the other. As they circled
the sprawling mass of tents, however, Kaptar steadily
inched his chariot closer to Gillus's. On sandy ground,
where high speeds were not possible, a man's skill with
the reins counted for more.

Gillus twisted his head and looked back at the competition. He lashed harder at his horses. Gillus's life
might not have been at stake in this race, but Kaptar
knew that Galar would not be pleased if he lost. And
Galar's displeasure was a risk one surely wanted to
avoid at all costs.

The Philistine soldiers had become aware that a
race was going on and ran to the edge of the camp to
watch and cheer. Kaptar felt a tingle of excitement that
had nothing to do with the fact that he was racing for his
life. The thrill of competition alone was enough to send
the blood pounding through his veins.

They were almost halfway around the camp now,
and he had all but drawn even with Gillus's chariot. For
a moment the sight of the open land beyond the city of

Ashkelon held his gaze. There was nothing to stop him from breaking away from the racecourse and heading out of the city—nothing but the fact that even if he and Nestor could elude the pursuit that would inevitably follow, they would still be in the middle of Philistia, long miles from where Kaptar wanted to be in Israel.

But if he won this race, he and Nestor could travel unhindered to Israel with Galar's army. Once they were there, their chances of successful escape would be much greater.

First, though, there was the matter of winning the race. As they entered the straightaway again, Kaptar's chariot was slightly ahead. If he could only maintain that lead . . .

Abruptly the chariot was rocked by a collision. Gillus had drawn up alongside and swung the right-hand wheel of his chariot into the left-hand wheel of Kaptar's. It was a dangerous maneuver, one that could have wrecked both vehicles and sent the men flying through the air. Kaptar glanced wildly at Gillus. The man's lips were drawn back in a snarl of desperation as his chariot swayed once more toward Kaptar's.

But before the wheels could clash again, Nestor leaned out from Kaptar's chariot, one long arm extended. He grasped the side of Gillus's chariot and held it off through sheer brute strength. The man riding with Gillus drew a short sword from its sheath at his waist and lifted it, preparing to slash at Nestor's bare arm.

Gillus was shouting curses at his opponents, but, Kaptar thought, he should have been watching the road instead of giving in to his anger. An instant later one of the wheels of Gillus's chariot hit a loose paving stone, and the chariot bounced into the air and came down with a crash. It stayed upright and intact—a tribute to Philistine craftsmanship—but Gillus's companion was thrown from the vehicle. Gillus himself barely hung on. The chariot slowed dramatically as the reins slipped out of Gillus's hands and the horses slackened their pace.

Kaptar kept going as fast as he could, opening up a large lead. He saw Galar up ahead. The general's face

was flushed with anger, and yet, as Kaptar brought the
chariot to a halt directly in front of him, he thought he
saw a glitter of satisfaction in Galar's eyes. The Philistine military leader had found perhaps the best charioteer this land had ever seen in the unlikeliest of places:
among the slaves of Ashkelon.

Kaptar stepped down from the chariot, trying to
bring his breathing under control. Nestor was a bit un-
steady on his feet as he leaped down beside him.

"Well, my lord?" Kaptar asked. "Do we go with
you to fight the Hebrews?"

"You do, both of you," said Galar. "And I almost
pity the Hebrew who has to stand against you. I want
you both in a special mercenary unit under my direct
command." He clasped Kaptar's arm. "With such warriors as you against them, this so-called King David and
his rabble will be destroyed!"

Kaptar smiled and nodded, but he was musing on
how surprised Galar was going to be when he discovered the real reason his two new recruits were so anxious to go to Israel.

He hoped he was there to see the general's face.

CHAPTER
THIRTEEN

Urnan bent over and lifted a hand to his mouth, racked by yet another violent coughing spasm. Jerioth, who sat across the room mending one of Leah's robes, rose and started toward him, but he managed to motion her back. A moment later the coughing subsided enough for him to gasp, "Do not trouble yourself, my wife. It . . . it is nothing."

"It *is* something and you know it, Urnan," Jerioth said worriedly. "In the months since you returned from the battle against the Philistines, your health has grown steadily worse. You should not have gone off to war."

"It was a short war," Urnan said wryly. "Less than a day, in fact. And I was not even wounded. No, Jerioth, I grow old. There is no escaping that fact. From now until the end of my days, my health will do nothing but grow worse."

"You cannot know that," Jerioth protested. "You may grow stronger—"

Urnan shook his head but said nothing, because there was nothing to say. Both he and his wife knew the truth of the matter, even though she might not want to admit it. But he had seen and done much in his life, and if his days were indeed drawing to an end, such was the will of the Hebrew God he had adopted.

Leah ran into the room then, followed by Sunu and Mara. All three were laughing. At moments like this, Sunu and Mara looked like children themselves, Urnan mused. Sometimes it was difficult to believe they were married and expecting a child of their own. The rounding of Mara's belly belied her girlishness. And although Sunu was gentle as he scooped up his half sister and tickled her, Urnan remembered all too well how he had looked with a sword in his hand, his body spattered with his own blood and that of his enemies. Young and innocent Sunu might appear, but he was a warrior, too, through and through.

Grandfather Urnan, help me!

Urnan looked up. Leah was still in Sunu's arms, held tightly as Sunu and Mara poked her in the ribs. She was laughing breathlessly. No one else in the room seemed to have heard her cry.

That was probably because they had not, thought Urnan. The call had been meant for him alone, and it had come directly from Leah's mind. Until recently such a notion would have sent a cold ball of fear into Urnan's belly, but he was becoming more and more accustomed to Leah's ways. Often she seemed to know what he was thinking before he spoke, and, too, whenever he was around her, no matter how troubled he was, his spirit eased and became content. At such times he recalled the wild dogs in Hebron and could not help but wonder if their spirits had been soothed the same way, simply because Leah had willed it so.

Urnan pushed himself to his feet, ignoring the painful popping in the joints of his hips, legs, and back. "Unhand the child," he said in a mock growl to his grandson.

"You want her?" asked Sunu. "You are welcome to her!"

With that he tossed Leah in the air toward Urnan. Jerioth cried out in alarm, but Urnan deftly caught the little girl and hugged her to him, enjoying the warmth of her arms as they wrapped tightly around his neck. "I would not allow any harm to come to her," he said to Jerioth.

She made a clucking noise of disapproval and said to Mara, "I hope that when your child is born, you do not allow her father and great-grandfather to toss her around like a bag of grain!"

"Israelite children are strong," said Mara. "But I hope Sunu will wait for the little one to grow a little before he does such things."

"If the child is a boy," said Sunu, "I will give him a sword for his first birthday, so that he can begin to learn how to slay his enemies."

Jerioth sighed, shook her head, and turned away, going back to her mending. Trying not to show his own concern, Urnan sat on the bench with Leah. Mara was not so discreet. She said, "You will do no such thing, Sunu. A child should have time to be a child and not worry about slaying enemies."

"If you think Philistine children are not taught to fight, I believe you are mistaken," Sunu said stubbornly. "We must always be ready to fight anyone who comes against us! That is why I ride out tomorrow with the mounted patrol for King David."

Mara's head jerked up, and she stared at her husband in surprise. "What? I knew nothing of this!"

Sunu walked to the bench and sat down heavily. Urnan knew he wanted to avoid another argument with his wife. "David and Joab fear the Philistines will return to avenge their defeat in the Valley of the Giants," Sunu said. "My father agrees with them. So David has decided that we must continue to patrol the hills between Jerusalem and the land of the Philistines."

That was sound strategy, thought Urnan, although he hated to see his grandson leave the city and his family again. Mara clearly had no use for military strategy; she stood glaring at Sunu, arms crossed, saying nothing —for now.

"Why do the Philistines hate us so?" Leah asked in her high, childish voice.

"That is a long story, little one," said Urnan, patting her on the shoulder.

"I have plenty of time."

Urnan wished he could say the same for himself. He felt his time slipping away from him, like water flowing down a stream. Instead of trying to explain the long history of hostility and hatred between the Israelites and the Philistines, he drew Leah closer and said, "I have time only for another hug."

"Then you shall have one!" she cried in delight as she wrapped her arms around his neck again.

Despite what Sunu might believe, thought Urnan, wars really mattered very little in life . . . especially compared to the hug of a small child.

"You think only of your own glory!" Michal's voice was shrill and accusing. "You feel joy when you hear the songs your people sing about you!"

"I wish only to be a good king," David replied evenly, "and the people of Israel are the Lord's, not mine. I am but a servant, to both God and the people."

"Spare my ears the sound of your false humility," Michal snapped. "I believe it not."

"It has been a long time since you believed anything I told you, has it not, wife?"

The guards standing outside the door of the king's bedchamber kept their eyes straight ahead and gave no sign that they heard the argument coming clearly from within. Eri tried to do the same as he waited for his audience with David, but it was difficult to pretend. He wished David had not sent for him, but to be fair to the king, it was likely he had not known he would be confronted by his angry wife just when Eri arrived. Michal came and went as she pleased in the palace, answering to no one—not even, it appeared, to the king himself.

The bickering continued for long, embarrassing moments before Michal finally emerged from the room, sweeping past Eri with barely a glance.

He was shown into the chamber, where David greeted him with a rueful smile. "Ah, women!" he sighed. "A man cannot dwell with them—nor without them—to any great degree of satisfaction."

"I have found only satisfaction with my wife, Baalan," Eri protested mildly.

"What about your first wife?" David shot back. Before Eri could answer, the king waved off the question, looking apologetic. "I beg your forgiveness, my friend. I had no right to say that. I know that great unhappiness has visited you in the past."

"Yes," Eri agreed, somewhat stiffly. "Yet I still say, I have known only happiness with Baalan."

David clapped a hand on his shoulder. "Then you are a very fortunate man, my friend. Come, have a cup of wine with me."

The king poured the wine himself; there were no servants in the chamber. Obliquely he asked his friend, "I suppose you heard my argument with Michal?"

"I heard," Eri admitted. "What did it concern this time?"

"Nothing important. She heard some of the women of the city singing a song about me this afternoon, and it irritated her. She is quickly roused to wrath these days." David gave Eri an intense, questioning look. "What should I do about this, my friend?"

For a long moment Eri said nothing. Then, feeling distinctly uncomfortable, he replied, "I am but an armorer and a warrior, my lord. I can be of no help to you, because this is a battle that cannot be won by force of arms."

David tilted his head back and drained the wine from his cup. When he lowered it, he said wearily, "I fear you are right." He turned away sharply and strode to the window to look out at the splendid city that some people were already calling the City of David. Rubbing his temples, he went on, "I almost wish the Philistines would return. I would rather face an enemy of flesh and blood, one who bleeds when struck by a sword, than to grapple with the anger of a cold-hearted woman."

"The Philistines . . ." Eri said quietly as he moved to the side of the king. "I have never known them not to nurse hatred in their hearts for our people. Be cautious with your wishes, my lord. I fear that, sooner or later, they will be granted."

Kaptar had not realized how much he hated being a slave until he breathed the air as a free man once again. He felt a fierce exhilaration knowing he had finally left the slave pens of Ashkelon behind. Laboring on the docks had hardened and strengthened his muscles, but it had taken a toll on his soul and mind. He swore he would never again allow himself to be forced into such a miserable existence; he would die before he would let anyone enslave him.

Of course, he realized that as a mercenary in General Galar's army he was still as much a prisoner as he had been in the pens, but he knew, too, that this time was a stepping-stone on his path to true freedom: When the army reached Israel, Kaptar and Nestor would desert at the first opportunity and join the Israelite forces.

As soon as the two men had had a private moment after the chariot race, Kaptar had explained his plan, and Nestor had agreed without hesitation to accompany him.

"I will be especially pleased if we can slay some of those Philistine curs before we leave," Nestor had growled.

Kaptar had assured him that was a likely prospect.

With the rest of the army they spent weeks training for the return to the land of the Hebrews. Galar was determined not to be defeated again. The ranks of the army continued to swell until the Philistine force was of such a size that Kaptar worried about the Israelites' ability to defend themselves. This time Galar might be able to sweep all the way to Jerusalem and crush the resistance. If that happened, Kaptar's own plans would be jeopardized.

But he could do nothing until the two armies met, so he concentrated instead on teaching Nestor the fundamentals of chariot warfare. Nestor had used a bow before, and his great strength made it a formidable weapon in his hands. He could drive an arrow through a thick piece of wood, so Kaptar was confident he could as easily penetrate a war shield. Nestor quickly learned how to spread his feet wide and balance himself in the chariot as it raced along. Kaptar at the reins and Nestor wielding the bow would make dangerous opponents for any enemy they faced.

One evening, as they returned to the tents where the mercenary units slept, they found themselves in company with one of the Philistine officers who commanded their group. The officer had closely observed their training drills that afternoon, and he complimented both men on what he had seen.

"You handle a chariot as if born to one, Egyptian," he said to Kaptar, "and your friend is a magnificent archer. You will kill many Hebrews when we go again unto their land."

"Why do your people hate the Hebrews so?" asked Kaptar, deciding to indulge his curiosity. "Is it because they control land that is coveted by the lords of the Five Cities?"

The officer waved his hand. "The land is but one reason. All Philistines hate the pigs of the hills. It is a natural thing." He paused, then added, "None hates them more than Galar."

"Did they do him a wrong?"

"Only by their pathetic existence." The officer smiled savagely as he continued, "I have been under Galar's command for many years. I recall a time, long ago, when he was but a captain and led me and the other men under his command into a Hebrew village called Shiloh. We killed many of the people there and put the village to the torch. The villagers gave us little trouble . . . save for the blacksmith. He returned to his shop just as we were having our way with his wife, and he seemed to go mad at the sight. He might have killed us all, or at least tried to, had he not been knocked senseless. Then he was taken off into slavery, he and his son. Galar could have had both of them killed, but he was a younger man then, and more merciful. The only one we killed in the blacksmith's shop was the smith's wife. But the smith came back years later and somehow infiltrated our camp. He killed the man who had been our sergeant on that long-ago day. Galar has never made that mistake again. Now every Hebrew who falls into his hands meets death—and that is as it should be." The Philistine officer glanced at Kaptar and found him pale and drawn. "What is wrong, Egyptian?"

Quickly Kaptar shook his head. "Nothing. I am a little weary from our training."

The officer slapped him on the back. "Sleep well tonight, then, and tomorrow practice killing Hebrews. It is a skill that will stand you in good stead!"

The words seemed to come from far away, muffled by the blood pounding inside Kaptar's head. He managed to smile and conceal both his revulsion for the officer and the effect the man's idle reminiscences had had on him.

For Kaptar had been told by his mother, Princess Tania, that his father had been a smith in the land of the Hebrews—in a village called Shiloh, where the Philistines raped and murdered his first wife, Shelah. That was the day Urnan was taken into captivity and thence into the slavery that ultimately led to his escape from Kittem with Prince Kemose and his journey to Egypt.

So the captain in charge of the soldiers that day had been Galar himself, who had risen through the ranks to command the entire Philistine army. For a moment Kaptar could not believe that fate had brought him so close to the very man responsible for so much tragedy in his father's life. Yet, in a way, Galar was also responsible for Kaptar's very existence. Had Urnan not been forced into slavery by the Philistines, he would not have been sent to the isle of Kittem to work in the copper mines. He would never have met Kemose or journeyed to Egypt, where he met and married Tania and fathered Kaptar. Looking at it in that light, Kaptar thought bitterly, he owed his very life to Galar.

No matter. For what Galar had done to Urnan and Urnan's family on that day long in the past, he deserved to die.

And what more fitting way for him to die, Kaptar thought balefully, than for Kaptar himself to strike the fatal blow?

CHAPTER FOURTEEN

Sunu pulled back on the reins and brought his mount to an abrupt halt. The other scouts riding with him did the same. They peered down into the Vale of Elah, angered—but not particularly surprised—by what they saw.

Philistine chariots were moving through the pass in the hills and proceeding straight toward the Valley of Rephaim.

Sunu motioned his companions back into the shelter of the outcroppings that dotted the hillside overlooking the pass. Already one thought was uppermost in all their minds: King David, and everyone else in Jerusalem, had to be warned of the approach of the Philistine army.

For surely it was the entire Army of the Five Cities that was advancing through the hills, taking the same path it had used in the first invasion several months earlier. Had the Philistines learned nothing from the defeat they had suffered then? Sunu wondered.

As he peered around a large boulder and gazed back along the ranks of soldiers that stretched into the distance, he realized that the Philistines had indeed learned something: This force was larger, perhaps by three times, than the army David had routed in the Valley of the Giants.

Sunu and his patrol had been riding regularly through the hills west of Jerusalem for several weeks, and they had seen no sign of the enemy before today. Some of the men, Sunu suspected, had been lulled into complacency by the peace that seemed to have settled over the land. But all along Sunu had known better—known that the Philistines could not be trusted, known that sooner or later the bloodthirsty inhabitants of the coastal plain would return to the hills of their longtime enemies.

Now the Philistines were here, and it was imperative that David be informed of their presence as soon as possible.

Sunu drew back, well out of sight of the forces passing below. The ranks of chariots had gone by, and now row after row of Philistine infantrymen were marching through. He whispered to two of his men, "Circle around the Philistines and then ride for Jerusalem as fast as you can. You must not allow yourselves to be captured. David must be told about this!"

The scouts nodded. Despite Sunu's youth, his experience as a warrior made him a natural leader, and the men of the patrol looked to him for all decisions. The messengers turned their horses and moved up the hillside, disappearing over the top of the slope. Sunu and the other men waited, giving their comrades plenty of time to be well on their way before taking any action of their own. Sunu lifted his arm and pointed at a thin spiral of dust to the east, in the valley.

"Scouts for the Philistines," he said quietly. "They do as we would under the same circumstances. Doubtless they intend to probe Jerusalem's defenses."

"We should stop them," said one of the other men.

A thin smile curved Sunu's mouth. "The same thought came to me, my friend." He gestured for his companions to follow him. "Come. We will see if we can intercept them."

As the couriers had done, Sunu and the others made their way to the top of the hill behind the cover of the rocks. Once they were out of sight of the pass, they prodded their mounts to a gallop. The Philistines were making more than enough noise to drown out the pounding of the Israelites' horses.

Sunu leaned forward as he urged his mount on to greater speed. If he and his friends could prevent the Philistine scouts from crossing the Valley of Rephaim, they might be able to cripple the invasion before it got completely under way.

The dust trail that marked the path of the Philistines drew closer. Unfortunately, Sunu thought as he glanced behind him, the patrol's horses were kicking up quite a bit of dust, too. But that could not be helped. Stealth was no longer possible; now it was a race to intersect the path of the enemy scouts.

Far in the distance to the east, Sunu saw a smaller tendril of dust rising into the air, marking the passage of the two messengers he had dispatched to Jerusalem.

"We must slow the vanguard of the Philistines," Sunu called to the other men. "They cannot be allowed to cross the valley unhindered!"

A short time later, the swift-moving cavalry that rode ahead of the main body of the Philistine army came into view. Sunu drew his sword from its sheath and, indicating the riders, dug his heels into his horse's flanks.

The Philistines wheeled around to meet this new threat. With shouts of rage and defiance on both sides, the two groups of riders came together. Iron clanged against iron as swords clashed. The Israelites were out-numbered, and their opponents were not only better armed but wore lightweight battle armor as well. But without armor and extra weapons, the Israelites were lighter on the backs of their mounts and were able to maneuver the animals more easily.

Sunu circled the first man he engaged in combat, and before the Philistine could turn, Sunu's sword flashed in the sun and cut a deep gash across the Philistine's shoulder. The man howled and dropped his sword. The next instant, Sunu's chopping blow nearly separated the Philistine's head from his shoulders.

An enraged cry from behind warned Sunu of new danger, and he twisted around in time to see a Philistine thrusting a lance at him. With a desperate flick of his sword Sunu deflected the lance, then whipped the blade in a backhand blow across the man's face. The Philistine bellowed in pain as he dropped the lance and clapped his hands to his suddenly bloody face. The next instant he fell silent forever as Sunu's sword cleaved his pointed helmet and shattered his skull. He toppled limply from his mount, dead before he struck the ground.

Chaos was raging all around Sunu, and the plain rang with the cacophony of battle. Then, suddenly, an eerie half-silence fell. Although he could still hear the harsh breathing of men and horses and the thin, mewling cries of mortally wounded men, the clanging of sword against sword had ceased abruptly. Not one of the Philistines was left standing. Those who were not already dead were leaking their life's blood on the ground where they lay.

But the Philistines were not the only ones who had paid a price. Three members of the Israelite patrol were sprawled on the ground, bloody, silent, and unmoving. All three were men whom Sunu had numbered among his friends, and a great cry of rage welled up his throat as he stared at their bodies. He raised his sword high over his head.

"Today we have struck a blow for Israel and the continued freedom of our people," he said to the other survivors, his voice shaking. "These scouts will bring back no useful information to the Philistine commanders. But their army yet advances toward Israel, and

David has not had time to prepare to meet it. We must do something to further slow their advance."

"We are yours to command, Sunu," declared one of the men.

"We must go to meet the Philistines ourselves," Sunu said grimly. "We will do what we can to occupy them while David makes ready for war. But to do so may mean our deaths."

His companions shouted as one that they were willing to spend their own lives in the cause of the land they loved. The sunlight glittered on first one bloodstained sword and then another as they were thrust into the air, symbols of the valiant ferocity with which Israel would meet any threat to its hard-won freedom.

Kaptar swayed easily back and forth in the chariot, paying only partial attention to what he was doing. It was no challenge to drive a chariot over smooth, level ground such as this plain. Guiding the team of horses over the more rugged path that led through the hill passes behind him had been much more difficult.

Kaptar was feeling increasingly frustrated. Ever since the Philistine army had left the coastal plain and entered the range of hills bordering Israel, he had been alert for an opportunity to slip away with Nestor, but none had presented itself. The Philistine officers were closely monitoring the mercenaries and former slaves, as if they feared just such a desertion as Kaptar planned.

The chariots were kept together in several ranks. Later, when the army finally confronted the Israelites, the charioteers would spread out so that they would not get in each other's way during the attack. That moment might be their best chance to get away and switch allegiances, thought Kaptar, but by waiting until then they ran the risk of being forced to fight the Israelites.

The plain gradually became more irregular. To a man's eye it still seemed flat, but through the body of the chariot Kaptar could feel subtle gradations as the vehicle rose and then descended on long, gentle slopes.

The terrain was still too level to conceal any dangers, however.

At least that was what Kaptar thought—just before the small troop of mounted Israelites suddenly materialized, seemingly out of the very ground itself.

The riders were among the chariots before anyone knew what was happening. They slashed with their swords at the horses and at the drivers and archers. Several of the mercenaries fell, and horses screamed in pain. One chariot, its driver slumped over, toppled as its team bolted. The archer was thrown clear of the wreckage, but one of the other chariots could not turn aside in time and ran over him. The man's scream was cut short as the heavy, iron-rimmed wheel crushed his throat.

"Charge them! Charge them!" shouted a Philistine officer. Kaptar had no choice but to whip his team to a gallop. He turned his head and said to Nestor, "These are the men we seek, but we cannot go to them now. Try not to slay any of them with your arrows." Kaptar did not worry about anyone else hearing what he was saying, for the air was filled with too much noise and confusion.

Nestor nodded his understanding and drew an arrow from the quiver strapped to the side of the chariot. He nocked it on the bowstring, lifted the bow, and let fly. The arrow whistled past the head of an Israelite, missing him by a handbreadth. Nestor was making it look as if he and Kaptar were indeed loyal to the Philistine cause.

The chariots broke through the ragged line of Israelite attackers with ease, but the damage was already done. Half a dozen mercenaries lay dead, one chariot was wrecked, and several horses had been crippled. Now the Israelites scattered, galloping in all directions. The Philistines had no hope of pursuing them.

Following the shouted orders of his commander, Kaptar pulled back on the reins and brought his horses to a halt. He turned to watch the fleeing Israelites, one of whom glanced back at the same instant. The young warrior had long black hair that blew wildly around his head, and he appeared to be laughing. Kaptar recognized the symptoms. The young Israelite was intoxicated with battle. Kaptar hated to think of those fierce, handsome features stilled in death, of eyes staring up sightlessly at a gray sky, but such was the fate that might await him.

Such was the fate that might await them all.

The chariots remained where they were, forcing the rest of the army to come to a halt behind them. General Galar was not traveling in the front ranks, of course; as the commander, he was farther back where he would be safer. But he came to the front now, the wheels of his chariot raising billowing clouds of dust as the vehicle came to a stop. "What in the name of all the gods happened here?" he bellowed at the officers who had led the advance.

"The Israelites attacked us," replied an officer. "They were hidden somewhere, and they came at us on horses."

"You allowed a few pigs of the hills on horses to stop my elite force of chariots?" Galar said incredulously.

"They struck quickly, and then they fled. There was no time—"

"There was time for some of our men to die," Galar said coldly. "Why did our scouts not warn us there were Israelites in the vicinity?"

"The scouts have not yet returned, General," explained the officer, sounding as if he would rather have had any other answer to Galar's question.

But Galar did not shout at him. Instead, he frowned in thought for a moment before a shrewd look stole over his face. "David must have patrols of his own out," he said, as much to himself as to anyone else, although Kaptar could hear him plainly. "Our scouts must have been attacked by the Israelites, perhaps even wiped out." Galar lifted his head, peering into the distance as if he could see all the way to Jerusalem. "Even now, riders are probably on their way to David with warnings of our arrival here. But no matter. Nothing will change." He turned to face his men and raised his voice. "All the Israelites will still die!"

The soldiers and mercenaries responded with lusty shouts of agreement. To avert suspicion, Kaptar and Nestor had no choice but to join in the wild cheering.

But if the fiery daring of the Israelites that Kaptar had witnessed today was any indication, Galar and the Philistines might have made a bad bargain. They might have purchased for themselves a great deal more trouble than they realized.

Urnan picked up the copper sheath and slid the sword from it. His eyes traveled approvingly along the smooth edge of the blade, and then he tested its keenness on the ball of his thumb. A faint smile touched his mouth. He had no use for false modesty; he had done a fine job when he forged this blade. The sword had stood him in good stead before, and it would again.

But this was the last time. He had already made that decision.

"Must you go?" asked Jerioth, her voice strained. "Surely David has enough men in his army without you."

"This is my land, and I must help defend it." Urnan did not look at Jerioth as he replied. He dared not, for fear his resolve might weaken. He went on, "My son is going to do battle against the Philistines, and my grandson is already out there somewhere in the Valley of Rephaim. Doubtless he and his patrol have already engaged the enemy. Otherwise he would have returned to Jerusalem with the messengers he sent to David."

"You cannot know that for certain."

Urnan slid the sword back into its sheath, then touched a hand lightly to his breast. "I feel it here."

"Do you feel as well the fact that you are an old man?" Jerioth asked bluntly. "You are not well, Urnan."

He experienced the familiar tightness in his chest that presaged another bout of coughing, felt as well the familiar burning and tearing in his belly. Ignoring the pain, he said, "I am well enough to slay Philistines."

"You are a stubborn old fool," Jerioth snapped. Then her expression softened, and she came closer and put her arms around him. "But I suppose that is one of the reasons I have always loved you."

Still holding the sword and sheath in his left hand, Urnan put his right arm around Jerioth's waist, drew her close, and brought his mouth down on hers in a long, intense kiss. As he reveled in her soft warmth, passion surged through his belly. He was old, yes, and even sick—he could admit that to himself—but he was not yet dead. He loved Jerioth and wished there was time to take her to their bed.

But the king—and the Philistines—awaited. The army would march forth from Jerusalem this very hour to meet this latest threat.

Elsewhere in the house, Eri was saying his farewells to his own wife, and Urnan was sure Baalan was every bit as concerned as Jerioth. Worrying when their men went off to war was part and parcel of a woman's life, he thought. There might come a time when that would no longer be necessary—he hoped so—but for now there was no avoiding it. The Philistines had to be turned back, or they would attack Jerusalem itself.

Jerioth stepped back as Mara came into the room, leading Leah by the hand. Mara's lovely features were tightly drawn today, because she knew that Sunu had not come back to Jerusalem with the messengers from his patrol unit. Of all the women in the house she had the most to worry about at this moment, because her husband's whereabouts were unknown. With Sunu's fate a mystery—and her belly swollen with his child—Mara could have been forgiven had she chosen to weep and wail. Instead she was making a visible effort to be strong, and she even smiled as she said to Leah, "See, I told you Grandfather Urnan had not yet left."

Urnan put his sword on the table and held out his arms to the little girl. She ran to him, and he lifted her for a hug. As her arms went around his neck, she said solemnly, "Be careful when you fight the Philistines, Grandfather Urnan."

He managed to laugh. "I am always careful, little one, but especially when I fight Philistines. You do not have to worry about me."

"Yes, I do. I have seen things—"

A cold tremor traced a path down Urnan's back as the child stopped short. With all the strange powers she had manifested, never before had she foretold the future. Yet who was to say she did not possess that skill, too? Urnan would believe almost anything where Leah was concerned.

"You must watch behind you, as if you had eyes in the back of your head," Leah said solemnly.

"I would look very strange with eyes in the back of my head," Urnan said, trying to keep his tone light.

"Please remember, Grandfather Urnan." Leah stared at him with eyes much older than her years.

"I will," he promised quietly.

She clung to his neck. "I hope you never have to go away again."

Urnan repeated the pledge he had made earlier to himself. "This is the last time. After this, our king will have to fight his battles without me."

"Urnan . . ." said Jerioth, her voice a husky whisper. She laid a hand on his shoulder.

They stood like that for a moment before Urnan bent to put Leah down. He smiled at Mara and said, "I will find that grandson of mine and tell him to hurry home to his wife. I will tell him that soon he will have a fine child of his own. A great-grandson for me."

Mara rested a hand lightly on her belly. "I pray that it is so."

"It will be," Urnan assured her.

Eri came into the room, followed by Baalan. "Are you ready to go, Father?" he asked.

Urnan picked up his sword. "I am ready," he lied.

Although he knew he had to, he would never be truly ready to leave his family, for it was the most important thing in the world to him. Political allegiances

might change over the years, but the family was the bed-
rock. Urnan prayed to the God of the Hebrews—his
God, now—that this was the last time they would ever
be parted.

Joab stared across the valley at the Philistine army.
"They are too many," he muttered. The statement was
perhaps unexpected, coming from so fierce a warrior,
but the odds against the Israelites were such that no one
in the small group of men clustered around King David
seemed surprised.

David looked at Ittai, the leader of the mercenaries, who had originally come from Philistia. "Your
General Galar has put together quite a formidable
force."

Ittai's mouth twisted in a grimace. "He has not
been my general for a long time. We worship different
gods now."

Eri, who stood nearby, knew what Ittai meant: The
mercenary worshiped at the idol of gold coins now. But
the Israelites were not about to complain, for Ittai and
his men were good fighters and loyal to their employers.

The Philistines were well advanced into the Valley
of Rephaim. David and his men were camped on the
same heights as during the Philistines' first invasion.
The confrontation was developing exactly as it had before, with one important exception: The Philistine army
was more than three times as large this time.

"Has there been any sign of our scouts?" David
asked Joab.

"None," he replied. "The messengers who brought
the word to Jerusalem believe that Sunu and the others
planned to attack the Philistine column and try to slow
it down. If they actually attempted such a thing . . ."
Joab shook his head. "It is doubtful they could have
survived for long."

Eri heard the words, but he refused to believe
them. He would not accept that Sunu was dead until he
saw the body himself. Yet he knew that Joab spoke the
truth; it *was* doubtful that Sunu and the other scouts

could have engaged the Philistines in battle and lived to tell of it.

"I say we pull back to Jerusalem and allow the Philistines to lay siege to the city," Joab suggested. "I do not like it, but we must be practical. If we meet them head on, we will be crushed, and the city will be defenseless."

David gazed out at the sea of Philistine soldiers filling the valley below. "You may be right. But I do not wish to retreat before the Philistines. That would only embolden them, and they might try to fall on us before we return to the city. For now, they seem to have stopped to see what we are going to do."

"And what *are* we going to do?" Joab pressed, peering intently at the king.

David called for the two priests, Abiathar and Zadok. "We three will remain here," he decided. "I wish to see if God will speak to me and tell me what course to follow."

No one could argue with that decision. As the men turned to go back to their tents, Eri suddenly said to David, "Look there, my lord."

David looked out over the plain once more. Three men were walking toward the hillside. They came slowly, because one of them was limping and the other two were helping him. As the three drew closer, Eri's heart leaped. He recognized the tall, broad-shouldered form of one of the men.

"Sunu," Eri breathed.

Indeed, the three men were Sunu and two of his companions from the mounted patrol—mounted no longer, however, because the horses had all been killed in their skirmishes with the Philistines.

Sunu told the entire story later, when night had fallen, as he and his exhausted comrades sat by the fire and eagerly sipped broth from wooden bowls. "We struck all along their column, attacking quickly and then pulling back, again and again. In this way we hoped to slow their advance and gather information about their strength and numbers at the same time."

"You did slow them down," David told the three, pride in his voice. "You gave us the opportunity to move into position to oppose them. What did you learn of their strength?"

"They are . . . formidable," Sunu replied, unknowingly using the same word to describe the Philistine army that David had employed earlier. "I could not count the number of men in their ranks. A thousand, two thousand?" He shook his head. "I know not. But they have many chariots, and archers, and lancers, and men with slings. We lost men each time we attacked, and horses as well. Then, the last time we slipped away, we saw the army of Israel here on the hill and knew it was time to join you, my lord."

David put a hand on Sunu's shoulder. "God will honor your bravery, my friend."

"Would that we could have killed more of them."

Joab said, "You would have been occupied for many seasons before you killed enough to make our force equal to theirs."

Eri leaned forward and asked his son, "How is it you were able to get away when you struck them in the rear of their column?"

Sunu smiled grimly. "We took them by surprise, and by the time they realized what was happening, we were gone and there was nothing for them to do but count their dead."

David looked thoughtful. "A sound strategy," he mused. "I shall have to think on it myself."

The other men exchanged meaningful glances. No one was more brilliant than David when it came to military tactics. If there was a way to turn the overwhelming power of the Philistine army to the advantage of the Israelites, David would devise it.

For tonight, though, Eri was glad simply to have his son back—bruised, footsore, tired, covered with minor wounds, but alive.

David picked his way carefully over the rocky ground into a small grove of trees, Abiathar following behind. They had left the camp so that David could pray without distraction, their destination a steep hillside overlooking both the valley where the Philistines waited and the lower hill on which the Israelites were encamped.

In the fading light of dusk David looked out over the plain. The brightly glowing dots of the Philistines' fires were too numerous to count, and the Israelite camp seemed almost dark in comparison.

Abiathar came up beside him, breathing heavily. "I am no soldier," he said after catching his breath, "but I would know what you are thinking, my king."

"What young Sunu said tonight is the key," David replied gravely. "We must take the Philistines from the rear. Yet how can we do that without giving them warning?" He sank to his knees beside a large rock and bent his head. "Oh, Lord, help me!" he cried out. "Show me the way!"

Abiathar stood back respectfully as David waited for a sign.

Suddenly David seemed to hear a voice bidding him to raise his head. He did, then peered again across the valley. The moon was rising behind him, and as its silvery rays washed over the plain, his gaze fell on a line of darkness that ran along one edge. His heart leaped when he realized what he was looking at: a long, narrow stand of olive trees known as the Grove of Weeping. David did not know why it had been called that, but the name seemed particularly inappropriate at the moment, for the grove had given him a reason to celebrate. The olive trees grew so close together that they formed a nearly impenetrable screen behind which men could move—many men—and not be seen. If a band of men were to follow the grove, they could get behind the Philistines and fall on them from the rear, exactly as David had visualized. But timing was crucial; the attack had to begin at exactly the right moment.

"The wind in the trees," David murmured. He looked up, startled, then smiled broadly. Although he had no idea where the words had come from, he knew what they meant. When the morning breeze sprang up just before dawn and rustled the tops of the olive trees, that would be the time to attack. He was sure of it—as he was sure now how the idea had come to him: The Lord had put it there. David had been given the sign for which he had prayed, the sign that would lead him in his quest to defeat the Philistines for all time.

CHAPTER
FIFTEEN

Some said the most difficult part of being a soldier was waiting for a battle to begin, but Urnan no longer believed that. He savored every moment that no one was trying to kill him and he was not being forced to kill someone else. But he understood Eri's and Sunu's impatience during the next day and the night that followed.

"The time for killing will come soon enough," he said to his son and his grandson as the three warmed themselves by a fire that evening. "And doubtless there will be enough blood spilled to water the grass in the valley for a long time."

"As long as it is Philistine blood, that is all right," Sunu grunted.

But it would not be only Philistine blood, thought Urnan. Many Israelites would die, too.

As one of David's most trusted advisers, Eri was privy to the plan of attack, and he had shared it with

Urnan and Sunu. Even as they spoke, part of the army,
under the command of Ittai, was moving quietly along
the edge of the valley, concealed from the Philistines by
the dense grove of olive trees. They would be in position
before dawn. The remainder of the force, under David
and Joab, would move down the hill while the sky was
still dark, then launch an attack on the Philistines' front
line but then call a retreat as soon as possible. With this
maneuver they would draw the entire Philistine army
into the valley so that the forces under Ittai could strike
from behind when the dawn breezes sprang up. The
Israelites would still be outnumbered, but with the ele-
ment of surprise on their side they would at least have a
chance against the superior numbers of the Philistines.

Urnan thought it was a good plan. He could feel in
his bones that it might work. But he felt as well a
strange dread, as if this day might bring personal tragedy with it. He looked at his son and his grandson, their
faces strong and handsome in the glow of the fire.
Would Eri and Sunu survive the battle? Urnan could
not say, of course; no man could. According to the
Hebrews, their God was aware of every sparrow that fell
from the air. Was He aware, as well, of every man who
fell defending the homeland of His chosen people?

A part of Urnan wished he could foretell the future
precisely rather than suffer this nameless foreboding.
And yet, in its own way, that would be an even greater
curse, he thought. To know the future and yet be helpless to prevent its tragedies would be the greatest burden of all.

Better to wait, to breathe deeply of the night air, to
embrace life and all it held. Death would come soon
enough on its own.

As did the morning, inexorably. In the predawn
darkness Urnan, Eri, and Sunu moved together down
the hillside with the rest of the army.

"We will fight side by side," Eri said.

"Side by side," Sunu repeated.

Urnan only nodded. He knew how difficult it would
be to keep that pledge. In the chaos of battle there was

no way to know where a man might be forced to go, and he could not always stay close to his companions. But for the time being they were together, three generations of the Children of the Lion, and Urnan took comfort in their camaraderie.

The sweep of gray in the eastern sky took on a reddish tinge. In less than an hour the sun would rise. When it climbed above the horizon, the battle would be well under way.

Following the low-voiced orders passed back to them by their officers, Urnan, Eri, and Sunu came to a halt with the rest of the company. Although Eri was one of David's inner circle, in the battlefield he was no more than a common soldier of Israel, like his father and his son. That was the way he wanted it, and no one had denied him that right. The three men stood quietly, each gripping a sword that he himself had forged, and waited for the order to advance once more.

It was not long in coming. A great shout went up from the men in the front ranks as they charged toward the Philistine camp. A moment later the momentum engulfed the Children of the Lion, and they, too, ran forward, bellowing war cries.

The Philistines no doubt had sentries posted, but with or without guards they would have known the Israelites were coming. The plain echoed with their raucous shouting.

The sky was still too dark to see clearly, but Urnan had no trouble distinguishing the familiar pointed shape of a Philistine helmet on the figure that suddenly loomed in front of him. He heard a sword whistling through the air and dropped into a crouch, letting the deadly blade swing harmlessly over his head. With a quick lunge he buried his own sword in the man's midsection, below the chest armor, then yanked the blade free as the Philistine cried out and fell.

To either side of him, Sunu and Eri were similarly engaged. Urnan had no time to spare them more than a glance before another Philistine appeared to take the place of the one he had just killed. Urnan desperately parried a blow and thrust forward. What felt like a finger of flame raked his ribs, and he knew his opponent had cut a long gash in his flesh. But he ignored the pain and, summoning up the strength he had developed over years of working the iron forges, overpowered the Philistine's defense and slashed his throat with a swift sword stroke.

Even in the midst of battle, memories came flooding back of that horrible day, many years in the past, when he had returned to his shop in Shiloh and found his son a prisoner and his wife being raped by the members of a Philistine patrol. Urnan's incompetence with weapons that day had led to Shelah's death and his and Eri's enslavement—at least in his own mind. Since then he had vowed to learn how to do more with swords than simply forge them, and he had become proficient, if not expert, in their use.

He recalled, too, the face of the Philistine captain in charge of that patrol. *Galar.* For years Urnan had yearned to take his revenge on the man but had never had the chance, although he had managed to kill Galar's sergeant. But a capricious fate had spared Galar himself.

Galar was a general now, and Urnan knew he commanded this army. If there was a God in heaven, Galar would meet his death this day, in this battle.

Urnan pushed aside those thoughts now and returned to the business of defending himself. The air was full of the clashing of swords and the shrill screams of dying men. Urnan realized suddenly that he could no longer see Eri and Sunu. As he had feared, they had become separated in the heat of battle. The cold fist of foreboding gripped him again. What if both of them had already gone down under Philistine swords and were dying at this very moment? Urnan fought with renewed vigor as he searched for his son and his grandson.

Among the olive trees of the Grove of Weeping, Ittai and the mercenaries waited impatiently, listening to the sounds of battle. Every man itched to be in the midst of the fighting, but still they waited for the signal. The eastern sky grew lighter and lighter. Would the breeze never come?

Ittai felt something on his face, a touch as gentle as the caress of a woman, and looked up. The treetops were swaying gently, and he could hear the soft rushing of the wind.

. Lifting his sword over his head, he cried out to his men and charged forward. They followed him, sweeping out of the trees and smashing into the milling confusion that was the rear ranks of the Philistine army.

Kaptar and Nestor witnessed Ittai's attack as their chariot skirted the battlefield. They had been doing their best to avoid the fighting, as neither man had any desire to kill even one Israelite. So far they had been successful.

Kaptar was filled with admiration for the tactics of the Hebrews. The Philistines were taken completely by surprise, and within moments the rout was on. Although the Philistines vastly outnumbered their opponents, they were confused and even frightened by the unexpected attack from behind.

Kaptar kept the reins of the team drawn taut. The horses, even bred and trained for battle as they were, were frightened by the smell of blood and the screams of dying men. Kaptar knew he could not let them bolt. He had to keep them under control.

Twisting his head around, he shouted to Nestor, "We must find a way out of the fighting!" If they could reach the Israelite army, they could explain what they were doing and might be safe, assuming the Israelites did not kill them first. That was a risk they would have to take.

Nestor tapped Kaptar's shoulder with a big hand and pointed. Kaptar saw the opening in the melee and swung the chariot toward it. Beyond the battlefield lay their freedom, so close Kaptar could almost taste it.

*   *   *

The sun was up now, Urnan realized, a giant ball of
fire rising slowly above the horizon. That meant the attack from the rear had already been launched. He could
see now that some of the Philistines seemed to be retreating and that the Israelites were pressing their advantage. A fierce exultation filled Urnan's breast. He
and his adopted countrymen were going to win. Now, if
he could only find Eri and Sunu and be sure they were
all right . . .

The pounding of hooves behind him warned him
that something was wrong. He twisted his head to look
over his shoulder and saw a Philistine chariot bearing
down on him. He had no time to do anything but fling
himself to the side and hope he landed out of the way of
the careening vehicle.

Urnan slammed hard into the ground and rolled
over. The horses seemed to be right on top of him, but
their hooves missed his head. One of the wheels rumbled close by his ear but missed as well. Then the chariot had passed.

It did not go much farther, however. The wheels
struck a rock, and suddenly the chariot was tumbling
over, throwing out its lone occupant. The Philistine
crashed to the ground and rolled over several times before coming to a stop. Urnan pushed himself to his
knees as he watched the officer lift his head and shake it
groggily.

Galar!

Urnan would have known him anywhere. Those
lean, cruel features were burned into his memory. Galar
had aged, but he was still the same man who had stood
by, watching and smiling, as Urnan's beloved Shelah
was raped and murdered.

Urnan came to his feet, clutching his sword in both
hands. "Galar!" he screamed. Then he ran toward the
Philistine general, sword upraised.

Galar rolled frantically to the side as Urnan's blade
swept down. The blow missed, and the sword struck the
ground instead. The impact shivered up Urnan's arms,
but he managed to hang on to the weapon.

Galar, seemingly uninjured by his fall, came to his feet in one lithe motion and whipped out his own sword. "The smith!" he exclaimed in amazement. "The smith of Shiloh!"

"God has delivered you into my hands," Urnan growled.

Galar lifted his sword. "Now I shall do what I should have done years ago. You can finally follow your pig wife into death, smith."

An eerie silence had descended around the two men, for most of the fighting had moved away from this part of the plain. That was as it should be, Urnan thought. He and Galar would settle this old grievance themselves.

He lunged forward, striking with the sword. Galar parried the blow and shot out a thrust of his own. Urnan barely avoided the blade. He stepped back to give himself some room, then attacked again.

For long moments the fight went back and forth, iron ringing against iron. Neither man was an expert swordsman, so they were evenly matched. Galar drew first blood when sweat dripped from Urnan's brow into his eyes and blinded him for a crucial instant. Galar's blade cut a shallow furrow in the outside of his right thigh. Urnan stumbled back, blocked a thrust aimed at his groin, and inflicted a gash on Galar's left arm.

Urnan felt his arms growing weary, his wounded leg throbbing and threatening to collapse under him. Jerioth had been right: He *was* too old for this. But nothing was going to stop him from finally taking his vengeance on Galar, not even death itself. He would greet God happily, if only he knew that Galar had preceded him. Of course, Galar would never reach the heaven of the Hebrews' God.

Suddenly Urnan stepped on a stone, turning his left foot under and throwing all his weight on his wounded leg. He cried out as pain shot through him; he felt himself falling but could do nothing to prevent it. A look of savage triumph flashed across Galar's face as he lunged, sword uplifted for the killing stroke.

Urnan's foot found itself between Galar's ankles, and Galar's expression turned to one of panic as he, too, lost his balance and fell. Urnan twisted his sword, trying to bring the tip around so that Galar would impale himself on it, but he failed to do it in time. Still, the edge of the blade dug deeply into Galar's stomach as he fell atop Urnan. For an instant the faces of the two old foes were mere inches apart, and the hatred that blazed between them was an almost tangible force. Then, with a heave and an arching of his back, Urnan threw Galar off.

Galar fell to the side, bleeding heavily from the wound in his stomach—which was not, Urnan knew, fatal or even incapacitating. Urnan had to press his advantage, so he struck quickly, aiming his sword at Galar's arm rather than his body. The blade sliced through flesh and grated on bone, and the Philistine's sword fell from suddenly nerveless fingers.

Breathing heavily, his pulse hammering madly in his head, Urnan lurched to his feet and stood over his enemy. His hands were trembling, but they would be steady enough to guide his blade as he struck the final blow. "Prepare to die!" he growled at Galar.

The general's wide-eyed, horrified gaze jumped to something beyond Urnan. "Help me!" he screamed. "Help me!"

Urnan did not want to fall for the trick, but he could not keep from glancing back.

To his horror he saw that another Philistine chariot was bearing down on them.

Kaptar heard the cry for help and could hardly believe his eyes when he realized where it had come from. General Galar was lying wounded and helpless at the feet of an Israelite who was obviously about to deliver the killing thrust. Kaptar did not want Galar to die without knowing who he really was, so he swung the chariot in that direction.

The old Israelite lifted his sword in defiance, unwilling to step aside. Kaptar had no wish to harm the man, so he hauled the chariot to a skidding stop. "Come with me!" he called to Nestor as he leaped from the vehicle. "It is time we settled our score with Galar!"

Kaptar drew his sword and advanced toward the Israelite. "I have no wish to fight you, old man!" he called. "Step aside, and let me have that dog of a Philistine!"

The Israelite's eyes suddenly widened as he stared at Kaptar with something like recognition. Kaptar was certain he had never seen the old man before, but as the Israelite lowered his sword, a name came from his lips that struck Kaptar like a bolt of lightning.

"Tania . . ."

It was impossible, yet unmistakable. Peering into the face of the young man who had leaped down from the Philistine chariot, Urnan saw the features of his dead wife, Princess Tania. This man was no Philistine, despite the chariot he drove. Was he—could he be—an Egyptian?

Urnan said, "Tania" and saw the man stop, confusion and incredulity flaring in his eyes. Could it be true? Still staring, Urnan jerked his torn, bloodstained tunic aside, revealing the birthmark on his hip, the print of the lion's paw.

The young man almost dropped his sword in shock. "Urnan!" he cried. He pulled up his own tunic, and there on his hip, as plain as the rising sun, was the match to Urnan's birthmark.

"My son," whispered Urnan.

Then they were in each other's arms, pounding each other on the back, crying tears of joy. The meeting that neither man had ever thought would take place had occurred in a most unlikely setting: the middle of a battlefield. But Urnan did not care. He was filled with joy. After all these years, to finally hold his other son in his arms, to see in the young man's features the face of his own lovely Tania . . .

It was then he remembered Leah's warning.

*   *   *

Kaptar was shaken to the core by a whirlwind of emotions. To find his father at last, and in this place—it was almost more than he could believe. Yet he knew the workings of destiny were often beyond the understanding of mere men. He embraced Urnan and did not know whether to laugh or cry . . . so he did both.

A flicker of motion caught his attention. He looked past Urnan's shoulder and saw to his surprise that the wounded Galar had somehow managed to get to his feet.

Not only that, but he had picked up a lance that had been dropped in battle.

And he was lunging straight at them, the sharp point of the lance poised to drive into Urnan's back.

"No!" Kaptar shouted. He had not found his father at last only to lose him. With a desperate surge of strength he shoved Urnan aside, out of the path of the lance.

The point of the weapon slammed into Kaptar's side.

The impact knocked him back a step. Pain flooded through him, and his vision blurred. But he managed to lift the sword he still held and drive it forward, feeling the blade slice deep into Galar's belly. Galar released his hold on the lance and stumbled back, shrieking in agony as he pawed at the sword buried in his stomach. Kaptar slumped to the ground, fighting for consciousness.

The Philistine's suffering was mercifully short. With a roar of rage Nestor released an arrow from his bow. The shaft thudded into Galar's chest with such force that the tip passed completely through his body and ripped out his back. He stood there, swaying slightly, eyes wide with horror and pain.

Urnan had regained his balance, and when he saw his son lying on the ground with the lance in his side, more rage than he had ever felt before exploded inside him. With a shout that might have shaken the walls of

Jerusalem, he planted his feet and swung the sword he had forged himself in one final, mighty blow.

Galar's head toppled from his shoulders and thudded to the ground, the eyes staring sightlessly now. His body, spouting blood from the severed neck, followed an instant later. Never again would he bring his evil to the people of Israel. Indeed, his life's blood was now watering the soil of their land.

Kaptar felt himself lifted in strong arms. Nestor said, "You will not die, my friend. Do you hear me? You will *not* die!"

Kaptar reached out toward Urnan, felt the older man's fingers clasp his tightly. "After . . . finding my father at last? No, I . . . I do not think so. This is a time . . . to live."

Then a great darkness closed around him and bore him away, as surely as if it had been the waters of the Nile.

"Father!" Eri shouted. He and Sunu were searching the battlefield for Urnan. They had been looking for him since the Philistines had begun their retreat to the hills. Eri suspected the soldiers would not stop running until they reached their coastal cities, and neither would they return to Israel, not after the crushing defeat they had suffered this day.

The battle might be won, but Eri and Sunu were both frantic with worry about Urnan. They had not seen him since early in the fighting. They stopped to check every Israelite body, dreading what they would find with each corpse they rolled over. So far they had not found him.

Sunu suddenly grasped Eri's arm and, with a touch of awe in his voice, said, "Look."

Limping toward them across the plain of death came Urnan of Shiloh, Urnan the smith, Urnan the friend of kings . . . and their father and grandfather. Eri felt tears sting his eyes. Urnan—old, bloody from his wounds, slowed by his infirmities—was unbent. Undefeated.

A great man.

But who were those with him? Urnan was followed by a huge, black-bearded man who carried another man in his arms with as little effort as if he were holding a babe. The second man was wounded; Eri saw a blood-stained cloth wrapped around his midsection. But he was alive and awake and evidently not too happy about being carried. The big, bearded man was clearly not going to put him down.

Eri and Sunu rushed forward to greet Urnan. "Father!" cried Eri as he embraced Urnan. Sunu threw his arms around both of them. "We thought you had been killed."

"Not today," Urnan said in a stronger voice than Eri had heard in many months. "Not the day when my family is finally reunited."

Eri raised his eyebrows in question.

Urnan turned to indicate the other two men. "The big one is Nestor, a good friend," he said. "And this is Kaptar, Eri. Your brother."

"Brother . . . ?" Eri repeated.

"Put me down, Nestor," Kaptar demanded, and this time the big man complied, although he kept an arm around Kaptar to hold him up. Kaptar held out his hand to Eri.

"Child of the Lion," he said.

"Child of the Lion," Eri repeated numbly, still overwhelmed. But he took his brother's hand anyway, then drew Kaptar into his embrace. Explanations could wait. Both men shouted in joy. Sunu joined in the hugging and backslapping with his father and uncle.

Urnan looked at Nestor. Although they were not related by blood, he sensed that the big man was a kindred spirit. "I know not why the Lord spared me," Urnan said quietly. "But I know now it was not my day to die."

"That is enough," said Nestor.

"Yes." Urnan nodded emphatically. "That is enough." He turned to his sons and his grandson. "Let us go home."

CHAPTER SIXTEEN

Nefernehi paced back and forth impatiently across the anteroom. She knew that Sheshonk awaited her in the chamber on the other side of the ornate doors. No doubt he wanted to slake his lusts with her body again; that was the only reason he ever summoned her. He would remove her thin robe and sandals as soon as she entered the room, then fall on her and quickly find release, as if he were some sort of animal. She shuddered.

Composing herself again, she reached down and rested a hand on her belly. It was still taut and flat, but it would not remain so for much longer.

She was with child.

It was difficult to assess how advanced the pregnancy was. Kaptar had been gone from Egypt for several weeks, and she thought it unlikely that he was the father. That could only mean it was Sheshonk's seed that had taken root inside her. When that terrible possibility first struck her, she had considered killing herself.

She could not bear the thought of carrying the child of anyone save Kaptar—and particularly not of his own brother—and a simple dram of poison would free her from that loathsome fate.

But after she had gotten over the initial shock, it had occurred to her that there was a chance—a small chance, to be sure—that the child *was* Kaptar's. And as long as she was unsure, she decided grimly, she could not do away with herself, for she might be killing Kaptar's child as well.

No, she would have to wait, would have to bring the child into the world. If it was a boy, and if Kaptar was the father, the baby would bear the mark of the lion's paw on his hip. There would be no doubt he was a Child of the Lion.

If the child was a girl, however, Nefernehi might never know her true parentage, but she supposed she could bear that. On the other hand, if the child *was* a boy and did *not* have the lion's paw print, then she would know for certain.

Another shudder shook her now at the thought that had haunted her dreams and robbed her of all rest and tranquility. She tried to force it out of her head now.

Behind her the door swung open. She turned, and one of Sheshonk's servants ushered her into the chamber and left her. Chin lifted, she faced Sheshonk.

He was seated in a wicker chair with a high, arching back, slumped down so far he was almost sitting on his spine. Through hooded eyes he studied her for a long moment. Finally he said, "You are as lovely as ever, Beautiful One."

Nefernehi said nothing. She no longer felt any need to respond to his compliments.

With a sigh Sheshonk pushed himself upright. He looked and sounded weary, and Nefernehi was suddenly struck by how much older he looked. He had aged in the past few weeks.

He stood up and held out his hand. "Come to me."

Without hesitation she crossed the room. There

was no point in dragging her feet now. He took her hand and pressed it to his lips in a kiss that was unusually gentle. "Nefernehi," he breathed. "Your beauty has pierced me to the core."

"I serve my pharaoh," she said quietly and noncommittally. If he expected her to whisper endearments now, he was mistaken; their relationship had progressed past the point of pretending. They both knew what he wanted from her, and they both knew he had the power to take it at will.

Power. That was what this was about. Love had nothing to do with it, and even lust had dimmed as a driving force.

He pulled her into his arms and kissed her, then stripped the robe from her body and began caressing her. Nefernehi responded as little as possible, since he no longer demanded that she simulate passion for him. When he pressed her down onto the bed and began to make love to her, however, she sensed a new urgency about him that made it difficult not to feel *something*. His movements were tender yet agitated; he was like a man who had been in the desert for days and had just been handed a skin full of water with the warning that he would receive no more, ever. The emotions warring within him were all too evident.

After he had spent himself in a series of trembling lunges, his head fell on her shoulder, and a sob escaped his lips. Now Nefernehi was struck by how *young* he truly was—little more than a child, in spite of his grownup appetites. Against her own better judgment she found herself putting her arms around him and caressing his back. Perhaps her maternal instincts were blossoming because of the child growing within her, she mused. If the baby was Sheshonk's, it would be the child of a child.

She wished fervently that Kaptar had never left Egypt.

Sheshonk sobbed for only a moment, then stiffened in her embrace, obviously embarrassed that he had given in to his childish impulse in her presence. He rolled off, stood up, and pulled on his garments, keeping his rigid back to her.

\-   Nefernehi remained where she was, nude, legs still parted. If he were to look at her, he would see her in the position to which he had forced her and be reminded of the cruel power he exerted over his brother's wife.

But Sheshonk would not look at her. Over his shoulder he said, "Get up and clothe yourself."

"If that is your wish, my lord," she murmured.

"It is," he snapped.

Was it possible he felt . . . guilty? Nefernehi would not have guessed that he was capable of that emotion. Accustomed as he was to having his every whim catered to, he had never developed a conscience, a sense of right and wrong or of boundaries that should not be crossed. At any rate that was what Nefernehi *had* believed—but judging from his behavior tonight, she might have misjudged him.

She got up from the bed and wrapped herself in the thin gown, then asked impassively, "How else may I serve you, my lord?" She hoped he would require nothing else of her tonight so she could return to her own quarters and rest.

At last he turned to face her, his features set in a stony mask. "I have made a decision," he announced. "You will return to your home in Waset."

Nefernehi's breath caught in her throat. Such a declaration was perhaps the last thing she would have expected from him. "What . . . what do you mean, my lord? Have I not pleased you?"

"Not pleased me?" he said, his voice trembling. "Indeed, you have pleased me, Beautiful One. You have pleased me too much. Your loveliness has blinded me to the fact that you are my brother's wife."

He *did* feel guilty! Nefernehi could barely credit her senses. This was a totally unexpected development. Yet, what did she really know of Sheshonk? She seldom saw him, save on the nights he summoned her to his bedchamber. She did not know what demons tormented him when he was alone.

Still, to be sent away like this . . . It struck her like the blow of a hammer. As much as she despised him, she had grown accustomed to her life here in On. She had no wish to return to Waset.

Besides, there were political considerations. "Are you certain that would be a good idea, my lord?" she asked. "You and my father, before his untimely death, arranged for me to marry Kaptar to strengthen the ties between Upper and Lower Egypt, but the relationship is still somewhat strained—"

"Do you think I do not know this?" he broke in. He looked away with a grimace, annoyed, she guessed, at the reminder that he was partially responsible for her marrying his brother in the first place.

"But if I go back to Waset now, there is no guarantee that the priests who rule there will ever allow me to return to On." *I might never see Kaptar again,* she added to herself. Even in the depths of her misery, when Sheshonk had rutted with her like an animal, she had clung to the hope that someday she would be reunited with her husband.

"I am aware of that, but I do not believe the priests would forbid you to return," Sheshonk said. "Regardless, it is a chance I must take. I can no longer have you here."

Nefernehi took a step toward him and lifted her hands, hating herself for being reduced to pleading. "You must not do this," she said. "My father is dead, and I have no other family in Waset. I would be alone."

Alone save for the child growing within me . . .

Sheshonk shook his head stubbornly. "I have made up my mind."

For a moment she considered telling him about the baby. He would have learned about the pregnancy soon enough, if she remained in On as she wished, and he would have assumed it was his. She realized suddenly that this turn of events, while perilous in some respects, would allow her to give birth and determine whether or not the child was Kaptar's while keeping Sheshonk completely ignorant of her condition. In her darkest moments she had fretted over the possibility that Sheshonk might have the baby killed if it turned out to be Kaptar's.

When she considered the situation in that light, the idea of returning to Waset was suddenly more appealing. Still, she did not want to appear too eager, nor did she like the idea of Sheshonk casting her aside so casually. Pharaoh or not, he owed her an explanation.

"Why are you doing this?" she asked.

He frowned at her. "You would force me to explain?" Then his expression softened, and he sighed heavily. "Very well. Although you have no right to question a decision of the Lord of the Two Lands, I will tell you."

"I wish to know."

With his hands clasped behind his back, Sheshonk began to pace. Nefernehi suspected he was avoiding looking directly at her. The very idea that the Lord of the Two Lands might be nervous about anything puzzled her, but she had learned that not even the most powerful people were immune to human failings.

"As I said, your beauty blinded me," Sheshonk began. "I have always loved Kaptar. I loved him long before the two of you were wed. He is my brother."

Nefernehi said nothing.

"I would never do anything to harm him," Sheshonk went on. "The threats I made to you were hollow ones. I was overwhelmed by . . . by lust when I spoke them." He turned toward her as if pulled by a force he could not resist. "I have never seen a woman as lovely as you, Nefernehi. I fell in love with you the first moment I laid eyes on you. Your beauty filled my mind and my heart and my soul and left no room for anything else. I could not think of Kaptar and the harm I would do him by taking you. I could not even think of your own feelings. All I knew was that I had to have you."

"Did . . . did you send Kaptar to the land of the Israelites just so I would be left alone with you?"

"I was jesting when I said that, but there was some truth in it," he admitted miserably. "Only some, though.

I do intend to expand our empire, and it is vital that I have reliable information about the situation in Canaan. I trust Kaptar more than anyone else to bring me that information. But . . . I knew that what I really wanted would be easier to obtain were Kaptar far, far away from On."

Nefernehi took a deep breath. "Had he been here when you sent for me, he would have killed you."

Sheshonk laughed humorlessly. "He would have *attempted* to kill me. And then my guards would have slain him, and I would have the guilt of my own brother's death on my head." He looked at her. "Instead I have the guilt of taking my brother's wife. It is difficult to say which one is worse."

Nefernehi knew the answer to that. As horrible as her experience with Sheshonk had been, evidently it was now over. She could put it behind her and never think of it again, and Kaptar would never have to know about it—assuming, of course, that the child was Kaptar's and not Sheshonk's.

If the pharaoh had impregnated her, everything would be different.

But the question of parentage could not be resolved for some time yet, perhaps not ever. Sheshonk was right; it was best for her to leave On and journey back to Waset.

"If you stay here," Sheshonk went on, "every time I see you I will be reminded of my crime against my brother. I can no longer bear that. That is why you must leave."

Nefernehi bowed her head in acquiescence. "As you wish, my lord," she murmured.

"Tonight I . . . I say farewell to you. You will gather your things and sail tomorrow on one of the royal barges up the Nile. You may take with you anything from the palace you wish, as a reminder of me."

"I wish nothing," Nefernehi said bluntly. She might already be taking something of Sheshonk's with her as a reminder of what had passed between them.

He nodded. "Very well. I will send for you as soon as Kaptar returns from the land of the Israelites."

"I pray that is soon."

Sheshonk turned away without saying anything else, and Nefernehi knew she had been dismissed. Her affair with the Lord of the Two Lands was over, and she could only wish that it had never begun. The time to dwell on what had happened was past, she told herself as she left the royal bedchamber. Now she must look only to the future, to the return of Kaptar, to the birth of her child. She placed her hand on her belly again.

The child was Kaptar's. It had to be.

CHAPTER SEVENTEEN

Urnan could not believe he had been so blessed. Against all odds he had his whole family around him. There was no doubt in his mind that it was God, the Hebrew God, who had answered his prayers; capricious fate alone could not have brought Urnan together with the son he had never seen.

The men had returned to Jerusalem with the victorious army of the Israelites. David had welcomed Kaptar and Nestor, offering to find quarters for them in the palace as honored guests.

"No, they will stay with me and my family," Urnan had insisted. "Kaptar is my son, and his place is with me. As his friend, Nestor is welcome as well."

"Of course," David agreed. He smiled and clasped wrists with both visitors. "Urnan has been my strong right arm for many years. If there is anything you wish, you have but to request it."

"Thank you," Kaptar murmured. "I would enjoy a

173

tour of your magnificent city, but on another day, when I have had a chance to rest. My injuries have weakened me."

"I understand," David had said. "Go now with Urnan to his house and rest, Kaptar. We will meet again, as you say, on another day."

The women of the household were pleased beyond measure to see their men returning from battle. Urnan, Eri, and Sunu were not unscathed, by any means, but none of them was badly wounded. Jerioth, Baalan, and Mara threw their arms around their husbands and greeted them warmly. Only then did they notice the two strangers.

"And who is this?" asked Jerioth, nodding toward Kaptar.

"This is my son," answered Urnan, his voice choking with emotion. "Show them, Kaptar."

Kaptar turned and pulled his tunic aside so that the mark of the lion's paw was visible. Jerioth gasped in surprise. "A Child of the Lion!" she exclaimed. "But where . . . how . . ."

"Kaptar's mother was Princess Tania of Egypt," Urnan explained. "I took her to wife when I visited that land after escaping from the slavery of the Philistines— something Kaptar and Nestor have also experienced."

"I remember the story," said Jerioth, still wide-eyed with wonder. "But how did he come to Jerusalem?" She turned to Kaptar, who still wore a bloodstained bandage around his midsection. "Are you badly hurt?"

Kaptar smiled. "Not so badly that I will not recover, especially when I am surrounded by my own family at last."

It was true; the wound in Kaptar's side that Galar's lance had made appeared to be a clean one. Nestor, who had some experience caring for similar wounds, had examined it and judged that it would heal rapidly. Abiathar had concurred.

The first evening after the return of the army, the entire family was gathered for its first meal together. As

Urnan looked around the table, he felt doubly blessed. His beloved wife was at his side, as were both his sons, his grandson, and his granddaughter. Baalan's placidly lovely face shone with joy as she sat next to Eri; Mara, her stomach gracefully rounded, virtually glowed as she clung to Sunu's strong arm.

Leah was bright and animated as she asked Kaptar and Nestor innumerable questions about their home-lands. Urnan listened in fascination to Nestor's tale of an island nation beyond the Great Sea. It seemed almost impossible that such a place could exist, so far away, yet he had to admit that things had happened in his life and the lives of his ancestors that were easily as strange and wondrous. In this world, who was to say what was possible and what was not?

"Will you ever go back to your home?" Leah asked Nestor when he had concluded his story.

The bearded man's massive shoulders rose and fell in a shrug. "I do not know that I can ever return there," he said. "But I would like to try."

"Take me with you when you go! I want to see it. I know what an island is, but I have never seen one."

Nestor laughed. "Perhaps, little one, perhaps."

Kaptar leaned forward and said, "I, too, would like to see your home someday, my friend. I would learn more about those who live there who bear the sign of the lion's paw."

Urnan spoke up. "They must be kindred of ours. Sometime in dim ages past, Nestor, some of them must have journeyed from your homeland to ancient Ur, where Belsunu, the founder of our line, was born."

"Perhaps." Nestor nodded sagely. "Perhaps some-day we will know."

Eri cleared his throat. "We are all here together. My brother Kaptar is recovering from his wounds, as are my father, my son, and I. Soon my son's wife will present me with a grandchild. We have much for which to be grateful, and we should all give thanks to God." He lifted his cup of wine. "And I say we should drink to the Children of the Lion."

"To the Children of the Lion," echoed the others.

Yes, thought Urnan as he sipped his wine, he was a lucky man indeed.

Several days later, Eri was summoned to the palace, where he found David stalking back and forth in great agitation.

"My friend!" exclaimed the king when Eri entered the room. "I have been thinking, and I wish your advice."

"I am here, my lord."

David put a hand on his shoulder and smiled. "Of course you are. Always you have been there for me when I needed you. No man could ask for a more faithful friend."

Discomfited somewhat by the praise, Eri said gruffly, "I am but a smith and a warrior."

David laughed. "You are so much more than that, Eri, whether you know it or not." He waved a hand, putting the matter aside. "But on to the thing that preys on my mind night and day since we returned to Jerusalem. I think God is leading me to find a symbol of some kind with which to celebrate our victories over our enemies."

"That sounds like a good thing," Eri said thoughtfully.

"There is no greater symbol to the people of Israel than the Ark of the Covenant."

Eri's eyes widened. The Ark, a heavy chest wrought of acacia wood, was said to contain the stone tablets Moses had brought down from the mountain with the laws of God inscribed on them. There was no holier relic in all Israel. More than once had it been the spoils of war.

Many years earlier, when the Philistines had possessed it, Eri and his friend Saul had convinced the priests of Baal that a curse on the Ark had been the cause of a particularly painful, embarrassing ailment that had afflicted them. The priests had been quick to accept that explanation rather than the truth, which was

that their own perverted practices had brought on their
extreme discomfort. For months, while Israel was still
under Philistine control, the Ark was sent from town to
town, but bad luck seemed to follow it. That bad luck
had been instigated primarily by Eri and Saul, who de-
lighted in secretly harassing the invaders who had occupied their land.

David's mention of the Ark brought back a flood of
bittersweet memories. Eri said, "Where is the Ark now?
Is it still in the village of Kiriath-jearim?"

"Yes, in the house of Abinadab, a righteous man,"
replied David. "I wish to bring it to Jerusalem and build
a temple for it here, where we can give it the honor it
deserves."

"And you would honor God at the same time."

"Yes," David said fervently. "Such is my wish."

"It is a worthy one." Eri knew instinctively that
David had hit upon a plan that would please not only
God but also the people of the city and the nation. The
Israelites would be happy to see the Ark of the Cove-
nant settled in a proper home—and what more proper
home than the new capital, the glorious City of David?

The king clapped him on the shoulder again. "I am
glad you approve. I must speak to Abiathar and Zadok,
and we will make plans for bringing the Ark to Jerusalem. But one thing I already know, my friend—I want
you and Urnan and Sunu to accompany me when I go to
Kiriath-jearim to get it."

Eri stared at the king. "Why, my lord? We are only
smiths, not priests."

"You are my friends," David replied solemnly.
"None have supported me more in my times of need
save the Lord God Himself. You deserve to walk alongside the Ark when it comes to Jerusalem."

"You . . . you honor me. I know my father and
my son will be honored as well."

"You will tell them for me?"

Eri nodded. "Of course."

David turned and walked to the window. "This will

be a good thing," he declared, gazing out at the city, "and the Lord will be pleased."

Eri could only agree. There was certainly no reason to believe otherwise.

The idea met with an enthusiastic response from the priests and the populace. The city buzzed with anticipation as David made ready to journey to Kiriath-jearim, which was only a two-hour walk from the city. Before leaving, David had his servants erect a huge, luxurious tent to serve as a tabernacle in which the Ark would rest until a temple had been built to house it permanently.

When the day arrived, Eri and Sunu came to the palace to join David's party. The king greeted them warmly, then asked, "Where is my old friend Urnan?"

"My father is not feeling well, I am sad to report," replied Eri. "He begs your forgiveness for not accompanying you today."

David looked concerned. "Urnan has no reason to beg my forgiveness for anything. No one has been a more faithful friend to me over the years, save perhaps you yourself, Eri. Is there anything I can do to help? Perhaps a visit from the royal physician?"

Eri shook his head. "What ails my father is the passage of years, and nothing can be done about that. None of us has the power to turn back time itself."

"This is true," David sighed. "What about your newfound brother, Kaptar?"

"He is still recovering from the wound he received at the hands of General Galar, and his friend Nestor will not leave his side."

"Very well." David gave a decisive nod. "You and Sunu shall represent the Children of the Lion today. No finer representatives could any family wish to have."

Eri and Sunu walked proudly behind David as the royal party set off for Kiriath-jearim amid much ceremony and celebration. The cheering citizens of Jerusalem lined the streets of the city to watch the departure.

Soon the group—which consisted of David, Eri,

Sunu, several priests, including Abiathar and Zadok, Joab, other army commanders, and more than a score of other good men from the city—left Jerusalem behind and walked in the open air and sunshine. It was a glorious day, and the warm breeze felt good on Eri's face. Ahead of him, horses pulled a newly constructed cart on which the Ark would be transported.

At midday the group arrived at the house of Abinadab, where they were treated to a feast prepared by Abinadab's wives before the Ark was brought out and loaded onto the cart. Only the priests, under the direction of Abiathar, were allowed to touch the Ark itself. When the party was ready to leave, one of Abinadab's sons, Ahio, climbed onto the seat of the cart and took up the reins. Another son, Uzzah, took a position beside the cart.

Abinadab bowed before the king. "Ahio and Uzzah have been charged with guarding the Ark while it resided in my house," he explained. "They do not wish to relinquish their duty until it has been placed safely in the tabernacle in Jerusalem."

David nodded. "So shall it be."

The rest of the group fell in around the cart and began the journey back to Jerusalem. David walked proudly in front of the vehicle, and Eri and Sunu took their places with Uzzah beside the cart.

Villagers from the settlements between Jerusalem and Kiriath-jearim stood along the road watching the procession, singing, dancing, and playing flutes and cymbals to celebrate the passage of the sacred Ark. Glancing at David, Eri saw that he was profoundly affected by the joyful outpouring of affection. David looked as if he wanted to join in the singing and dancing himself, though to do so, of course, would be unseemly for a monarch.

The procession had covered perhaps half the distance back to Jerusalem when it passed a threshing floor to which farmers brought their grain. A large stone jutted from the road surface. Ahio did not see it in time to avoid it, and one of the wheels struck the stone and rolled over it, causing the cart to lurch violently. The Ark slid toward the side of the vehicle.

Instinctively Eri put out a hand, intending to steady the Ark and keep it from falling. Before he could touch the holy relic, Uzzah, acting on a similar impulse, rested his hand against the side of the Ark for a moment.

But only for a moment. As if he'd been struck, Uzzah cried out and staggered back a step, clutching at his chest.

Eri hurried to his side, calling out, "David! My lord! Something is wrong!"

As the entire group came to an abrupt halt, Uzzah fell to his knees, features twisted, both hands pressed to his chest, then toppled over, sprawling facedown on the ground.

"Uzzah!" Ahio cried as he leaped down from the cart and rushed to his brother's side. He rolled Uzzah onto his back. It was obvious to everyone crowding around that Uzzah was dead, struck down by some terrifying, mysterious force. Ahio looked up at them, grief-stricken, and moaned, "Why? Why did my brother fall?"

A deep voice from somewhere in the crowd answered him. "He touched the Ark. He displeased the Lord by his audacity."

David straightened and turned around to face the onlookers. "Who said that?" he demanded.

The crowd parted, and a tall man with a gray beard and dark, intense eyes strode forward. "I did."

"And who are you?"

"My name is Nathan. I am a prophet of the Lord."

Eri was paying little attention to this exchange. He was upset and bewildered by the death of Uzzah, whom he had considered a good man, but he was even more shaken by the realization of how close he himself had come to touching the Ark.

The words of the gray-bearded man finally penetrated his consciousness, and he looked up angrily. "Do you mean to say that God struck down Uzzah because he tried to keep the Ark from falling off the cart?"

Nathan regarded him calmly. "This is what the Lord has told me."

Eri took a step toward the prophet. "That is wrong—"

David stopped Eri's advance with an outstretched hand and said quietly, "It is not for us to judge the workings of God's will, my friend."

Eri's anger did not subside, but he controlled himself and settled for glaring at Nathan. David turned back to the prophet and asked, "What would the Lord have us do? Is it possible He does not want the Ark returned to Jerusalem?"

Nathan considered the questions for a long moment, then replied, "There is near here the house of a Levite priest named Obed-edom. Let us leave the Ark there while we ponder and wait for God to provide an answer."

David agreed. It was a solemn group now that took the Ark to the house of Obed-edom, who agreed to take care of it for the time being. Uzzah's death had saddened everyone in the procession.

Eri was still outraged as he turned his steps toward Jerusalem with Sunu and the others in the party. He had long since accepted the God of the Hebrews as his own, but he could not help but question what had happened today. David might accept on blind faith the rightness of Uzzah's death, but Eri found he could not. He realized he might never find the answers he sought, but the questions would stay with him always.

Months passed, and other things occupied Eri's mind. Urnan's health continued to worsen even as Kaptar recovered from his wound. More than once Eri saw Leah sitting with her Egyptian uncle, happily chatting with him and Nestor about that distant land, and whenever Kaptar seemed to be in pain, Leah could ease it simply by placing her hands on his side over the injury. Leah had demonstrated strange powers in the past, and Eri was not pleased by these displays. He shared Jerioth's concern about the girl.

At the same time he wished Leah could soothe Urnan's suffering as easily as she did Kaptar's. It appeared that she could not, however. Urnan's coughing grew worse, and there were times when he looked so haggard and drawn that Eri knew he must be experiencing great pain, although he never complained.

It was not right, Eri raged to himself. Just as Uzzah's death had been unfair, so, too, was it wrong for a man who had endured so many tragedies in his life to suffer as Urnan was now suffering. What was the point? Eri asked himself. Why should anyone suffer through life—when all that awaited at the end was death? The question tormented him night and day, and only in hard work at his furnace could he escape it for a time.

One day Eri was summoned once more to David's palace. The king greeted him by saying excitedly, "The Lord has given me an answer!"

Eri wished he could make the same claim, but so far he had gained little insight into the things troubling him. He waited for David to continue.

"Carrying the Ark in a cart was not the proper way to transport it," David declared. "We angered God by not showing Him the proper respect. I have ordered that two sturdy staves be hewn to slide through the rings on either side of the Ark. That way it can be carried by hand, two men on each side, without anyone having to touch it. Thus will we bring the Ark to Jerusalem. Nathan agrees with me that this way will please God." David laid a hand on Eri's shoulder. "I would have you be one of the men to carry the Ark."

Eri surprised both himself and David by shaking his head. Never before had he refused to do anything David had asked of him. "I am sorry, my lord, but I cannot. I am still too troubled by the death of Uzzah and the illness of my father."

"You are certain?"

Eri nodded. "I am afraid so."

"Well, so be it, then. I would not force you to do this. We have been friends for far too long. I will respect your wishes, Eri."

"Thank you, my lord."

"I only hope that God is as understanding of your reluctance as I am, my friend."

The comment was well-meaning, Eri knew, but it angered him nonetheless. He no longer understood God. Why should he hope that God would understand him?

The Ark returned to Jerusalem as David had decreed. A raucous celebration swept through the city when the holy relic arrived, borne by four men. Once again David led the procession, and this time he yielded to the fervor that gripped the crowd. Wearing only the thin robe of a priest, he joined the wildly singing and dancing throngs that preceded the Ark on its journey to the tabernacle. Once the Ark had been carried into the huge tent, priests were assigned to watch over it, and David returned to the palace. His face was flushed, his eyes sparkled, and his dark hair, damp with sweat, curled into tight ringlets.

When he entered his quarters, he found Michal waiting for him. Disdainfully she looked him up and down, her mouth twisting in a sneer. In a mocking voice she said, "How glorious was the king of Israel today, who uncovered himself in the eyes of the handmaids of his servants."

David's face darkened with anger as he said, "I but sang the praises of the Lord."

"And pranced nearly naked in front of the crowd," she snapped peevishly. "I saw you, David. How has the king of Israel come to this? My father never would have done such a thing."

"No. What Saul did was split the nation in twain and try to kill me time and time again—me, who had been his most faithful follower." David turned away from her, furious that she had spoiled what should have been a joyous occasion. "Leave me," he said coldly. "Never again will I come to your bed. We are without issue, and so shall we remain."

For a moment Michal regarded his stiff back, her

own demeanor as chilly as his, before she turned and stalked out of the room.

The breach between the king and his first wife, long a festering sore, was now complete. Never would it be mended.

CHAPTER EIGHTEEN

Iron rang against iron, and sunlight flickered on the two blades as they danced around each other and then met with a resounding clash. The swords sprang apart, darted to the left and right, came together again with blinding speed as the two men sparred. Urnan leaned back against the wall of the house, grateful for the shade it cast, and watched Sunu and Nestor at play.

For play it was to the two warriors. A strong friendship had sprung up between them in the months that Kaptar and Nestor had lingered in Jerusalem, and nearly every afternoon they could be found in the small yard behind the house honing their swordsmanship. Nestor was the more experienced warrior, and already Sunu had learned a great deal from him.

Kaptar came out of the house and sat on the ground beside the stool on which Urnan rested. Glancing up at his father, he smiled and said, "It is almost like watching two kittens at play, is it not?"

"Two very large, strong, and dangerous kittens," agreed Urnan, returning the smile. He felt fairly good today, especially compared to the past few days; he had not been struck by coughing fits, and the pain in his belly had subsided to a level he could tolerate.

"I would never have survived my captivity by the Philistines had it not been for Nestor," Kaptar said fondly. "I am reminded of the stories my mother told me about you and my uncle Kemose."

Urnan nodded. "Kemose was a great man. I have never known his like. But I sense some of his strength in you, my son. Since I could not be with you when you were growing up—which I will always regret—I am glad Kemose was there to guide you on the proper path."

"He was devoted to Egypt. He dreamed of the Two Lands being reunited in fact as well as in name."

"You share his devotion to Egypt, do you not?" Urnan asked quietly.

"I do."

"This is your way of telling me that you must return to the land of your birth." Urnan's words were a statement, not a question.

Kaptar nodded. "I am fully recovered from my wound. Despite the joy I feel at being united with you and the rest of my family, Father, my homeland is calling me."

Urnan reached down and put a hand on Kaptar's shoulder, squeezing lightly. "And you must answer the call." He spoke quietly, but Kaptar could hear him over the clang of the blades and the grunts of the two warriors.

"I wish I could stay here with you—" Kaptar began.

"You made a promise to my friend Kemose and to your beloved mother," said Urnan. "You vowed to support your brother while he sat on the throne and to work to return Egypt to its former greatness. You must keep your pledge." He smiled. "And you have told me of the wife you left behind, this Beautiful One of the South. No man can blame you for wanting to go back to her. But who can say? Perhaps you will return here someday, and we can be together again."

Both of them knew how unlikely that was, for Urnan's days were drawing to a close. He would not live to see Kaptar return to Israel.

"I can stay for a short time yet," Kaptar said gruffly. "My brother can wait, and so can Nefernehi."

"Do not linger too long," Urnan advised. "One generation's day passes, and the next generation must have its time in the sun. This is your time, Kaptar. Do not waste it. The sun will set, no matter what we do, and rise again on a new day."

Kaptar nodded solemnly. "Thank you, Father," he said, his voice little more than a whisper.

Urnan leaned back against the wall again and smiled as he watched his grandson and Nestor whirling around each other tirelessly. They were young; they had no idea just how quickly the sun rose and fell each day. But they would learn, if they were lucky enough to live that long.

Oh, yes, thought Urnan, they would learn.

He awoke early the next morning and felt a hollowness inside him. Something had gone out of him, and Urnan feared he knew what it was. There was no pain, but still he knew. He felt light, almost empty.

Somehow he found the strength to move his legs. He pushed them out of the bed and let his feet fall to the floor, moving slowly and quietly so as not to disturb Jerioth, who slumbered beside him. When he stood, he felt for a moment as if he would float right up off the floor and keep rising forever. But the sensation of weight returned to his feet, and he shuffled across the room toward the door, struggling for each breath as he willed himself to keep moving.

It was not yet dawn when he stepped outside. Although he knew the early morning air was chilly, he did not feel it. He went to the stairs on the side of the house that led to the roof and, bracing one hand against the wall, began to climb them slowly and carefully.

"Grandfather Urnan?"

The voice came from behind him, tentative and worried. He looked back and saw Leah standing at the foot of the steps, frowning up at him. Urnan smiled and said, "Go back to bed, child. Go to sleep."

"No," she said. "I want to come with you."

"You do not even know where I am going."

Leah shook her head. "It doesn't matter. I want to go with you."

"You cannot. Please, Leah . . ."

She ignored him and came up the steps with the vigor of youth, slipping her smooth little hand into his gnarled, callused one. "I will go up to the roof with you. I want to watch the sun rise."

Urnan suddenly realized that was why he was climbing these steps, too. He squeezed her hand, drawing strength from her touch. Somehow it made him feel more real, more rooted in the world.

Stars shone faintly in the sky overhead when the two of them reached the roof, but a band of light in the eastern sky told them dawn was approaching. Urnan sat down with his back against the low parapet that ran around the edge of the roof and turned his eyes toward the east, toward the lightening sky. Leah settled down cross-legged beside him.

"You must use your powers wisely, my child," he told her, his voice stronger now. "There are many in this world who would fear you, who would harm you, if they knew the things you can do."

"I have no power . . . save that of love."

Urnan leaned over and kissed the girl's forehead. "We both know better. In ages past, the Children of the Lion suffered much because of their knowledge of iron. Though you do not know it yet, your knowledge is even greater . . . and your tragedies could be greater, too. But not if you are careful."

"I will be," Leah promised in a whisper.

"Good." Urnan looked up and watched the stars dim as the glow in the eastern sky grew brighter. "Go down to the others now, quickly. I would speak with them."

"Are you sure? I do not want to leave you."

"Please, Leah. There are things I must say to them."

She released his hand and stood up, then scurried to the steps, cast one more glance at him, and disappeared.

Eri came to him first, running up the steps and across the roof. He dropped to a crouch beside his father and caught hold of his hand. "Father . . . ?"

"It is all right," Urnan said, wishing he could explain to Eri just how right this was. His hour was over; the time had come to move on. But Eri could not see that. He was still too young. Urnan squeezed his hand and said firmly, "Remember everything I have taught you. There is much power in the work we do, and even though our skills at the forge make it easier for others to wage war, they accomplish many good things as well."

"I will remember," Eri whispered.

"Take care of the family. You are the patriarch now. Love them, guide them, care for them."

"This I will do, Father." Eri's voice shook with emotion.

Then he stepped aside for Kaptar, who gripped Urnan's hand tightly.

"Though we met late in the day," Urnan said to his second son, "you have given me great joy, Kaptar. You are a fine man. No father could ask for a better son."

Kaptar swallowed hard. "I wish—"

"There is no need," Urnan interrupted. "My wish has been granted. Once more have I seen the face of my beloved Tania, for every time I look at you, I see her. Return to her land, to your homeland, just as you planned. Make it a great land."

"I will do my best."

"Remember and never doubt that your father loved you, and loves you still."

Sunu stepped up next and threw his brawny arms around Urnan's shoulders. "You cannot leave us," he said in a choked voice. "There is still so much you have to teach me."

"I have taught you already to love your family and to honor the traditions of the Children of the Lion. This you must do."

Wordlessly Sunu nodded, unable to speak through the tears that ran down his face.

"And one more thing," Urnan continued. "Be not blinded by the blaze of glory you think you see in war. There is much more glory . . . in an honorable peace."

Urnan's voice was weakening now. The hollowness inside him was growing, and once more he felt as if he were going to float into the air, up and up and up. . . .

Baalan and Mara came to him then and hugged him, holding him there a few moments longer. Urnan knew he could depend on Baalan to be a good wife to Eri, as she had been for so many years. To Mara he said, "Be patient with my grandson. He has much to learn. But he is a good man, and he will be a good husband to you and a good father to your children."

Mara hugged Urnan again and whispered, "If Sunu is half the man his grandfather is, he will be great indeed."

Then Jerioth was beside him. She sat down, put her arms around him, and brushed her lips across his in a gentle kiss. "I know I was not your first love, nor even your greatest," she murmured, "but our love was real. It was the most honest thing I have ever known."

"Jerioth . . ." Urnan breathed. The hollowness had almost completely engulfed him now. There was little of him left. "You are my heart, my soul. From the moment I met you . . . you have always been so to me."

He was too weak now to hold his head up. He rested it on her shoulder, barely conscious of the tears that slid down her cheeks onto his face. Leah slipped to his other side and held his hand in both of hers, squeezing tightly.

We will be together again, Grandfather Urnan. This is not the end. This is only a beginning. . . .

He heard the words, although he knew she had not spoken them aloud. His gnarled old fingers linked with her young ones, and a great peace flooded through him. He felt no pain at all.

He lifted his eyes to the horizon and saw the sun rise. There! There it was, the light of a new day shining on him one more time, so bright, so bright. . . .

Urnan was laid to rest in a tomb on the side of the hill on which Jerusalem stood. Leading the mourners was King David himself, clad in sackcloth, his face smeared with ashes. Joab and other members of the army came to mourn, too, all carrying swords forged by Urnan the smith.

The body, wrapped in several layers of linen, was reverently carried through the narrow opening in the tomb by Eri, Kaptar, Sunu, and Nestor. By the light of a single torch they laid it on a slab carved out of the rock wall, Urnan's sword and one of his hammers close beside him. Jerioth came into the tomb then and placed an empty jar beside his head, so that he would have something in which to pour wine in the afterlife. She had cut off her hair in mourning, as had all the other women in the family, even Leah.

The little girl contrived somehow to be the last one in the tomb to say farewell to her beloved grandfather. When at last Urnan was alone in his final resting place, his sons and grandson closed up the entrance with large rocks, in front of which Nestor rolled a massive boulder.

After the burial, family and friends returned to Urnan's house for the funeral feast, the first time any of them had broken their fast since his death. It was a solemn yet curiously joyful occasion—for Urnan had lived fully and honorably, and though he himself might be gone, life would go on.

After all the visitors had departed, Kaptar and Eri strolled out on the roof. The sun had already set, but a reddish-gold glow suffused the western sky.

Kaptar looked wistfully at it as he said, "Our father

warned me how quickly the sun can set. I understand now what he meant."

"Life is fleeting," murmured Eri. "I have been much troubled of late by that very truth. Why are we here, Kaptar? Why do we suffer and struggle in life, only to be rewarded with death?"

"It is said there is a better world on the other side of the grave."

Eri nodded. "I have heard this. But I have never been told so by anyone who has returned from that world."

"Perhaps someday that will happen, my brother. Perhaps someday we will have proof . . . or at least something stronger on which to hang our faith."

For several moments the two men stood silently, watching the colors of sunset fade and the first stars appear in the heavens above.

"I must go back to Egypt," Kaptar said finally. "I promised my wife, and Urnan as well, that I would return."

"When will you go?" asked Eri.

"I will wait for a suitable time. It is not proper to travel so soon after the death of a loved one. But when the time comes, Nestor and I will leave."

Eri threw his arms around Kaptar in a rough embrace. "We will miss you, brother. Would that we could have grown up together. Will you ever come back for a visit?"

"If I can," Kaptar promised.

But even as he spoke the words, his heart was heavy. From his conversations with David and Joab and others, he knew a great deal now about Israel's political and military strengths and weaknesses and would have much to tell Sheshonk when he returned to Egypt. But Sheshonk might use that information to launch an invasion of Israel, to bring it once more under the control of the Two Lands.

Kaptar fervently hoped that would never happen. He had just pledged to his brother that he would return to Israel someday—but not as part of an invading army.

*   *   *

"Are you sure you must go?" asked Sunu. His hand rested on the hilt of the sword sheathed at his waist.

"I am pledged to the service of your uncle Kaptar," Nestor replied. "In my homeland my family always served those who bore the mark of the lion's paw. I can do no different."

With a whisper of metal against metal, Sunu's sword slid from its sheath. "Have at you, then!" he cried, lunging at Nestor and swinging the blade with almost blinding speed.

But the big man, meeting the challenge, drew his own sword and parried the blow. Grunting with effort, the two warriors traded thrust for thrust, feint for feint, their movements difficult to follow even for trained eyes.

Eri and Kaptar watched the exchange as they leaned against the rear wall of the house. With a smile Eri said, "My son will miss these times. Your friend has taught him much of the swordsman's art."

"I fear that Nestor will be sad to depart, too," said Kaptar. "This place has been more of a home to him than any since he left the island beyond the Great Sea. Just as I have found a new family, so, in a way, has Nestor."

"We would be happy to have him stay," Eri pointed out. "And you know that invitation extends to you as well, brother."

Kaptar shook his head. "I am a Child of the Lion, but I am also an Egyptian. I must return to my home and my other brother."

Several months had passed since the death of Urnan. During that time, Mara had given birth to a son, whom she and Sunu had named Jubal. Like every other male in the line, the baby bore the mark of the lion's paw on his left hip. He was healthy and growing rapidly, and as Sunu liked to point out, there was nothing wrong with his lungs. His squalling could fill the house when he was unhappy, but he had also begun to laugh when he was pleased.

In the interval Eri and Kaptar had grown closer, and now they felt as if they had known each other all their lives. More than once Eri had found Kaptar looking distracted and uneasy, but despite his urging Kaptar steadfastly refused to acknowledge that anything was amiss.

Now that the period of mourning had passed, Kaptar was ready to begin the long journey back to Egypt. He and Nestor would take their leave the following day, but tonight the women were planning a farewell feast.

"How will you travel?" Eri asked as he and Kaptar watched the two swordsmen.

"David has been kind enough to offer us two horses to ride and two donkeys to carry our supplies. He has also promised to send a small force of guards with us as far as the western boundary of the land of the Amalekites, in case we encounter any more Philistine slavers."

Eri snorted in contempt. "I doubt the Philistines have slavery on their minds these days. They are still recovering from the defeat of their army and the death of Galar. Still, I am glad David is sending guards with you."

Kaptar instinctively put his hand on his side, where Galar's lance had pierced his body. The wound had healed cleanly, leaving an impressive scar that was sometimes tender to the touch. "I am glad our father had the chance to see Galar die before his own days ran out," he said softly.

Eri nodded. "As am I. It was a vengeance long delayed. There were times when I feared justice would *never* find Galar."

"I once had a debt of vengeance of my own to pay," Kaptar mused, "but fate did not allow me to pay it." He offered no more details, and Eri did not press him. "I have always regretted the workings of destiny in that instance."

"Ah, but that is something over which none of us has any control." Eri put a hand on his brother's shoulder and gestured with his other hand at Sunu and Nestor. "It grows warm out here. Come, let us go inside and leave these two to their exercise."

Kaptar grinned. "A good idea, brother."

The feast that evening was a bittersweet affair. Leah settled herself on a cushion next to Nestor and peered up at the big man.

"I meant what I said," she told him, "about wanting to go to your homeland someday."

"I know you did, little one," he rumbled. "But it is very far away, and I cannot take you there. I do not know if I myself will ever be allowed to return."

Leah gazed solemnly at him. "You will return . . . in a way. And I will go, too. This much I can see, but no more."

Though the evening was warm, a tiny shudder went through Nestor, as if he were cold. But Leah seemed satisfied now, and instead of peppering him with more questions about his homeland, she merely smiled every time he looked at her. Nestor took a deep breath and wondered what exactly it was about this little girl—who was a fraction his size and hardly a warrior—that made him so nervous.

The party that left Jerusalem the next day numbered almost a score of men. Kaptar, Nestor, Eri, and Sunu were accompanied by more than a dozen guards provided by King David, who came to the eastern gate to bid farewell to the visitors.

"I pray the two of you have a safe journey," David said, clasping wrists with Kaptar and Nestor in turn. "You did the nation of Israel a great service when you killed General Galar."

"The Philistines were already defeated and retreating," Kaptar said modestly.

"Yes, but with Galar dead, it will take them a long time to rebuild their army—if indeed they are *ever* capable of rebuilding. Galar's death will keep Israel safe from the Philistines, at least for a while."

"It is my hope that Israel remains safe for a very long time," said Kaptar.

"Oh, there will be more wars," David declared with a wave of his hand. "We are a small land, surrounded by enemies. The Ammonites, the Moabites, the Edomites, the Assyrians—all are hostile to our empire. We shall have no choice but to fight them. Perhaps we may even take the war to them."

Kaptar tried not to show his concern. This was the first time he had heard David use the word "empire," and his speculation about expanding the war to the surrounding lands sounded uncomfortably like a plan of conquest. If Kaptar were to tell Sheshonk what David had in mind, that information might prompt the pharaoh to plan an invasion even earlier than he might otherwise do, before Israel had a chance to grow too strong.

Kaptar shook his head slightly. He would have a great deal to think about during his journey back to Egypt.

With waves and calls of farewell, the group departed.

For several days they rode in a southwesterly direction, then turned and headed west. This route brought them ultimately to the seacoast village of Raphia, through which Kaptar had passed so many months earlier. Little had changed since then, including the suspicions of the Amalekites.

The Israelites reined in their horses and dismounted on the outskirts of the village. They were under orders from David to avoid hostilities if at all possible.

"So this is where we part," Eri said to Kaptar, his voice choked. "From here you and Nestor can follow the coast back to the delta of the Nile."

"The Nile . . ." Kaptar murmured, lost for a moment in visions of the great river. But his anticipation of being home once more was tempered by his sadness at leaving behind Eri and Sunu, who were more than brother and nephew. They were good friends.

Sunu grinned at Nestor. "You can still come back to Jerusalem with us, Nestor. Joab would make you a commander in the army. There are still many battles to fight."

"They will have to be fought without me, although I shall miss them." Nestor drove a fist against Sunu's shoulder, staggering the younger man a little. "Do not forget the things I taught you."

"I shall not forget," vowed Sunu.

Eri and Kaptar embraced, and then Kaptar swung up onto his mount once more. With a wave he said, "The Children of the Lion were reunited once. We shall meet again, brother." Then he dug his heels into the flanks of his horse and sent it trotting toward the sea.

"We shall meet again," Eri called after him.

Nestor mounted up and rode alongside Kaptar. Neither of them looked back. But in a quiet voice Nestor asked, "Do you really think we shall come back here someday, my friend?"

Kaptar nodded. "I am certain of it."

"The little girl—Leah—said that I would return someday to my homeland, and that she would go with me. She said she had seen that much. She must have . . . visions."

"Eri told me that from time to time she does exhibit certain powers." Kaptar smiled. "Perhaps she is right. Perhaps she *can* see the future. But you and I cannot, Nestor. Like everyone else, we can only wait and see what the gods have in store for us."

CHAPTER NINETEEN

Several weeks later, two weary travelers rode into a small Egyptian fishing village on the Nile delta, leading a pair of donkeys behind them. Kaptar felt his heart leap, felt a fresh surge of strength and optimism at the knowledge that he had returned at last to the Black Land. He was home.

"Ah, it is good to be back!" he exclaimed to Nestor, then immediately regretted it. Nestor was still far from his own homeland.

When he tried to apologize, Nestor waved off the words. "There is no need to be sorry. Where you are, there will I be, too, and it shall be as home to me."

"You will certainly be made welcome here in Egypt," Kaptar assured him. "Come, we will find a boatman to take us up the Nile to On."

Securing passage proved to be more difficult than Kaptar had expected. He had no way of proving he was a prince, brother to the pharaoh. Had he found a boatman who knew him, Kaptar could simply have ordered the man to take them to On, but under the circumstances he had to barter for passage. The few supplies he and Nestor still had were insufficient for that purpose, and none of the boatmen wanted their horses or donkeys. Kaptar was about to admit defeat and decide that they would have to ride the horses all the way to On when Nestor, finally losing his patience, grabbed the boatman with whom they had been haggling.

"Are you saying that you doubt the word of my lord Kaptar?" he growled, one massive hand around the boatman's throat. One good shake would have snapped the man's spine.

"Release that man, Nestor," snapped Kaptar. "You cannot go around killing people just because they do not recognize me."

Nestor sighed heavily. "No, I suppose not." Then his expression brightened, and he went on, "But I could squeeze this dog's neck for several minutes so that he cannot breathe, and when I finally release him, he will be little more than a drooling idiot for the rest of his days."

Kaptar considered for a moment, then shrugged offhandedly. "It is true I merely told you to release him. I said nothing about *when.*"

The boatman managed to croak a few words past the iron grip of Nestor's fingers. "I . . . I will take you . . . to On."

"Truly? How good of you. I shall make certain Sheshonk hears of your generosity. Let go of him now, Nestor."

The man nearly fell to the dock when Nestor released him. He rubbed his sore neck and gulped down great drafts of air. Although Kaptar did not like treating a fellow Egyptian that way, he was anxious to return to the capital city. Besides, the man should not have been so greedy.

A man who traded in animals approached just then, and Kaptar quickly sold him the horses and donkeys and gave the boatman some of the money. The coins seemed to assuage somewhat the pain in the fellow's neck.

The boat cast off, and its crew rowed steadily through the sluggish waterways of the delta. When they reached the Nile itself, a thrill went down Kaptar's spine. There was nothing to compare to it in the land of the Israelites; the River Jordan was but a trickle to a man who had sailed up and down the mighty Egyptian river.

Cultivated fields stretched along both banks. Kaptar watched them gliding past and pointed out various landmarks to Nestor, who seemed impressed by the lushness of the fields. "If there were smoking mountains in the background, this would remind me of my homeland," Nestor commented.

"Smoking mountains?" Kaptar repeated. "I have heard of mountains like that. It is said that far upriver, past the great cataracts, past the very source of the Nile itself, there were such mountains in the past."

"In my land, the earth rumbles from time to time, and a man can feel it trembling beneath his feet. It is a sign that the gods who live inside the smoking mountains are unhappy."

"And well they should be, forced to live inside mountains like that." Kaptar was smiling, but he sobered quickly and changed the subject when Nestor appeared not to find humor in his comment.

In less than a day the fishing boat arrived in On. Kaptar's pulse quickened when he saw the capital city of Lower Egypt, sprawling on the riverbank. The city seemed not to have changed during his absence; it appeared as bustling and prosperous as ever. His gaze darted from building to building and finally settled on the royal palace.

Somewhere in there was his wife, the Beautiful One of the South. Kaptar could hardly bear the wait. He wanted to leap overboard, swim ashore, and run through the streets toward the palace shouting her name. He forced himself to remain patient. He knew that when he reached the palace, he could not go immediately to Nefernehi; he must first see Sheshonk and give him a preliminary report.

Then . . . then he could go to Nefernehi, and his reunion with her would be sweet indeed.

When they had docked, Kaptar said to the boatman, "If you will stay here, I will send a messenger from the palace with proper payment for your assistance."

"You truly are the brother of the pharaoh, aren't you?" the boatman said grudgingly.

"He told you he was," Nestor growled. " 'Twas your own fault you did not believe my lord Kaptar."

The boatman bowed humbly. "It was a pleasure to serve you, my lord. I will wait here at the docks until I have been given leave to depart for my village."

Kaptar and Nestor gathered their belongings and stepped from the boat to the stone pier. They walked along it to the shore, then strode through crowded streets toward the palace.

Nestor gazed in awe around him. "I have not seen such a city as this, nor so many people in one place since I left home."

"Yes, even Jerusalem is but a village compared to On," Kaptar said proudly.

Nestor stared at a herd of camels inside a rope corral and shook his head slowly. "I have never seen such beasts. What are they, and what are they good for?"

"They are camels, and better suited for desert travel than horses," Kaptar replied with a smile. "Much better, in fact, because of their strength and the fact that they can go much longer without water. Traders use them to carry goods all across this part of the world, from Libya to the Arabah."

"Do men ride them?"

"Oh, yes. One must be careful, though. They are rude creatures at times, and they like to bite and spit."

Nestor laughed heartily. "Give me a good horse— although I suppose brutes such as these have their uses."

The two men moved on toward the palace. A few

minutes later they reached the huge, ornate structure with its palm-studded courtyard. Guards stood at the entrance, holding spears almost as long as the men were tall.

One of the guards stared in shock as Kaptar and Nestor strode up. "My lord Kaptar?" he exclaimed.

Kaptar, vaguely recognizing the man, smiled. "That is right. I come seeking an audience with my brother, Pharaoh Sheshonk."

"It has been said that you were dead," said the guard, still staring. "There were rumors that you were killed while on a mission to a far land on behalf of our king."

"As you can see, I am very much alive." Kaptar suppressed his impatience. "This man is my friend and companion, and we must see Sheshonk as soon as possible, to let him know that I still live."

"Yes, of course." The two guards quickly swung open the gate, and Kaptar and Nestor were admitted to the courtyard.

One of Sheshonk's servants met them inside. Kaptar remembered that the man was a scribe, although he could not recall the fellow's name. "Take us to my brother," he commanded.

The scribe bobbed his head but was slow to obey. "My lord Sheshonk will see you shortly. I have already sent word to him of your arrival." He looked Nestor up and down. "Who is this foreigner? Can he be trusted in the presence of the pharaoh?"

"I would trust him with my life," snapped Kaptar. "I have done so on more than one occasion."

"I meant no insult, my lord," the scribe said quickly.

"Take us to my brother." Kaptar was tired of waiting. The journey from Israel had been a long and arduous one.

"That I, ah, cannot do at this moment," said the scribe. "But I am certain that Sheshonk will see you shortly."

Kaptar's impatience grew as he and Nestor were

forced to tarry in an anteroom. Food and drink were brought, but Kaptar had no appetite save for a reunion with his wife. Nestor, on the other hand, ate and drank copiously.

Although he knew it would be improper, Kaptar was considering delaying this meeting with Sheshonk and demanding to be taken immediately to Nefernehi's quarters. But the scribe finally reappeared then and said, "Sheshonk will see you now." He ushered them into the pharaoh's chamber.

The heavy odor of incense filled the air, causing Nestor to grimace in distaste. Kaptar did not care for it, either, but he was evidently more accustomed to such niceties of civilization than Nestor. Sheshonk was lounging on a pile of cushions, surrounded by several young women, all of them beautiful, all of them nude or nearly so. The pharaoh was taking his pleasure with his concubines.

He bounded to his feet, rushed forward, and flung his arms around his brother. "Kaptar! You have returned! I was beginning to despair of ever seeing you again."

"And there were times when I despaired of seeing you, or Egypt, again, my brother," Kaptar replied. Despite his irritation at being kept waiting while Sheshonk dallied with his concubines, he felt an undeniable warmth toward his young brother.

"And who is this?" Sheshonk asked, stepping back and looking at Nestor, running his gaze from head to foot over the big man as the scribe had done.

"My good friend Nestor," said Kaptar. "He saved my life while we were both in the slave pens of the Philistines and then accompanied me to the land of the Israelites."

Sheshonk looked sharply at him. "Slave pens? You were a captive of the Peleset?"

"For a time, before Nestor and I joined their army for an invasion of Israel."

"An invasion of Israel?" Sheshonk repeated. "I believe you have much to tell me, brother."

"Indeed I do, but first there is one thing you can tell me: How fares my beloved Nefernehi?"

A shadow seemed to pass over Sheshonk's face, leaving a worried frown behind it. "I have . . . news of Nefernehi," he said hesitantly.

A cold wind seemed to blow through Kaptar's soul. Forgetting for a moment his brother's royal station, he seized his shoulders and demanded, "What is it? What is wrong? She is not . . . is not dead, is she?" He knew that illness could strike suddenly in this tropical climate, sometimes killing with little or no warning.

Sheshonk shook his head. "No, of course not. The health of the Beautiful One of the South is fine . . . as far as I am aware."

"What do you mean by that? Is she not here in the palace?"

"She is not even in On, my brother," said Sheshonk. "She has returned to her homeland of Upper Egypt to dwell in the city of Waset."

Kaptar blinked rapidly as he struggled to comprehend what Sheshonk was telling him. "Returned to Upper Egypt?" he repeated after a moment. "But . . . but why?"

"She did not say," Sheshonk replied softly. "I fear that she thought you were dead. It seemed that she was also angry with you for undertaking the diplomatic mission for me. She said that if you ever did return, I was to tell you that she does not wish for you to follow her."

"And you allowed this? You are the pharaoh! You could have stopped her."

Sheshonk's eyes hardened. "Yes, I could have forbidden her departure," he admitted. "But I did not feel it was my place. It was because of you she left, brother, and I would not interfere with the relationship between you and your wife, despite my royal prerogatives." He glanced down at Kaptar's hands, which still tightly gripped his shoulders. "Now, I think you forget yourself."

A shudder went through Kaptar, and he dropped his hands from Sheshonk's shoulders. He closed his eyes and rubbed his temples, where a pounding ache had sprung up. "I . . . I cannot believe this," he said. "I must go to her."

"Despite her wishes?" said Sheshonk. "That would not heal the rift between you, Kaptar. Such a course would only widen it. What you must do is wait. Perhaps one day Nefernehi will come to her senses and return to you."

"Perhaps," muttered Kaptar. "Gods, I never dreamed how unhappy she was!"

"I am sorry, my friend," Nestor rumbled. "Would that I could advise you in this matter, but I fear I know little about affairs of the heart. I am schooled in war, not love."

Kaptar laughed humorlessly. "It appears that the same could be said of me."

Sheshonk took hold of Kaptar's arm. "Come. Do not think about this now. You have visited the land of the Israelites. Tell me about them, and the Peleset, and this business of slavery and war. It sounds like quite a tale."

"Yes," said Kaptar, distractedly. "Quite a tale."

He only wished it had had a happier ending.

CHAPTER
TWENTY

Sunu crouched below the crest of the hill, being careful not to make any noise with his sandals in the gravel underfoot. He and the other members of his patrol were lying in wait as an Edomite caravan passed on the other side of the slope. The Edomites' donkeys carried supplies bound for their army, which had fiercely resisted the advance of the Israelites for several months. Edom had proved a difficult challenge, more difficult than the other small nations surrounding Israel, which had fallen relatively easily to David's army.

Motioning to his men to hold themselves ready, Sunu listened intently to the faint noises drifting over the hill. He heard the steady clopping of the donkeys' hooves and the voices of the Edomites growing louder and judged that the caravan was almost directly on the other side of the hill.

There were times—not often, but frequently enough to worry him—when Sunu reflected on what his grandfather had told him that morning several years earlier. Urnan had warned him not to be blinded by the glory of war. Sunu wanted to honor his grandfather's wishes, but conflict was inevitable. If Israel had not gone to war against its enemies, it might have been destroyed by now. By slaying the enemies of Israel, Sunu was serving his nation, his king, and his God.

But of late he had been assailed by troubling doubts. He was a father—not only to Jubal, now a robust little boy, but also to a daughter, Rachel, who was still a toddler—and Mara was more and more outspoken in her desire that Sunu stay home and work in the smithy, where he and Eri still forged weapons for the army, rather than constantly ride off to use those weapons and risk his life on some distant battlefield. Sunu did not want to disappoint his wife; nor did he care for the possibility that he might be killed and not see his children into adulthood.

Sunu hated difficult decisions. They required too much thought, discussion, and compromise. He preferred simpler conflicts—man against man, sword against sword—in which his duty was clear and only one outcome was desirable: his survival.

Such a conflict faced him now. Sunu edged his head above the crest of the hill and saw that the Edomite caravan was in perfect position for the ambush. A dozen or so men were driving heavily loaded donkeys along the path. Sunu's patrol was outnumbered two to one, but he intended to cut down those odds now.

He picked up his bow and drew an arrow from the quiver strapped to his back. The other Israelites already had their arrows nocked. Sunu nodded curtly and said in a low voice, "Now!"

With a surge of powerful leg muscles, Sunu lunged upright, followed by the rest of his men. They could see the caravan now, and it took only a heartbeat to aim their arrows and release them. Whistling sounds filled the air as the shafts flew through the morning sunshine.

One of the Edomites gave a bubbling scream as an arrow caught him in the side of the neck and tore through his throat. Another man, struck in the side, curled up in a ball as he fell. All down the line, men staggered and fell under the ferocious and unexpected onslaught.

There was time for only one volley. As soon as Sunu had loosed his arrow, he dropped the bow, snatched his sword from its sheath, and ran down the slope toward the caravan. With the advantage of surprise on their side, Sunu and his men fell upon the hapless Edomites, slashing and thrusting with their swords. Sunu quickly cut down one of them before the man had even drawn his sword.

But his next opponent was not so easily dispatched. The Edomite attacked from behind, and Sunu ducked beneath the man's wildly swung sword just in time. He tried to thrust his blade into the Edomite's belly while the man was still off balance, but the Edomite recovered quickly and parried the blow. With a warrior's clarity Sunu realized he was facing a skilled swordsman—one more skilled, perhaps, than Sunu himself.

He had no idea how the other men of the patrol were faring; he was too busy defending himself from a relentless flurry of thrusts and lunges. Sword rang against sword as he parried desperately. The harsh clanging of metal blended with the braying of terrified donkeys, the grunts and yells of battling men, and the thin, keening cry of a wounded man that ended abruptly as death claimed him. It was a clamorous cacophony of sounds that might be heard in the very depths of Gehenna.

Outrage at being forced into a defensive posture suddenly filled Sunu. When he deflected a thrust and the blades slid against each other until the two swords locked hilts, he seized his opportunity. He was close enough to drive his left fist into the Edomite's belly. The blow doubled the man over.

Sunu twisted his sword savagely, and the maneuver jerked the Edomite's grip loose. The man frantically tried to hang on to his own weapon, but it slipped from his hand, and Sunu whipped his sword around in a backhand blow that caught the man on the side of the neck. Crimson blood spurted over Sunu's forearm. Soundlessly the man fell to the ground as his life pumped out onto the rocky soil of Edom.

Breathing heavily, Sunu straightened and looked around. The Edomites were all dead, and Sunu's five companions were still alive and on their feet, though two of them bore minor wounds. Sunu grinned wearily. "Well done, my friends. These supplies will not benefit our enemy now."

"Should we kill the donkeys?" one of the men asked.

"Only if you want to carry those packs to King David on your back," Sunu told him. "We will take them."

"The prophet Samuel once told Saul to slay everything that belonged to Israel's enemies, even the beasts of the field," another man pointed out.

"Samuel is long since dead, and I've no desire to sweat under a load such as these." Sunu's tone left no room for argument. "Fetch our horses. We will slip back through the Edomite lines and deliver these supplies to David."

As the men turned to follow his orders, one warned, "It will be dangerous."

Sunu's smile turned into the familiar reckless laugh of the young warrior who had penetrated the walls of Jerusalem, who had stolen through the mighty army of the Philistines to bring his king a drink of water from the well of Bethlehem. "Of course it will. Would it be worth doing otherwise?"

As he spoke, he tried not to think of what Urnan had told him on that sorrowful day far in the past.

The child would be a beauty, thought Jerioth as she and Leah brought water from the well to their house. Leah was still a girl, but she was fast approaching young womanhood. She had always carried herself with an air far more mature than her years, and she was displaying the same precociousness in her physical appearance. She looked three or four years older than she really was.

And that was just one more thing to worry about. Jerioth smiled wryly. By now she was all too accustomed to worrying about Leah, whose mysterious powers seemed to grow stronger and less predictable every year. Jerioth had learned to shield her own thoughts around the girl if she did not want her to know what she was thinking.

Although she could not explain those powers, she accepted them as real, as one of the many inexplicable mysteries of life. Had she herself not raised the spirits of the dead so that they could speak with the living, in years past when she was still known as the Witch of Endor? Those days had been fraught with peril. She could never be certain that an angry mob of villagers, frightened by her power, might not descend on her isolated hut with torches. The fact that that had never happened she considered a stroke of good fortune, nothing more; she had heard of one reputed necromancer who had been stoned to death by just such a mob. A similar fate could befall Leah if the people of Jerusalem knew the full extent of her eerie abilities.

Leah broke into her reverie. "You are frowning again, Grandmother. What is wrong?"

Jerioth glanced at the girl, noting that she had called her "Grandmother," as she had begun to of late, although they were not related by blood. She suspected that the bonding of their souls was as close or closer than that of flesh and blood, for she was the only one who had even an inkling of what Leah was experiencing.

She shook her head in response to the girl's question. "Nothing is wrong, little one. I was just thinking."

"Not so little anymore," Leah said proudly. "I have grown a great deal."

Jerioth looked at her, noting again the long, raven-black hair that cascaded down her back, the slender body with the beginnings of womanly curves at breast and hip, the large dark eyes that seemed not only to see things as they were but to see *through* them, too.

"Yes," Jerioth agreed affectionately. "You have grown."

Neither of them noticed the man who had come around the corner of a building toward them until it was too late to get out of his way. He was staggering slightly, and although it was early in the day, Jerioth suspected that he had been drinking wine all night in one of the taverns. He reeled toward Leah, who tried unsuccessfully to avoid him, and the two collided. The only damage was to the man's feet and sandals, which were soaked by the water that splashed out of the jug Leah was carrying.

"Here now!" the man slurred, his voice coarsened by drink. "Watch where you're going! You've spilled water on me!"

"I am sorry," Leah said quickly, even though the accident had not been her fault. "I will be more careful in the future."

"See that you are, girl." The man put his hands on his hips and regarded her imperiously, running his eyes over her body. Jerioth noted with displeasure that his gaze lingered on the small breasts swelling under the thin cloth of Leah's robe. As Leah started to go around him, the man reached out and grabbed her slender wrist. "If you wish to make up for this indignity," he went on with a leer, "I can think of a suitable way."

Jerioth did not know if Leah understood what the man was talking about, but she certainly did. Moving quickly, she put herself between Leah and the man. "My granddaughter has apologized," she said. "We will be going about our business now."

"Step aside, old woman," growled the man. "I wish to go about *my* business, and right now that includes this girl."

"No, it does not," Jerioth said firmly.

Snarling impatiently, the man put a rough hand on Jerioth's shoulder and shoved her aside. She looked around, hoping someone on the street would come to their assistance, but the only other people in sight were some distance away and paying no attention to them.

The man reached for Leah again. "Come here, girl," he ordered harshly.

His hand never touched her. Instead he stiffened, his eyes widening in surprise and pain. His mouth opened and his throat worked, but no sound came forth save a tiny croak. He shuddered violently.

At first Jerioth thought the man was having a seizure of some kind. But then she noticed Leah's eyes, blazing with fury as she focused on the man with the full force of her gaze. Jerioth looked back at the man, whose face was contorted with pain and drained of all color.

"Leah, do not do this," she said quietly. "Please, it is not worth it."

Now the man's eyes were bulging as if they were about to pop from their sockets, and his tongue had edged out of his mouth, trembling like the rest of him. Jerioth suddenly had an awful vision of the man's head literally exploding like a gourd dropped from a high roof. Leah *had* to release him from whatever terrible curse she had placed on him.

But despite Jerioth's pleas, her furious gaze did not waver.

"Never come near me, or my grandmother, or any of my family again," Leah intoned. "Always treat others with respect, for not everyone is cowed by your brutal manner. Get on your knees. I will loose your tongue so that you may give me an apology."

Abruptly the man fell loosely to his knees. His mouth worked again, and the words came out thickly. "I am s-sorry. I meant . . . no offense."

"I will release you now, but do not forget what has happened this day."

The man managed to respond with a jerky nod.

Leah stepped back and took a deep breath. The man sprawled forward, catching himself with his hands before he landed on his face, and remained there on hands and knees, trembling.

Leah stepped around him and looked back at Jerioth with an innocent smile. "Shall we go home now, Grandmother?"

"Yes," Jerioth said slowly. "Yes, let us go."

They moved off down the street. When they were some distance away, the man pushed himself upright and called in a hoarse voice, "Witch! Sorceress!" Jerioth looked back and saw him pointing a trembling finger at Leah. "God will curse you for your evil ways!"

"Ignore him," Jerioth said to the girl. "He is but a poor, frightened man."

"I have already forgotten all about him," said Leah, her voice light.

That was good if it was true, but Jerioth suspected it was not. In her rage Leah had tapped more deeply into her powers today than ever before—surely she would not forget *that*.

Jerioth knew that *she* would not forget. Not ever. The look of cold fury in Leah's eyes would live on in Jerioth's memory.

And she was afraid to ponder it too deeply. Very afraid indeed . . .

CHAPTER TWENTY-ONE

Sunu eagerly searched the crowds lining the road to Jerusalem for his wife, Mara. The throngs had come out a short distance from the city, which was visible up ahead on the hilltop, to celebrate with raucous cheering and singing the return of the army following the defeat of the Edomites. Edom had finally fallen to David and would henceforth be a vassal state.

Sunu and the other men of his mounted patrol were riding near the head of the column, behind the chariots that had been captured earlier from the Philistines and were now used by the army. Whenever he looked at those chariots, Sunu was reminded of his uncle Kaptar and his friend Nestor. It was a shame, he thought, that they had not remained in Israel, for they would have risen quickly in the ranks of David's army. Of course it was true that Kaptar was a prince in his homeland of Egypt. Sunu himself cared little for the privileges and accoutrements of rank; he was satisfied as

long as he had a good horse, a sharp sword, and enemies to pursue and dispatch.

A moment later Sunu spotted Mara's lovely face in
the crowd. She had Rachel in her arms and was lifting
the little girl high so she might catch a glimpse of her
father. Sunu grinned and waved at them. Then he saw
his father and mother standing behind Mara, a smiling
Jubal perched on Eri's shoulders.

Eri had not gone off to this war. He had finally
heeded the urgings of his wife and remained in Jerusalem, devoting himself to his furnace and forge. Eri was
well advanced into middle age now, and as the patriarch
of the family it was important that he stay home rather
than risk his life again and again in battle.

The column marched in triumph into the city, then
dispersed as soldiers hurried to their homes to be reunited with their loved ones. After leading his horse to
the military stable, rubbing it down, and giving it grain
and water, Sunu walked quickly to his family's house.

Mara practically flew into his arms, pressing her
mouth to his in a passionate kiss. He sighed happily and
tightened his arms around her. The warmth of his wife's
body in his arms, the sweetness of her lips pressed to his
—these things made all the hardships of war worthwhile. As did the laughter of his children, who greeted
him with hugs a moment later when Mara released him.
Sunu lifted Jubal and Rachel in the air in turn, tossing
them up and catching them as they squealed with delight.

Eri and Baalan were more restrained but no less
sincere in their welcome.

"It is good to be home," Sunu told them.

"Perhaps you shall not have to leave again," Eri
said. "There should be peace in the land now that the
Edomites have been defeated."

"Yes, peace," Sunu repeated. But he felt a strange
stirring inside as he spoke the word, a feeling of dissatisfaction, he decided. He tried not to frown.

For years now, he had lived with war. He had to ask
himself if he could live with peace.

*   *   *

Several weeks later, a servant from the palace arrived at the house with a message for Sunu and Mara: King David wanted to see them both as soon as possible. The servant professed not to know the reason for the summons, but Sunu did not believe him. David had probably instructed the man to plead ignorance.

"I hope nothing is wrong," Mara said worriedly as she dressed in her best robes.

"I know of nothing that could be wrong," Sunu assured her. "We have certainly done nothing to displease the king. I have served him loyally and well, and you— no one could be unhappy with you, Mara."

She shook her head. "I pray you are right, Sunu."

They hurried through the streets toward David's magnificent palace, where they were ushered directly into his presence.

David clasped the wrist of the young warrior. "My good friend Sunu. And Mara, you are as lovely as ever. The nation of Israel is blessed to have you among its subjects."

Sincere as it seemed, Sunu was unaccustomed to such flattery, and it made him uneasy. He asked bluntly, "Why were we summoned here, my lord? Is there some service we can perform for you?"

"Nay, the service this day shall be mine to perform." David turned to Mara and went on, "Despite everything that was said in later days, you know that I always bore a great love for your grandfather, Saul, and your father, Jonathan, do you not?"

"There was a time I did not believe it," Mara admitted warily. "But now I know it to be true. My grandfather was possessed of rages sent by demons known only to him, and it was my father's ill fortune to have been a victim of Saul's rages. All his subjects were victims, in a way, because my grandfather's state of mind helped lead to the nation's defeat by the Philistines."

Solemnly David nodded. "Those were sad times for our land. We should all praise God and thank Him that they are in the past."

"What has this to do with us, my lord?" Sunu asked with the same boldness that had carried him through many battles.

"Now that Israel is secure, I wish to do something to honor Saul and Jonathan, my fallen friends and comrades," David replied. "Without their sacrifices, our people might still labor under the yoke of foreign conquerors."

Sunu's anxiety eased somewhat, but his curiosity grew. "What do you mean, my lord?"

"I sent Zadok, the priest, to search throughout the land for a particular man. He was found living humbly in a small village and, on my orders, brought back here to Jerusalem." David smiled at Mara. "He awaits without."

Mara glanced at Sunu, who seemed as baffled by all this as she. Turning back to David, she said, "I do not know whom you mean, my lord."

David gestured to a servant. "Bring in our other visitor."

The servant went into an adjoining chamber, then reappeared a moment later. With him was a young man who stepped forward hesitantly on twisted, deformed feet. Mara took one look at the crippled man and exclaimed, "Mephibosheth!"

The young man looked at Mara as if he wanted to go to her, but he turned and faced David instead. Prostrating himself, he said in a voice quaking with fear, "I wish only to serve you, my lord. I make no claims on the throne of Israel."

David stepped forward and bent over to gently grasp Mephibosheth's arm and lift him to his feet. "You have no need to prostrate yourself before me, Mephibosheth," he said. "You are the son of my beloved friend Jonathan and the grandson of the man who was *my* king, Saul. You are an honored guest in this palace."

Mephibosheth blinked rapidly as he tried to take in what David was saying. After a moment he asked, "I . . . I was not brought here to be killed?"

"Never!" David gripped the young man's arms. "You can stay here for the rest of your life if you wish, and you will always be as welcome as you are now." Grinning broadly, he turned to Mara. "Come, greet your brother."

Unable to restrain herself any longer, she rushed to Mephibosheth and threw her arms around him, blending her tears with his as they embraced.

Sunu felt only joy for his wife as he watched them. Mara and Mephibosheth had been together when he first met them—she a young woman of fifteen whose burgeoning beauty shone through ragged clothes and dirty face, Mephibosheth a young lad, crippled by a fall in infancy. Sunu had appointed himself their protector during that perilous time when Israel was both divided internally and besieged by outside enemies, and he and Mara had grown to love each other. Then Mephibosheth was left with friends in an isolated village, for fear first that his relationship to Saul and Jonathan might put him in danger and then, later, that David might regard him as a rival for the throne and have him killed.

Now it was clear that Mephibosheth's assassination was the farthest thing from David's mind. He was displaying only respect and affection, almost as if the young man were his own brother.

"I would be pleased if you would live out your life here in Jerusalem," he told Mephibosheth, "either in the palace or with your sister and her new family. Or, if you wish, I will find you a house of your own."

"I have lived alone for some time now, my lord," said Mephibosheth. "I would go on this way, if it pleases you."

"So shall it be." David put both hands on the young man's shoulders. "This is a great day. The final wound is healed, the rift is closed. Israel is truly one land again. So may it remain, until the end of time."

"Amen," Sunu whispered. What else could any man wish? But once again he felt a restlessness gnawing at him.

*   *   *

David paced impatiently across the room, awaiting the arrival of the diplomatic party he had sent to Hanun, the new king of the Ammonites. Ammon, across the Jordan River to the northeast of Israel, was the largest and most powerful of Israel's neighbors. Peace reigned between the two nations for the moment, but with the ascension of Hanun, David worried about the stability of that peace. A new monarch often sought to solidify his power by waging war; David was familiar with that strategy himself. So he had sent messengers to the Ammonite king, hoping they would return with his assurances that he planned no aggressive action against Israel.

Waiting with David were Abiathar, Zadok, and Eri. At the sound of approaching footsteps David swung around anxiously. A grim-faced Joab strode in, and David was instantly at his side, asking, "Have my messengers returned from Rabbah?"

Joab nodded. "They have, my lord, and I fear the situation is the same as the reports that reached us in advance of their coming."

David grimaced and made a curt gesture. "Send them in. I would hear for myself."

Eri had no idea what David and Joab were referring to, and Abiathar and Zadok appeared equally puzzled.

A moment later the delegation that had journeyed to Rabbah, the capital city of Ammon, was brought into the chamber, and Eri understood immediately why David and Joab were so perturbed. The men of the party, which was composed of lesser priests, military commanders, and officials of David's government, all wore beards, but only on one side of their faces—the other side had been shaved clean. Their robes had been hacked off at the bottom as well, so that their spindly shanks showed. They had been deliberately humiliated by the Ammonites.

David trembled with rage. "Hanun did this to you?" he demanded.

One of the men stepped forward, his face wretched with embarrassment. "He did, my lord. And he said he would do the same to any Israelite who dared come to him begging for a dishonorable peace."

"A dishonorable peace!" Joab exploded, his hand moving instinctively to the hilt of his sword. "If he does not want that, we shall show him how Israelites wage an honorable war!" He looked at his king then, as if for confirmation.

For a long moment David said nothing, and Eri wondered what was going through his mind. Peace and prosperity had come to Israel at last with the conquering of the Edomites. David himself should have been a happy man, with a palace full of beautiful wives and fine children. He was older now, too, and after so many years of illustrious service to Israel, he deserved a respite from the strife and discord that were Israel's lot.

But the insult from Hanun could not be tolerated. Eri knew that, and so did everyone else in the room. So it came as no surprise when David finally said quietly, "It shall be war."

Joab nodded in fierce satisfaction. "We shall march to Rabbah and teach those Ammonite dogs a lesson they'll not soon forget!"

"*You* will march to Rabbah, old friend," said David. "I trust no one to conduct the business of war more than I trust you, not even myself, so I shall remain here in Jerusalem."

That decision *was* unexpected: Always before, David had taken an active part in every military campaign. But Eri was glad he had chosen not to fight this time. The king was right: Joab was fully capable of commanding the army and leading it to victory.

"As you wish, my lord," said Joab, barely concealing his surprise at David's decision. Abiathar and Zadok also spoke up in support of David's choice.

Only Eri was silent, and he could not have said why. He had grown less and less fond of war over the years, and he could understand why David would feel the same way. Yet he could not shake a sense of foreboding, a dread that what had happened in this chamber today might have unforeseen—and far-reaching—consequences.

David rolled from side to side in the bed. Even the soft cushions and cool, silky bed covers brought no respite from his restlessness. His mind was afire, leaping from one fevered thought to another, never settling long enough to allow slumber to overtake him. He tossed the covers aside and sprawled on the bed clad only in a short girdle, thinking that perhaps the warmth of the night was keeping him awake. But sleep continued to prove frustratingly elusive.

With a weary sigh he sat up and swung his legs out of the bed, then padded to the doorway, calling softly to the guard who was always on duty in the corridor outside his bedchamber.

"Send for Eri the smith," David told the soldier. "I would speak to him."

"But sire, it is very late—" began the guard.

"I know what time it is," David snapped. "I have given you an order. Summon Eri to the palace at once!"

"Yes, my lord," said the guard, hurriedly backing away.

David paced the room nervously until Eri appeared in the doorway.

"You sent for me, my lord?" asked the smith, suppressing a yawn.

David greeted him by grasping his arms. "My friend! Thank you for coming. Perhaps you can calm my troubled mind."

"I will try, my lord," said Eri. "What can I do to help?"

"I wish I knew, old friend." David sighed as he turned to pace the room again. "There is much on my mind these days. The war against Ammon . . ."

"How goes the siege of Rabbah? Have you had word from Joab?"

"Yes, just today. The siege is proceeding as well as can be expected. Rabbah is heavily fortified, and it will

be some time before we can wrest it from the Ammonites. In the meantime, Joab and the army will do what
they can to weaken their defenses—and their resolve."

"Surely you do not fear that we will be defeated."

"Of course not!" David exclaimed. "I have the ut-
most faith in Joab. He is the finest soldier I have ever
known." He waved a dismissive hand. "Besides, God is
on our side. He will not allow us to be defeated. No, I
fear it is other matters that roil my thoughts."

"I stand ready to listen," said Eri.

David halted his pacing as an idea occurred to him.
"Let us go up on the roof. Perhaps some night air will
cool my head and refresh my soul."

Eri nodded in agreement, and the two men went up
to the flat roof of the palace.

The cool night breezes David had hoped for were
nowhere in evidence; the evening, in fact, was uncom-
monly still and warm. He began pacing again, his hands
clasped behind his back.

"Why is a man troubled by unhappiness when he
should be content?" he asked in a tortured voice. Without waiting for Eri to answer, he went on, "I have everything. I am king of the land I love, the land God has led
me to serve and defend. I have served and defended it
well. The people of the land love me and would lay
down their lives for me. I have the most beautiful wives
a man could wish for, and the finest children. What
more is there?"

Eri shrugged. "I know not, my lord. Most men who
lived an existence such as you describe would be very
happy."

David chuckled humorlessly and turned to his
friend. "I can always trust you to be honest with me, Eri.
That is why I sent for you. You think me foolish, do you
not?"

"I think you are my king," Eri said quietly. "If you
feel as you say you do, there must be a reason. But I
cannot say what it is."

Again David paced nervously. "I have not composed a song in months. Did you know that? I, who have

always lifted my voice in praise of God, no longer sing. And it is all I can do to sit in judgment of all the petty squabbles that fill my days. Sometimes I think that if one more petitioner appears before me, I will leap down from my throne and throttle him!"

"It sounds to me, my lord, as if you need a war to fight," Eri suggested. "Perhaps you are upset because you placed Joab in charge of the siege of Rabbah and did not go to fight the Ammonites yourself."

David looked at him thoughtfully. "You think this may be so?" He sighed. "It could well be true. And yet . . . it seems there is something else disturbing me—" He broke off his musings with an abrupt shake of the head and strode toward the low parapet that ran around the edge of the roof, Eri following behind.

The king suddenly came to a stop and gazed out over the city. The palace was the tallest building in Jerusalem, and from here David had an unobstructed view of all the other rooftops.

"Who," he asked in a voice tight with surprise, "is that?"

His gaze was fastened on the rooftop of a house not far away. A lamp illuminated the scene: a woman taking her evening bath in a large wooden tub. As Eri moved up beside David, the woman rose to her feet and raised her arms. She was holding a jug in her hands, and as she upended it, water cascaded down over her long black hair and her lush, nude body. Eri turned away.

David stood as if rooted to the spot and continued to watch the woman at her bath.

She was the most beautiful woman he had ever seen. His eyes were as keen as ever, and he had no trouble discerning her lovely features in the lamplight. The soft yellow glow played over the proud thrust of full breasts crowned with large, rosy nipples. David felt a tightening in his throat and a hollowness in his belly as his gaze moved down the woman's body, tracing the graceful lines of her swelling hips and flat belly. His eyes lingered on the thick triangle of dark hair at the juncture of her thighs, and he could imagine how silky and

finespun it was, almost as if he were running his finger-
tips through it. Her thighs and calves were as sensuously
shaped as the rest of her body. Never had he seen a
woman like this, never! His pulse hammered madly in
his head, and his blood seemed to be on fire.

"Do you know who she is?" he asked again, his
voice hoarse.

Eri looked at the woman quickly, as if to confirm
something he already knew, then turned his eyes away
once more. "I know her," he said. "She is called Bathsheba. She is the wife of Uriah, a Hittite mercenary who
is even now serving with the army of Israel under Joab
at Rabbah. We should not be doing this, my lord."

The note of disapproval in Eri's voice made David
turn his head sharply, although he was loath to take his
eyes away from the woman called Bathsheba. "You presume to tell the king of Israel what he should and
should not do, smith?"

Eri's features grew taut in a mixture of anger and
hurt, but David barely noticed. Eri said, "Uriah is a
friend of mine. I have fought beside him against the
enemies of Israel . . . your enemies, my king. And
Bathsheba is a good friend to Mara, the wife of my son,
Sunu. That is why I presume to speak as I do. Besides,"
he added, "you would have me be honest, remember,
my lord?"

David grimaced at the reminder and turned his attention back to Bathsheba. He did not want to waste
time arguing with Eri while this vision of feminine pul-
chritude was displayed so openly and sensuously before
him.

"My mind is clearer now," he said shortly. "You
may return to your home."

Eri hesitated. "Are you sure, my lord?" His tone
made it unclear whether he was talking about his dis-
missal or something else.

"Of course I am sure. Thank you for your patience,
Eri. Good night."

Eri sighed. "Good night, sire."

Only vaguely aware of his old friend leaving the

rooftop, David watched raptly as Bathsheba finished her bath, stepped gracefully from the tub, and wrapped a cloth around herself. David felt a pang of regret when that beautiful body was hidden from his sight and Bathsheba, lamp in hand, left the rooftop.

The fire burning inside David was brighter than the flame of that lamp, brighter than the very sun itself. He turned away from the parapet and hurried down to his bedchamber, where he shouted for a servant, not stopping to reflect on what he was doing. If he hesitated, he might never have another opportunity like this.

When a servant appeared, David demanded, "Know you the house of the woman Bathsheba?"

The servant frowned in puzzlement and began, "You mean the wi—"

"I mean Bathsheba." At this particular moment David did not want to hear Uriah's name spoken aloud.

The servant nodded uncertainly. "Yes, my lord."

"Go there and bring her to me."

"My lord?"

"You heard me," snapped David. "Bring the woman Bathsheba here to me!"

The servant nodded again and backed toward the doorway. "Yes, my lord, right away."

David's pacing grew more frenzied as he waited for Bathsheba. The fire within him blazed hotter and hotter until he felt it would consume him entirely.

Finally the servant reappeared in the doorway and announced, "The lady Bathsheba, my lord." He stepped back to allow her to enter the room as David swung around quickly and faced her.

Bathsheba came in with her head held high, defiance and pride in every inch of her body. Her regal bearing served only to fan the flames of David's desire. She wore a dark blue robe that accented the midnight sheen of her thick, curly hair. Her dark eyes searched David's face, and her breath came rapidly through slightly parted ruby lips.

"Leave us," David said to the servant without even

looking at him. At this moment he had eyes only for the beautiful Bathsheba.

The man withdrew silently, closing the door behind him. David and Bathsheba were alone in the bedchamber. She returned his fevered stare coolly, saying nothing, almost as if *she* were the monarch and he the humble petitioner.

"Uncover yourself," he said hoarsely, as if she were a woman of the streets.

Bathsheba did not seem insulted by the command. She raised her hands, parted the robe, and drew it back over her shoulders, revealing the beginning swells of her firm breasts. She hesitated then, but only for an instant, just long enough to inflame the man who stood before her. Drawing the robe fully open, she let it fall around her hips, then past her thighs, to lie in a crumpled heap around her feet.

She stood nude before the king.

If she had been lovely before in her bath, she was utterly breathtaking now. The lamplight illuminated a body that was virtually perfect. Her breasts were so firm that they barely moved as she stepped out of the fallen robe and moved away from it. Her belly and abdomen were smooth, rounding to the mound covered by luxurious black curls. And her mouth . . . her mouth beckoned David with a power stronger than any he had ever known.

"You know why you are here," he said huskily, barely able to speak. He was almost overcome with desire.

"Of course." Bathsheba's voice was low, throaty, as perfect as the rest of her.

"Then come to me." David lifted his hands toward her. "Come to me freely, with everything that is yours."

"My lord . . ." she murmured.

She stepped forward and took his hands, allowing him to draw her into his embrace. David crushed his mouth to hers as his arms folded her against him, his hands roaming up and down the smoothness of her back and the curves of her buttocks. He felt her nipples prodding insistently against his bare chest, and his manhood prodded in return against the softness of her belly. She thrust her groin at his with all the skill of a trained courtesan, but there was nothing false about her response. She wanted him as much as he wanted her.

So he drew her to his bed, and in the hot, sultry night that hung over Jerusalem, both took what they wanted so badly.

CHAPTER TWENTY-TWO

Nefernehi smiled as she watched her son running along the sandy bank of the Nile. Birds of all kinds—egrets, herons, black kites, beautiful crested hoopoes—were congregating on the shore of the great river, but Khode, shrieking and waving his arms, sent them all flapping lazily into the sky. He threw back his head and laughed excitedly as he watched them.

"You should not chase them, Khode," Nefernehi called. "The gods have placed them here for a reason."

"For me to chase!"

Nefernehi laughed softly. She could not argue with his logic. Of course, she seldom argued with Khode over anything. He was a good child, strong and intelligent and mindful of others; he was everything she could ever have wanted him to be.

He was Kaptar's child.

In the heat of the Egyptian sun the young boy did not bother with clothing, choosing instead to go nude on these outings to the Nile above the great city of Waset. Whenever he turned his back toward his mother, she could see the distinctive, dark red mark high on his hip, shaped like the paw print of a lion. It marked him as the son of Kaptar, a true Child of the Lion, and Nefernehi never tired of looking at it. From the instant she had first seen it, only moments after Khode's birth, a huge wave of relief had flooded through her, and since then the sight of it always made her smile. It was definitive proof that Sheshonk's seed had not taken root inside her during their forced intimacy—had not taken root because Kaptar's seed was already growing there.

The only thing missing from her life was Kaptar himself.

She continued watching Khode from the shade of the tent her guards had set up. As a member of two royal families—the line in Waset by birth, the one in On by marriage—she could not travel about the countryside unaccompanied. Always there were soldiers with her, and it would have been simple to take one of them to her bed, as Kaptar's mother, Tania, had done during her marriage to the Libyan Musen in order to birth a pure Egyptian heir—Sheshonk. It had been years since Nefernehi had seen her husband, and sometimes she found herself overcome by a powerful yearning for the touch of a man, the feeling of a hard male body pressed to hers. After all, she was still a young woman. But she had not given in to that impulse.

Many years earlier, word had reached Waset that Kaptar had finally returned from his diplomatic mission to the land of the Israelites. He had been gone for more than a year, and many had believed him to be dead. But he was alive, and Nefernehi happily anticipated his arrival in Waset. Surely he would come up the Nile to be reunited with his wife and take her back to On.

Time passed, and Kaptar did not come. She wondered if he knew that he had a son. She waited a year, then another and another.

Now Nefernehi's emotions had settled into a bitter mix of longing, anger, and disappointment. He must have decided he was well rid of her, she decided; otherwise he would have come to her or at the very least sent for her. True, relations between Upper and Lower Egypt were severely strained, more so than before Kaptar's journey to Canaan, but Nefernehi knew the priests of Waset would have allowed her to return to On.

No, the blame for their separation could be laid solely at Kaptar's feet, and if that was the way he wanted things, then so be it.

Still, she missed him, and she would not dishonor the memory of what they had had by taking another man to her bed. Better to be lonely than to do that. Besides, with Khode around, she rarely had time to be lonely or to indulge in self-pity.

They had left Waset this morning on a small boat and come several miles up the Nile to a spot they had visited before, a smooth sandy beach bordered by a dense grove of trees. In the tent that had been set up just inside the grove, Nefernehi leaned against a backrest, comfortable in a thin garment that circled her waist and draped over her left shoulder, leaving her right shoulder and breast bare. She closed her eyes for a moment while Khode ran and played on the beach. The guards had assured her he would be safe, for there were no crocodiles in this section of the river. Besides, they would watch him at all times.

Nefernehi dozed off. She was unsure how long she had slept before suddenly being awakened by a guard, who had taken hold of her shoulder and was shaking her. He had dared to touch her!

Her initial reaction—outrage—faded instantly when she saw the fear in the soldier's eyes and heard the terror in his voice as he said urgently, "Wake up, my lady, wake up! Look there, in the river!"

Nefernehi sat up sharply, her first thought that something had happened to Khode. A crocodile could have exploded out of the water and seized him in its great jaws, whether crocodiles were supposed to be in this part of the river or not, or Khode could have waded out too far and been caught by the current, or—

She was shocked by what she saw in the river. Several small boats were cutting through the water, heading downstream; others had veered away from the main group and were coming toward the shore. Nefernehi could see the dark, savage faces of the men in the vessels.

Kushites!

She grabbed the guard's arm. "Where is Khode?"

"I told the boy to run back deeper into the trees," he answered. "He did not want to leave you, but I made him go."

"You did well." Nefernehi looked back at the approaching boats and shuddered. If Khode fell into the hands of the Kushites . . .

"You must run as well, my lady," the guard urged. "If the Kushites have not yet seen you, they will not pursue you into the trees." The man went to the rear of the tent and lifted the fabric. "Go out this way, so they will not see you."

Nefernehi hesitated. If the Kushites *had* spotted her, it was possible they could not see her clearly enough yet to tell she was a woman. The raiders had no way of knowing how many people had come ashore here. She could slip out, flee into the trees after Khode, and perhaps not be missed. But to do that would be to abandon the men who had come on this journey solely to protect her and her son.

If she did not get away, however, then Khode would be on his own, alone against these bloodthirsty natives from far up the Nile. Nefernehi could not allow that.

One last look told her the Kushite boats were still some distance from the shore. She had time to escape. She turned and hurried to the rear of the tent, bending over to stoop under the flap as the guard lifted it. "May the gods be with you," she said to the man.

"And with you and your son," the soldier replied.

Nefernehi plunged into the trees. They grew

densely here, watered by the great river, and she knew that the farther she went into the grove, the less likely it would be that the Kushite raiders would see her. As she ran, weaving around the trunks of the great palms and date trees, she called softly, "Khode! Khode!"

There was no reply. Nefernehi kept running, even as a greater fear washed over her. What if Khode had gone only a short distance into the grove and then stopped to hide? She might have gone past him without seeing him, and he might be too afraid to acknowledge her calls. She might be leaving him behind at this very moment.

Uncertain which course to follow, she hesitated again, listening fearfully to the savage yells and screams behind her. The Kushites had reached the shore and were attacking her guards, she knew. Khode was an intelligent child; the guard had told him to run, and she had to assume he was still running.

Anyone with any sense would flee from the Kushites. In the past the savage tribes that lived above the cataracts of the Nile had raided downriver, looting and killing, venturing almost as far as Waset itself. But it had been many years since they had dared come this far, so it had never occurred to Nefernehi that they might pose a threat on this outing.

She could still hear the shouting behind her. Slowing to a trot, she peered intently around as she made her way through the trees, calling her son's name every few moments.

Finally, with a surge of relief so strong it brought tears to her eyes, she heard Khode's familiar voice call, "Mother!" Turning toward the sound, she fought the impulse to shout his name and assure him that she was coming. An ominous silence had fallen behind her, and Nefernehi suspected that all the soldiers back on the shore had been killed.

"Khode!" she hissed. "Where are you?"

"Here, Mother," replied the boy. She saw his head emerge from a sandy hollow under the roots of a great tree.

Nefernehi looked back over her shoulder. She could no longer see the Nile because of the trees, and she was thankful for that. It meant that no one along the riverbank could see *her*—or her child. She slid into the hollow beside him and embraced him, feeling his small body shuddering with fear.

"It is all right now," she told him in a low voice. "No one will harm you."

"The soldier said to run," he babbled. "I did not want to leave you, but he said I had to—"

"You did the right thing, my son," Nefernehi said soothingly. "Now we are together again, and if we stay hidden here, we will be safe."

She hoped she was right. If she heard the savages approaching, however, she and Khode would have no choice but to flee again, for this hiding place would not conceal them for long, not from anyone determined to find them.

Would the Kushites realize the full import of that tent set up near the beach? If they knew a member of the Egyptian royal family was hidden in these trees, would they ever stop looking?

Nefernehi could not answer those questions. All she and Khode could do was wait, wait to see whether they would live or die.

Two days later, footsore and weary, Nefernehi and Khode trudged into Waset. They had walked down the river from the spot where their innocent outing had so nearly proved fatal. It was not a great distance, but neither of them was accustomed to walking very much, and Khode was only a child, after all. Also, they had hidden during the day and walked at night, so that when the Kushites returned upriver from their raid, they would not spy the two figures tramping along the bank.

Nefernehi held Khode's hand tightly as they walked. She had been clutching him thus since the hours of terror they had endured a couple of days earlier. Hidden under the roots of the tree, they had waited until Nefernehi was confident the Kushites had departed to rejoin their murderous brethren. When they emerged, she had gone back to the campsite, forbidding Khode to follow her. What she found there was even worse than she had expected: The soldiers were all dead, of course, but some of them had evidently been tortured before they were granted the release of death. All the bodies had been mutilated.

Nefernehi had found a broken spear with a perfectly good head and part of the shaft still attached to it and clutched the salvaged weapon now as she and Khode entered the city. She could tell from the confusion in the streets that the Kushites had terrorized the inhabitants, and she wondered if this raid was only the beginning of a fresh wave of violence.

Nefernehi went straight to the temple where the high priests who ruled Waset lived. As she and Khode entered the holy building, one of the priests, a man called Phasolt, noticed them and hurried over.

"Nefernehi, daughter of Nehri, honored is his memory," said Phasolt. "It was feared that you and your son had been taken by the Kushites!"

"It was a near thing, my lord," said Nefernehi. "My guards were all killed, and my son and I barely escaped with our lives. Did the Kushites come all the way to Waset?"

Phasolt nodded grimly. "They dared to invade our city! Our brave soldiers repelled them, but not before many Egyptians were killed."

"Will they come back?"

"No one knows." Phasolt shook his head. "But if this is to be a war, we cannot fight it alone. We have already sent emissaries to On, to ask for help from Sheshonk."

Sheshonk. How Nefernehi hated the name. But Upper Egypt would need the pharaoh's help to fend off a full-scale invasion.

Kaptar was in On, too. What would he do, Nefernehi wondered, when he discovered that his family might be in danger here in Waset? Given the history of the past few years, she thought bitterly, there was a very good chance he would do nothing at all.

The door of the throne room was violently thrust open, and Kaptar strode into the chamber with Nestor behind him, as usual. He stopped before the ornately carved wooden throne on which his brother slouched, hands clasped together in front of his face, a solemn frown creasing his brow.

"I take it you have heard the news?" Sheshonk grunted.

"I have heard that the Kushites are raiding as far down the river as Waset," Kaptar replied sharply. "Rumor has it that there will be war between them and Upper Egypt."

Sheshonk nodded slowly. "What you say is true. Emissaries from the high priests of Waset have visited me and begged my help to turn back the Kushites. What do you think I should do, Kaptar?"

"I care little for anyone in Waset . . . save Nefernehi."

It was true. Over the past years Kaptar had grown increasingly weary of the tensions and political maneuvering between Upper and Lower Egypt. Still mindful of the vow he had made to Kemose, he had done what he could to support Sheshonk's efforts to unify the Two Lands. None of it had been successful, of course; the friction between On and Waset was too old and ingrained to be easily overcome.

This crisis represented an opportunity to do just that, however, or at least to make some inroads in the process. The priests of Waset had requested Sheshonk's aid in repelling a possible Kushite invasion. What better chance than this to draw the Two Lands closer together?

"You must help the priests," Kaptar said bluntly. "Though they mean nothing to me personally, we cannot allow the Kushites to conquer them."

"I am of the same mind." Sheshonk's relief was plain. Kaptar had been his chief adviser these many years, and he was loath to go against whatever Kaptar believed was the wisest course.

"But first," Kaptar went on, "I must travel to Waset in advance of the army. Nestor and I will leave immediately with a small force."

"For what purpose?"

"To bring Nefernehi back to On."

Sheshonk blinked in surprise and sat up straighter. For a moment he seemed unable to say anything. Then he ventured hesitatingly, "When she left here, she asked that you not come after her. I told you this when you returned from the land of the Israelites, brother."

"True." Kaptar nodded curtly. "But this is different. I do not know what was in Nefernehi's mind when she departed On, but now she is in danger as long as she remains in Waset. I will not have this. She will come with me back to On whether she wishes to or not."

"Nefernehi is a . . . strong-willed woman, Kaptar. She may not like you making such a decision for her."

Kaptar's determination did not waver. "Then she can be angry with me . . . but she will be angry with me in On, where she is safe."

Sheshonk sighed. "Very well. Take as many men and boats as you wish, since I know I cannot stop you short of having you thrown in chains."

A faint smile touched Kaptar's mouth. "One boat and only a few men will be all that I require. Speed is what is important now. I must reach Waset as soon as I can."

"Then may Amon shine his goodwill on you in your journey, my brother," said Sheshonk.

Before the sun went down that day, Kaptar, Nestor, and a handful of Egyptian soldiers were on their way to Waset. Kaptar did not know what they would find when they arrived.

He only prayed that Nefernehi was still alive.

CHAPTER
TWENTY-THREE

Mara nestled her head on Sunu's shoulder, catching her breath. Their lovemaking had been as passionate as ever, and for a time Mara had been able to put aside all her fears and doubts.

But now, as her pulse slowed and she lay with her husband in their darkened bedchamber, her misgivings returned.

"Must you return to Rabbah?" she whispered.

Sunu's body stiffened beside her. Mara's question had disrupted the sensuous lassitude gripping him, and he sat up abruptly. In the faint light from the moon and stars that filtered through the open window, Mara could see the frown on his face.

"You know I must," he said. "Joab expects the siege to continue for many more weeks before the Ammonites are defeated. I would not be in Jerusalem tonight had he not sent me back to the city with messages for the king."

Mara sat up, her bare breasts brushing against his side. "You have done more than your share of fighting," she said fiercely.

Sunu swung his legs from the bed and stood up, his anger evident in his stance as he turned to face her. "As long as Israel has enemies, my share of fighting, as you call it, is not done," he declared. "You are the daughter and granddaughter of two of our land's greatest warriors. You know I speak the truth."

"I know." Mara, too, came to her feet. Her own anger prompted her to speak her mind, rash thought it might be. "But I hate to see the men of Israel dying before the walls of Rabbah while David is here in Jerusalem lying with the wife of another man!"

Sunu's breath hissed between his teeth. "You should not say such a thing! You dishonor our king by believing the gossip about him."

"It is *not* gossip," Mara insisted. "It is the truth, and I know it because Bathsheba herself has admitted it to me. You know that she and I are friends."

Sunu turned away, shaking his head. "Still, I would not hear—"

"You would not hear the truth!" Mara hurried around the bed and grabbed his arm. "Bathsheba is with child!"

"No!"

"It is true. And the child is David's—there is no doubt of that."

Sunu seemed finally to accept, albeit reluctantly, what his wife was telling him. He shook his head wearily and lifted a hand to massage his temples. "What will the king do now?"

"I do not know," said Mara, "but one thing is certain: More men will die at Rabbah while David's child grows in Bathsheba's womb."

David drew in a long breath. "How can this be?"

Bathsheba smiled as she watched him pacing back and forth across the royal bedchamber. "I think you know the answer to that as well as I, my love."

Curtly David waved off the comment. "What will we do?"

"You are the king. No one will dare punish you."

"You are wrong," he snapped. "I am not above the law. The punishment for adultery is death by stoning. Such is God's law, and the law of man."

Bathsheba moved in front of him to stop his pacing. Taking his hands in hers, she said tenderly, "I would not name you the father of my child. The punishment will fall on me alone."

David gazed down at her solemn, beautiful face, feeling more love for her than he had ever known before. "I could not allow you to make such a sacrifice."

"It would not be a sacrifice. Israel needs its king much more than it needs a foolish woman who allowed love to blind her."

David drew her into his arms, and she rested her head against his broad chest as he stroked her raven hair and said quietly, "When first you told me you are with child, my heart leaped with joy. I would write a song, I thought, a song for my son. Only then did I start to think about what it might mean."

"How could anyone condemn us, David?" she murmured. "I love you. What is between us is good, not evil."

"Not in the eyes of man . . . or God," David said. "We are but poor, foolish sinners, no better than multitudes of other men and women since the beginning of time."

"There must be a way." He felt her sobbing against his chest. "There must be!"

"Perhaps . . ." David said slowly. "Perhaps there is." He put his hand under her chin and lifted her head so that he could look into her eyes. "None could condemn us—if the child you are carrying was Uriah's."

"But he is at Rabbah with Joab!" cried Bathsheba. "He has been there for weeks!"

"I will send for him and have him come to Jerusalem to take a message back to Joab." The words came more quickly now as the idea took shape in David's mind. "While he is here, he will make love to you. What man would not? Then, as far as anyone will know, the child will be Uriah's."

"I . . . I must allow him to take me?" Bathsheba shuddered. "Uriah is a crude man. He appreciates the company of his fellow mercenaries more than he does that of his wife. I have never loved him."

"You must endure this," David told her. "It is the only way."

She took a deep breath and nodded. "It will be as you say. Send for Uriah."

Uriah the Hittite was a lean, bearded man with a permanently dour expression. But pride shone in his eyes as he stood before the king of Israel.

"We have heard much here in Jerusalem about your valor in the struggle against the Ammonites," David said from his throne. "That is why you have been chosen for the honor of carrying my message to Joab."

"Thank you, my lord," replied Uriah. "It is indeed an honor to have your trust. I will guard your message with my life and deliver it directly to Joab. I will leave tonight."

David managed to smile, but it was difficult. He could not put out of his mind the fact that Uriah was the husband of his beloved Bathsheba, and the image of the two of them together—as they would be tonight—haunted him. Forcing his thoughts back to the matter at hand, he went on, "It is a long journey from Rabbah. You need not depart until the morrow, Uriah. Tonight you may rest in your own home. I seem to recall that you are married?"

"Aye, my lord."

"Go see your wife, then. I am sure she has missed you."

Uriah nodded. "Thank you, my lord. You are most generous."

"Return to the palace tomorrow, and I will give you the message you must bear straight to Joab."

David leaned back on the throne as he watched

Uriah depart. His plan would work; he was sure of it. It was difficult to determine exactly when a child was conceived—Bathsheba herself was confident it had been only a few weeks since David's seed had taken root inside her. If Uriah went to her tonight, then later, when the child was delivered, everyone would assume that the mercenary captain was the father. Nothing could go wrong. Nothing . . .

"Uriah!" exclaimed Eri as he rounded a corner and saw the Hittite striding toward him. "I had not heard you had returned to Jerusalem."

In the manner of fellow warriors, the two men pounded each other on the back in greeting. They had known each other for some time, and during the siege of Rabbah Uriah had befriended Eri's son as well.

"I have been summoned to Jerusalem to take a message back to Joab," said Uriah, a note of pride in his voice. "Summoned by David himself."

"When are you leaving?"

"Tomorrow, after the king gives me the message."

"Splendid!" said Eri. "Then we have time tonight to share a jug of wine."

Uriah appeared to ponder the suggestion for a moment before answering. "Yes. I would like that very much."

The two men headed for a nearby tavern that was frequented by soldiers, mercenaries, and palace guards and soon found themselves seated at a table with a friendly crowd gathered around them. With wine and talk flowing freely, the time passed more quickly than Eri would have thought possible. It was quite late, he judged, when he stood up and announced, "I must take my leave. My wife will be wondering where I am."

His declaration met with a chorus of disapproval. "A warrior does not flinch before the stare of an angry woman," one of the men asserted.

Eri grinned ruefully. "You are not wed, are you, my friend?"

"No, but—"

"You need say no more, then." Eri turned to Uriah. "Are you not returning to your home? You, too, have a wife awaiting you."

"Later." Uriah lifted his cup of wine. "I would spend more time first with these good fellows."

Eri shrugged good-naturedly. "So be it, my friend. Good night."

Feeling a bit light-headed, he left the tavern. Spirits had little effect on him, but he would be glad to get home, he reflected, and get some sleep. He hoped Uriah would not stay in the tavern much longer, for the way he had been drinking, he might not be able to find his way home at all.

Stopping in his tracks, Eri wondered if he ought to go back and try harder to persuade him to leave. Then, with a shake of the head, he decided Uriah was capable of making his own decisions about when to go home.

And, after all, it was none of Eri's business.

"The Hittite did not go near his house—or his wife?" David's voice was strangled as he questioned the servant he had given the task of watching Uriah.

The man shook his head worriedly. He might not know why it was so important where a simple mercenary captain had gone—or what he had done—but he knew quite well that his lord and master was unhappy. "I am sorry, my lord. Uriah went to a tavern and spent the night there. He was drinking and singing with his comrades until early this morning, when he fell asleep on the floor." The servant swallowed hard. "He is outside now, waiting for a message that you are supposed to give him."

David could not believe his bad luck. It was all he could do not to tear out his hair at this turn of events. Too many witnesses could confirm that Uriah had not visited his home—no one would believe that he had fathered Bathsheba's child. As time passed and her belly swelled, the full weight of the scandal would crash on her head, and on David's as well, because he had meant what he told her—he would not allow her to carry the blame alone.

A shudder ran through him as he turned his face away from the servant. In his darkest moments since he had discovered that Bathsheba was carrying his child, he had been painfully aware of what he might ultimately be forced to do. He had dreaded making that decision. Now it looked as if he had no choice.

David drew a deep breath into his body, held it for a moment, then blew it out in a resigned sigh. "Bring me a scroll," he told the servant. "I would write the message for Joab myself."

"You do not wish a scribe?"

"I have already told you what I want," said David sharply. "Do as you are told!"

"Yes, my lord." The servant scurried away.

If Uriah were dead, David could take Bathsheba to be his wife. They would have to wait a short period of time, for the sake of appearances, before they were married, but then the child would be a prince or a princess, the true son or daughter of the king of Israel. Some might wonder about the length of time between the marriage and the birth, but no one would dare to say anything. Legally no crime would have been committed.

But all of that would come to pass *only* if Uriah were dead.

David knew what he would write to Joab. The general might disapprove, but he was loyal. He would obey.

Uriah would not know it, but he would be carrying back to Rabbah the orders for his own death.

Sunu crouched behind the breastworks that had been thrown up in front of the walls of Rabbah. Inside the walls, Ammonite soldiers sometimes jeered the besieging Israelite forces, but such arrogance was becoming more and more uncommon. Too many Ammonites had stood up to shout insults at the Israelites only to be brought down with an arrow launched by one of Joab's expert archers, Sunu among them.

He cared little for this sort of warfare. Sitting and

waiting for an enemy to starve or surrender was almost dishonorable, he had thought more than once during this siege. Only the fact that David and Joab had ordered this particular deployment made it right in Sunu's mind. He knew that neither his king nor his general would ever do anything less than honorable.

Still, he longed for the feeling of a good horse under him and the weight of a sharp sword in his hand. He was a warrior, and when he killed an enemy, he wanted to look into the man's eyes and watch the light of life fade away. That was the way he hoped to die someday, at the hands of a worthy opponent who had bested him in honest combat.

Thousands of men were ranged in a great circle around the walled city. No one could get in or out of Rabbah. The Israelites had tried shooting into the city arrows dipped in pitch and set afire. Great columns of black smoke had risen into the sky, but the damage was apparently not severe enough to force the Ammonites into surrendering. They were still holding on stubbornly, repelling all direct attacks. The city walls were sufficiently thick, strong, and well defended to allow them to do that for a long time. A siege was the only answer. As much as he hated the prospect of more waiting, Sunu was intelligent enough to understand that.

A commotion at the rear of the Israelite camp attracted his attention. Someone appeared to have just ridden in on a lathered horse. Now a group of men was approaching his position, and Sunu guessed they were looking for Joab, whose tent was nearby.

A moment later he recognized the man in the center of the group. Uriah had returned from Jerusalem. Sunu went forward to greet him. Uriah was unsmiling, as usual, but he clasped Sunu's wrist with a warm, strong grip and said, "How fares it with you, my friend?"

"Well, though I could use a battle." Sunu grinned.

"Perhaps you will get one." Uriah held up a scroll tied with a silken cord and sealed with the mark of the king. "I bear new orders for Joab."

Sunu felt his heart pound in anticipation. Perhaps

David had finally commanded Joab to launch an all-out assault on Rabbah. He joined the group of men, all officers, and a few moments later Uriah stood before Joab in his tent and handed him the scroll.

"This message comes directly from our king," he said.

Joab grunted, took the scroll, and broke the seal. Quickly he read the message. As he did, Sunu thought he saw his eyes widen with surprise for an instant. But they became hooded and unreadable again as he glanced up at the man who had brought him the message.

"Have you read this?" he asked.

"Of course not," Uriah answered haughtily. "David sealed it in my presence, and I would not dare break the seal of the king."

"No, of course not." Joab rolled up the scroll. "My apologies, Uriah. I was somewhat startled by the message, that is all."

One of the other officers asked, "What does our king command, if I may be so bold?"

"You may not," snapped Joab. "David's words are for my eyes alone. And his commands will be carried out in due course."

The officer stolidly accepted the rebuke. Sunu wondered what the message had contained that had upset Joab. For he was clearly troubled; he would not have spoken so to a friend and comrade otherwise. Joab took a deep breath now and addressed Uriah.

"Rest for a time. You must be weary after your journey." He hesitated, then added, "You were a faithful messenger indeed, Uriah."

"Thank you, General." The Hittite turned to Sunu. "I shared wine with your father in Jerusalem. He is well, and so are the other members of your family."

Sunu was glad to hear that. In recent days, thoughts of Mara, and of little Jubal and Rachel, had forced themselves into his mind more and more. He would be glad when this siege was over, for reasons other than simple boredom.

*   *   *

Sunu was in front of his tent with Uriah late that afternoon when one of Joab's lieutenants approached. "Come with me," he said to Uriah.

"Why?" Uriah asked. As a captain of mercenaries, he was of roughly the same rank as the other man.

"Joab has sent me to enlist you in my troop."

Uriah bristled. "I command my own troop."

"I have need of good fighting men," the officer said. The man seemed nervous to Sunu. "Before the sun sets this day, my men and I will attack the gate to the Ammonite city, and I would have you at my side, Uriah." He took a deep breath. "Besides, it is Joab's order."

Uriah and Sunu exchanged glances, and Sunu knew the Hittite was thinking the same thing: The gate of the city was the most heavily defended place of all, since it was also the most vulnerable. To attack it would be flying into the face of death.

And yet it was a chance for action at last, and if by some stroke of luck the Israelites were successful in overwhelming the defenses at the gate, the rest of the army could then pour into the city and put an end to the siege.

Sunu said to the officer, "I will go."

"You were not ordered to—"

"I will go with you anyway," Sunu interrupted. "What say you, Uriah?"

The mercenary shrugged. "If that is Joab's command, then that I shall do." He picked up his sword. "Let us go slay some Ammonites, my friends."

The force that had been hastily assembled for the attack was not a large one, but Sunu knew all its members. Good fighting men, every one of them, he thought as he looked around. They were gathered behind breastworks directly in front of the gate, and only a distance slightly greater than the range of an arrow's flight separated them from their objective.

Joab was there to order the attack itself, and Sunu thought he had never seen the general looking so grim.

No doubt he realized he was sending at least some of these men to their deaths. "Our archers will send volleys at the walls to give you a chance to reach the gate," he told them. "Go with God, my friends." Joab looked sternly at the officer he had placed in charge. "You have your orders. Remember them, and carry them out."

The man swallowed hard, then nodded. "Yes, Joab. I will."

Joab noticed Sunu then. With a frown he said, "You were not to be part of this attack."

"I volunteered to accompany these good soldiers," replied Sunu.

"It is not necessary—"

"Pardon me, my lord, but I wish to go."

For a moment Joab's eyes flared with anger, but then he nodded abruptly. "If such is your decision, so be it, Sunu. But be careful."

The warning struck Sunu as strange. Joab had not uttered it to any of the other men, and he knew as well as anyone how perilous this attack would be.

There was no time to ponder such matters, however. Joab gave the order to the archers, and volley after volley of arrows took flight toward the walls of Rabbah. As the deadly rain of shafts fell, Sunu, Uriah, and the other men in the attacking force scrambled out from behind the breastworks and charged toward the city.

This was not a surprise attack; the Ammonites could see them coming. But with the arrows flying around their heads, the defenders of Rabbah were too busy to stop them. Sunu's heart pounded with excitement, and he began to think that perhaps this strategy was going to work. He surged to the forefront of the attackers, shouting a battle cry.

The gate swung open, and Ammonite soldiers poured forth to meet the Israelite charge. At the same time, the archers atop the walls finally began to shoot in response, and the Israelite volleys lessened as some of the men fell and others sought shelter. Below, swords clashed as the two forces came together in front of the gate, which had been hastily closed again.

Even as Sunu threw himself into the battle, he knew that everything had suddenly gone wrong. The Ammonites had met the charge with more soldiers than he had expected, easily outnumbering the Israelites, and their archers were now loosing their shafts at much closer range.

The realization that he might well die here today, in front of the gate of Rabbah as the sun sank toward the horizon, only made Sunu fight more fiercely. He ran one Ammonite through, then twisted to disembowel another with a backhanded swipe of his sword. From the corner of his eye he saw Uriah locked in combat with several Ammonites and would have gone to help him had he not been busy at his own task.

Gradually Sunu became aware that the other Israelites were falling back toward the siege lines. He wondered if he and Uriah had missed an order to retreat but was certain they had not. Yet the others were turning and fleeing, almost as if they intended to leave Uriah and Sunu alone in front of the gate, surrounded by Ammonites.

"Sunu!" The shout came from the officer in charge of the attack, who had paused in his flight long enough to turn back and call to him. "Get out of there! The attack is over!"

Sunu did not waste his breath replying. He parried a blow, then struck one of his own, chopping deeply into the arm of the Ammonite soldier in front of him. The man fell, clutching at the hideous wound.

A scream brought Sunu's head around sharply. He saw Uriah staggering to the side, an arrow buried in his chest. "Uriah!" he shouted. It was too late to go to the Hittite's aid. An Ammonite drove a sword into Uriah's belly. The mercenary dropped his own blade and doubled over, then fell as the Ammonite ripped the sword free from his body.

Sunu started toward his fallen comrade, but he had taken only a step when something slammed into the side of his head. He felt a warm gush of blood down his face, and a red film covered his eyes. He stumbled, trying to see where he was going, but his senses were deserting him. He realized he was falling only when his knees slammed into the hard-packed earth. An instant later, his face struck the ground, but he was only vaguely aware of what had happened.

Then he knew nothing at all.

CHAPTER
TWENTY-FOUR

Sunu walked with only a slight limp along the street, Mara at his side. Although he did not know it at the time, he had suffered a fairly serious wound in his left thigh during the fierce fighting in front of Rabbah. His leg was still stiff sometimes, and on the side of his head was a long scar where an Ammonite sword had struck him. The blood that had flowed from the wound had saved his life, masking his features in crimson so that he had appeared to be dead when he collapsed. Sooner or later the Ammonites might have gotten around to thrusting a sword or a spear into his body just to make sure, but more arrows from the Israelite archers had driven them back into the city. Then Joab had sent men to recover the bodies of the slain, including Sunu, who was *not* dead.

But Uriah was, and Sunu had a bitter taste in his mouth whenever he thought of the Hittite and remembered too much about that day. He had never told anyone of his suspicions, but he was certain of one thing: David had meant for Uriah to die at the hands of the Ammonites. That was the message the king had sent to Joab. Uriah had been abandoned in front of the gate so that he would be killed, and there could only have been one reason such an atrocity had been committed: the king's new wife. *Bathsheba.*

Mara squeezed Sunu's arm, breaking into his bleak reverie. "It is so good to have you home, husband," she said.

"It is good to be home," Sunu told her truthfully. They were on their way to the market in the center of the city. "I intend to be here more often from now on."

Mara smiled up at him, and some of the coldness in his heart melted. He would learn somehow to accept what he had been through. With the help of Mara and his children and the rest of his family, he would be all right.

As for David, how he dealt with what he had done was not Sunu's concern. But he could not help but wonder what thoughts went through David's head during the darkest hours of the night when sleep would not come.

David rubbed his eyes wearily as he sat slumped on his throne. The night before, his slumber had been disturbed by a nightmare he could not recall when he awoke. All he knew was that he had sat up in bed with his heart pounding and his face clammy with a cold sweat. The rest of the night he had spent tossing and turning.

This morning he was in no mood to see petitioners, but that was part of a king's duty, after all. He would much rather have been with Bathsheba, who had her own apartment elsewhere in the palace. She had borne him a fine, healthy son following their marriage, and David visited the two of them often.

Bathsheba was more beautiful than ever these days. Musing on her loveliness made him smile, and he did not hear what his servant was saying to him until the man had spoken at least twice.

"—here to see you, my lord."

David looked up sharply. "What? What did you say?"

"My lord, the prophet Nathan—"

The tall, gray-bearded prophet with burning eyes strode impatiently into the throne room. "I must speak with you, David," he declared. "There is a tale you must hear."

David sat up straighter and waved a hand. "Speak, my friend. I am always interested in what you have to say."

Unlike some of the priests, Nathan dressed in a plain robe and was a blunt-spoken man. Without further preamble he began, "There were once two men who lived next to each other, a rich man with many sheep and a poor man with only one."

David leaned forward and nodded. This was going to be one of Nathan's parables, no doubt.

"The rich man cared little for his sheep, save as a means of proving how wealthy he was," Nathan continued. "But the poor man, with the one sheep, loved the animal and cared for it almost as if it were his child. The sheep meant more to him than life itself."

"I understand," said David.

"One day the rich man had visitors, and he wished to provide a suitable feast for them. He could have had his servants slaughter one of his own sheep, of course, but even though he had many, he was loath to lose even one of them, lest anyone think him less wealthy." Nathan paused, and his voice took on a richer, deeper timbre as he continued. "So the rich man went to his neighbor's pen and stole the man's only sheep, which he took back to his home and slaughtered for the feast!"

Rage flooded through David at the injustice perpetrated by the rich man. He came to his feet and lifted a clenched fist as he said, "Any man who would do such a thing deserves to die!"

Nathan's hand shot out, his finger leveled accusingly at the king. *"You* are the man!" he shouted.

David stared thunderstruck at the prophet. He saw now what Nathan had done, and he understood the parallels he had drawn. Bathsheba was the one sheep, and he was the rich man who had so callously stolen her. As guilt and grief washed over him, he slumped back in his chair. Shuddering, he buried his face in his hands, unable to face any longer the burning gaze of the prophet.

"You are the man," Nathan repeated in a quieter but no less outraged voice. "Others may speak only in whispers of such things, but I am a prophet of the Lord, and I shout out the truth. You have sinned, David, sinned against Uriah and against Bathsheba herself. And you have sinned against God. You *will* be punished." He folded his arms across his chest. "The child will pay for your sin. He will sicken and die."

"No!" The shout ripped from David's throat as he came once more to his feet. "No! The child did nothing wrong—"

"That matters not. The sin is yours, and so will be the punishment."

David's hand went to the sword buckled at his waist. It would be easy to draw the blade and strike down the prophet. Nathan would likely not defend himself.

And yet to do that would only deepen his sin. He could still the tongue of Nathan forever—but he could not still the voice of his own heart.

"Leave me," David said, turning away from the prophet. "I must pray."

"It will change nothing," Nathan intoned.

Perhaps not, thought David as he hurried from the room, but he had to try. If he could only make God understand how sorry he was, his child might yet live.

The entire city plunged into gloom as word spread that the young prince, the son of King David and his new wife, Bathsheba, had fallen ill. The best physicians in the land were summoned to Jerusalem to attend the child, and priests surrounded the bed of the infant night and day, sending up prayers to Yahweh that the babe might be cured of its illness. Nothing seemed to help. David himself prayed almost continuously, fasting during the day and lying on the ground outside the city walls at night as if he were nothing more than a beggar.

For, in truth, that was what he had become. He was begging God for the life of his son.

On the morning of the seventh day, Eri and Sunu went outside the walls to where David had prostrated himself. As they drew near, they could hear the feeble muttering of the humbled king. Although he was near unconsciousness, he never stopped praying.

Eri put out a hand to stop his son before they came too close. No one dared approach the king anymore, for it was rumored that he had gone mad with grief.

"To see him come to this," Sunu sighed. "None would have ever believed it possible."

"I am glad our enemies are far away in Rabbah, still under siege by Joab's forces," said Eri. "If Jerusalem were to be attacked now, there would be none to lead us, and the city would fall."

"Perhaps it is time Israel had a new king."

Eri looked sharply at Sunu. "Your thoughts have been led into the path of evil," he said. "No matter what his flaws, David is the anointed of God, the chosen leader of our people. He shall not be put aside simply because he made a mistake."

"He ordered Uriah's death," replied Sunu. "Everyone knows that now. I know it better than any, for I was there." He reached up and lightly touched the scar on his head.

"I know," said Eri, his voice gentler now. "Our king did a terrible thing . . . but he is still our king, and he is doing penance for his sin."

Sunu shrugged, obviously unwilling to argue anymore about the matter. He was not sure why he and his father had come here today, unless it was because of the same curiosity that had driven other citizens of Jerusalem to troop by all during the day and night. No one had ever seen a king brought so low, especially not by his own hand.

At the sound of footsteps behind them, Eri and Sunu looked around. The high priest, Abiathar, was approaching, and from the expression on his face they knew that the situation had just gotten worse.

"Eri," said the priest, "I am glad you are here. You must go to the king and tell him he must return to the palace at once."

"You were sent with this message?" asked Eri.

Abiathar nodded. "The physicians say it . . . it will not be much longer now."

"You fear to approach our king?"

The priest looked past Eri at David's recumbent form. In a whisper he said, "It is rumored that David has gone mad."

Impatiently Sunu turned away. "I will go to the king," he said. "I fear him not."

"Sunu, wait—" Eri began, but it was too late. Sunu was already taking long strides toward David, his limp hindering him but little.

"My king," Sunu said in a strong voice as he drew near, "you must arise and return to the palace. You are needed there."

David lifted his head and peered up unblinkingly at Sunu, his eyes dark, set in deep hollows in his haggard face. His gaze was that of a man who had been staring into his own tomb. In a harsh voice he rasped, "My son . . . ?"

Sunu shook his head. "I know not. I am told only that you must return to the palace."

For a long moment David did not move. Then he raised a hand and extended it to Sunu, who hesitated, then helped him to his feet. In a stumbling gait David started toward the city gate.

People on the streets moved aside nervously to give the king room as he walked toward the palace. Eri, Sunu, and Abiathar followed him. When they reached the palace, David went straight to Bathsheba's apartment, where he found her weeping. A group of grim-faced physicians and priests stood around the tiny cradle in which the infant lay.

"I am sorry, my lord," said one of the physicians. "There was nothing we could do."

Eri and Sunu watched from the doorway of the room as David whispered, "Is my son dead?"

"Yes, my lord," replied the physician.

David stepped to the cradle and stared down at the dead child. He lifted his hand, as if to touch the child's face, then stopped and drew a deep, ragged breath. Without a word he turned and stalked from the room, brushing past Eri and Sunu. Eri watched his old friend's retreating back, wishing he could follow and say something to assuage the king's grief. But there was nothing to say now, and Eri and Sunu both knew it.

"David went to his own apartment and bathed, then had himself massaged with fine oils and dressed in his best robes," Eri explained to his family that night as they all sat around the table in their house. "Then he went to the tabernacle to worship."

"And then," said Sunu, picking up the story, "he gave orders to his charioteers and his personal guards. They are to be ready to travel tomorrow. David is going to Rabbah to conduct the siege of the Ammonites himself."

Baalan raised her eyebrows. "He is not staying in Jerusalem to mourn his child?"

Eri shook his head. "Abiathar summoned up the courage to ask him the same question. The king replied that he has fasted and prayed and, yes, even mourned during the seven days when the infant was ill. Now the child is dead. It is too late for his prayers to do any good, David said."

"That poor man," said Baalan. "And Bathsheba—she is a good woman at heart. I am filled with sorrow for her."

"As am I," said Mara, who was closer to Bathsheba than any of them. "I wish I could have done something to help her."

"Once David reached his decision, there was nothing anyone could do to help," said Sunu. "Unless I had been able to save Uriah that day before the gates of Rabbah."

Eri put a hand on his son's shoulder. "It was not to be," he said quietly.

Sunu sighed and nodded. He looked at his own small son and daughter and thought about how much he loved them. He knew he would be racked with guilt were he to make a decision such as David's—a decision that brought down the wrath of God on an innocent child.

"So David is going to Rabbah," said Mara. "He could not defeat God, so now he will smash the Ammonites in His stead." She looked intently at Sunu.

He heard the concern in her voice and understood the reason for it. "David will go to Rabbah without me," he declared, "even though my injuries have healed. I am done with war. My forge—and my family—are enough for me now."

Her eyes glittering with tears, Mara reached across the table and clasped his hand. Eri and Baalan smiled in satisfaction, pleased at the decision Sunu had finally made.

Then a light touch fell on Sunu's shoulder, and he turned his head to see his young half-sister, Leah. She was smiling, too, but her smile was tinged with regret. "I wish we were all done with war," she said softly.

But something in her eyes told Sunu she knew it would never be so.

CHAPTER
TWENTY-FIVE

Kaptar stood at the prow of the ship as it cut steadily through the waters of the Nile. The oarsmen rowed in a brisk rhythm against the current of the great river, not daring to slow their pace lest the black-bearded giant who stood beside Kaptar turn and glower at them. There was enough force in Nestor's potent gaze to make any man quake.

"From what you have told me, we will be there soon, my friend," he said to Kaptar. "Until we reach Waset, there is no need to worry. It serves no purpose."

"You are not married, Nestor." Kaptar did not take his eyes off the lush landscape unfolding before them. "When I think of Nefernehi in the hands of the Kushites—"

"I would tell you not to think of such things, but I suspect it would do little good." Nestor squeezed Kaptar's shoulder briefly but said no more.

Kaptar knew that Nestor was right; until they

reached Waset, there was nothing he could do to help Nefernehi. In fact, he did not know if Nefernehi even *needed* his help. It was possible the Kushites had made no more raids on the city; perhaps their initial foray had also been their final one.

But that was unlikely, and Kaptar knew it. If the Kushites believed themselves strong enough to attack Waset once, they would do it again.

Suddenly Nestor gripped Kaptar's arm. "Look there," he said, pointing upriver. "Is that . . . smoke?"

Kaptar's breath caught in his throat as he studied the column of black rising in the distance. There was no mistaking it—what Nestor had seen was indeed smoke.

"They have set the city afire," Kaptar breathed, barely able to grasp the horror of what he was seeing. He turned and shouted to the oarsmen, "Faster! Row faster, you fools! Can you not see that Waset is ablaze?"

The oarsmen responded valiantly, and the boat fairly flew over the water. Kaptar stood at the prow, his fingers wrapped tightly around the hilt of his sword, his heart pounding almost painfully.

As the boat drew nearer to Waset, Kaptar could see the great buildings rising along the shore. The column of smoke had become billowing clouds. Kaptar felt a tightness in his chest as he thought of Nefernehi somewhere in that maelstrom of destruction. She might be dead already. He might be too late.

Drawing a deep breath into his lungs, Kaptar forced those thoughts out of his mind. If he gave in to despair, Nefernehi was truly doomed. He and Nestor and the small force of soldiers with them represented her best chance for survival.

The sounds of battle floated from the streets of the city as the boat grounded on the sandy shore just north of the stone piers that extended into the Nile. The area around the pier was swarming with Kushites. Kaptar could see their feathered headdresses waving in the breeze. As he leaped down from the boat and motioned for the others to follow him, a great shout went up from the Kushites. He and his group had been seen, Kaptar realized. A sizable number of savages ran toward them, shrieking and waving spears above their heads.

"Follow me!" Kaptar ordered, darting toward a street that appeared deserted, at least for the moment.

That was about to change. The Kushites caught up with the rear of Kaptar's force, and the Egyptian soldiers turned to face them with courage and valor that would have made Kaptar proud had he time to think about it. As it was, he was thankful his companions were conducting a delaying action. He had to find Nefernehi.

Nestor's long-legged, loping stride enabled him to keep pace easily with Kaptar. As he glanced back over his shoulder, a wistful expression on his craggy, bearded face, he asked, "Do you know where we will find your wife?"

"It has been years since I visited Waset," replied Kaptar, "but I believe I can still find my way to the temple of Amon. If any of the priests are there, they will know where Nefernehi can be found." He hoped fervently that was true. As a member of the royal family of priests, it was possible she had quarters in the temple itself.

The city of Waset was in chaos. As Kaptar, Nestor, and the handful of men still remaining with them penetrated deeper into the heart of the city, small bands of roving Kushite raiders sprang out at them from alleys and buildings. Nestor roared his defiance as he hewed a bloody path through the marauders with his sword, swinging it with both hands and all the power in his brawny arms and shoulders. Entrails spilled, heads flew, and the paving stones of the street were soon awash with blood. Kaptar fought at Nestor's side, barely noticing the gashes he received from Kushite knives and spears.

Nestor pointed with his bloody sword to a massive building. "Is that the temple?" he shouted to Kaptar.

"Yes!" Kaptar felt his heart sink as he gazed down the broad avenue. Smoke was billowing from inside the temple. Although the structure itself was built of stone and would not burn, its furnishings and accoutrements would. If Nefernehi was in there, she might be in mortal danger.

Nestor hacked aside the last of the Kushites blocking their way, and he and Kaptar sprinted toward the temple of Amon. They were alone now, Kaptar saw as he glanced over his shoulder. The soldiers who had come with them were all gone—some dead, others probably still fighting the Kushites along the path that had brought them here.

But Nestor was worth three or four men by himself, Kaptar thought gratefully, and he himself had fought with a frenzy that was unlike him. He would allow nothing to stop him from reaching Nefernehi's side. *Nothing!*

They bounded up the great steps leading to the temple entrance and pounded through. From the corner of his eye Kaptar saw a Kushite lunging at him, spear outstretched. Kaptar jerked himself aside, and the spearpoint raked a long finger of pain across his torso. At the same time, he swung his sword with both hands, and as the edge of the blade met the Kushite's neck, Kaptar was rewarded with a solid impact that shivered up his arms. The sword cut through muscle and bone, and the Kushite's head toppled wide-eyed from its perch.

Kaptar kicked aside the falling body and bounded on. Another figure staggered out of an alcove ahead of him. Kaptar was ready to run the man through when his battle-fevered brain told him he was looking at one of the priests who lived and worshiped in this temple. The man collapsed before Kaptar could reach his side. While Nestor guarded his back, Kaptar crouched beside the mortally wounded priest, grasped his shoulders, and raised him so that he could speak.

"Nefernehi!" Kaptar shouted in the face of the dying man. "Know you the lady Nefernehi?"

The priest lifted a trembling arm and pointed in the direction of a staircase on the opposite side of the great temple. "H-her apartment . . ." he rasped. "Up there . . . top of the stairs . . . save her."

That was exactly what Kaptar intended to do. But

before he could assure the priest of that, the man's head slumped loosely to the side. Kaptar quickly but gently lowered him to the floor, then snatched up his sword. "Up those stairs!" he called to Nestor, pointing with the blade.

As they dashed across the room to the stairs, Kaptar saw flames leaping from other alcoves that surrounded the main chamber. There was still time to reach Nefernehi before flames blocked all the exits to the building, he believed, but they had to move quickly. At least she was still alive, and that knowledge made his heart sing. The dying priest would not have urged him to save her were she not alive.

Kaptar and Nestor were halfway up the narrow staircase when angry shouts from below made them turn around. As Kaptar whirled to face this new threat, a spear flew past his head to clatter against the steps. Nestor snatched it up and threw it with such force that it passed completely through the body of a Kushite who had appeared at the bottom of the stairs.

But others swarmed up toward them. Kaptar and Nestor met the charge with keen-edged iron. Although there was not enough room to swing a sword properly, the two men managed to thrust their blades with skill and force, and one by one the savages tumbled back down the stairs, dead or dying.

At last Kaptar and Nestor were free to resume their climb, but the delay had cost them precious moments. The fires had spread, and dense black smoke was clogging their lungs.

At the top of the stairs the air was a bit clearer. Kaptar took a deep breath and bellowed, "Nefernehi! Nefernehi!" He looked around wildly for the entrance to the apartment the dying priest had said was there and finally spotted it on the other side of some drifting tendrils of smoke. With Nestor at his heels, he plunged toward it.

As he ran through the arched entrance, he cast around for any sign of his wife but saw none. Suddenly a small figure darted toward him, sword held aloft. Kaptar barely had time to realize he was being attacked by a child before the lad was on him.

"Khode! No!"

The voice sounded puzzlingly familiar, but before Kaptar had time to ponder it, he instinctively parried the boy's sword thrust and knocked the weapon from the child's hands. He bent down and with his free arm scooped up the kicking, struggling child.

"Stop that!" he told the boy sternly. "Stop that, I say! I am here to help—"

He was shocked into silence: On the boy's hip, revealed when his tunic had ridden up his side, was a dark red birthmark shaped like the paw print of a lion.

"Kaptar . . . ?"

The astonished voice made Kaptar's head jerk up. He saw her then, emerging from a curtained alcove across the room, as spectacularly beautiful as ever, though her features were taut with fear and she clutched a dagger in her hand. He stared at her for a timeless moment, drinking in the sight of her, then turned and looked at the boy. "Is he . . . ?"

A smile touched Nefernehi's lips. "Your son," she said. "His name is Khode."

"Khode!" Kaptar said to the child. "Stop fighting now. I am your father. I have come to help you and your mother."

Kaptar's mind was spinning madly. He had expected, or at least hoped, to find Nefernehi here, but he had no idea she had had a son. *His* son. A Child of the Lion.

Nefernehi came partway across the room, then stopped short and peered past Kaptar in alarm. "Kaptar, who is *that?*" she hissed.

He cast a glance over his shoulder and saw Nestor, holding a bloodstained sword, arms and torso spattered with gore, eyes glaring savagely. Kaptar grinned and turned back to Nefernehi. "A friend," he told her. "A good friend who has stood beside me for many years. His name is Nestor."

"I do not wish to rush this reunion, my prince,"

said Nestor, "but parts of this temple are on fire. I believe we should depart as soon as possible."

Kaptar put his sword arm around Nefernehi and drew her close to him, being careful not to touch her with the blood-smeared blade. For a moment they stood together, her face pressed against his chest, his face resting against the top of her head. Then he said, "You are right, Nestor. Come, Nefernehi."

She did not budge. "Why?" she asked. "Why have you come for me now, after all these years?"

"To save you from the Kushites, of course."

"But why never before?"

He could tell by the look in her eyes how important this was to her, so he told the truth. "You did not want me to follow you when you left On," he said. "I but respected your wishes."

"Did not want you to follow me?" she repeated. "I never said—" She stopped suddenly, and a flash of anger glittered in her dark eyes. "Sheshonk," she breathed.

"We will discuss this later," Kaptar promised. "Right now we must leave, before it becomes impossible."

With Khode still in his arms and Nefernehi at his side, Kaptar followed Nestor back down the stairs to the main room. The fire had engulfed even more of the temple, and it was impossible to see farther than the length of a man's arm through the smoke. But somehow Nestor led them to the entrance, and a few moments later they staggered out to the street. Even coughing and choking, Kaptar and Nestor held their swords at the ready and looked around with watering eyes for Kushite raiders. At Kaptar's side, Nefernehi, dagger in hand, was also prepared to defend her family; the fire in her eyes burned as fiercely as any warrior's.

But no Kushites were to be seen. Indeed, a troop of Egyptian soldiers was approaching down the broad avenue. Some Kaptar recognized from the group that had accompanied him and Nestor, and he was glad they had survived the battle. The other soldiers were strangers, and Kaptar wondered where they had come from.

The officer in charge of the troop informed him that boats full of reinforcements had been sent up the Nile by Sheshonk shortly after Kaptar and Nestor had departed. They had arrived in the city in time to force the marauding Kushites to take to their boats and flee before wreaking any further damage.

"The savages never would have penetrated so deeply into the city had they not employed a ruse," said Nefernehi. "They have been attacking us from the river for many weeks, but our soldiers repelled all their raids. Today, though, some of them brought their boats ashore upstream and circled around to the east of the city, so that they could come at us from inland. We were expecting an attack from the Nile. But once our soldiers turned to face the threat from the land, the rest of the Kushites swarmed ashore at the docks."

Kaptar grunted. "They have learned military strategy from somewhere. This is not a good thing."

"We will drive them back beyond the great cataracts," boasted the young officer in charge of the reinforcements. "Henceforth, On and Waset shall work together to drive any invaders from the sacred Black Land. So says Sheshonk."

Nefernehi shuddered slightly at the mention of the pharaoh's name. Kaptar noticed her reaction and wondered at it. He had already surmised that Sheshonk had lied to him about her departure from On. She had never said that she did not want Kaptar to follow her.

But all that could be discussed later. For now, he wanted to take a good look at his son. He placed Khode on the ground and said, "You seem to be a fine lad."

"I am," the boy said boldly. "Are you really my father?"

"Of course I am," said Kaptar. "Have you seen the print of the lion's paw on your hip?"

Khode nodded.

Kaptar drew his tunic aside to reveal his own birthmark. "That is one of your legacies from me and my family. You are a Child of the Lion."

"A Child of the Lion," Khode repeated in a hushed voice. "What does it mean?"

"It means that trouble may follow you, my son . . . but so will glory." Kaptar put a hand on Khode's shoulder and gazed around him at the chaos and destruction. Smoke was still rising into the late afternoon sky, the avenue was littered with sprawled and bloody corpses, and in the distance he could hear the sobbing and wailing of women.

But he was alive, reunited at last with his Beautiful One of the South, and his good friend Nestor was here with him as well. He looked down at his son, perhaps his greatest gift, and said again, "So will glory."

CHAPTER
TWENTY-SIX

The Kushites were in full retreat up the Nile, but the Egyptian soldiers pursued them anyway, seeking to deal them a blow powerful enough to ensure that they would raid Waset no more. Nestor accompanied the Egyptian forces while Kaptar remained in Waset to present Sheshonk's proposal for mutual defense to the ruling priests. While reluctant to agree to a full alliance with Sheshonk, the rulers of Upper Egypt were persuaded to strengthen their political and economic ties with Lower Egypt.

Through Kaptar's efforts, his uncle Kemose's dream of reuniting the Two Lands was one step closer to reality. Kaptar was justly proud.

But he was even prouder of his son, and reuniting Upper and Lower Egypt meant less to him than his own reunion with his wife.

"For some reason, Sheshonk must have wanted us to be apart," he said to Nefernehi one day when they were discussing their lengthy separation. "He has long depended on me for counsel. Perhaps he thought you were distracting me from my duties to him—and he would have been right, because visions of you fill my thoughts every hour of the day."

"Perhaps," Nefernehi said, but she did not sound convinced of his theory. She offered no reason of her own for what Sheshonk had done, however. "It would be best if you said nothing of this to Sheshonk," she went on. "Now that we are together again and have our son with us, we should put these past years behind us."

"Yes," said Kaptar, "everything save my sojourn in the land of the Israelites. I would not forget being brought together with my other family and finding my father at last."

Their only point of contention arose when Kaptar announced that Nefernehi and Khode would accompany him back to On when Nestor returned. "I thought to stay here in Waset," Nefernehi protested, "now that the threat of the Kushites has passed."

"We cannot be certain it has," Kaptar countered. "My home is in On, and I would have my wife and child with me."

Nefernehi did not argue for long, finally yielding to his wishes with a distracted sigh. Obviously there was something about On that bothered her—the presence of Sheshonk, perhaps? Kaptar did not press her.

Nestor arrived in Waset several days later with the Egyptian soldiers, and he reported success to Kaptar. "The Kushites have been driven far past the great cataracts, and we inflicted casualties on them the entire way. I do not think they will return to plague this land anytime soon." A grin stretched across his bearded face. "Ah, you should have been with us, Kaptar. There were great battles, the likes of which I have not seen since we smote the Philistines together. You would have enjoyed yourself immensely."

Kaptar looked at his wife and son and smiled. "I passed the time here quite pleasurably," he said.

The next day, the boat that would carry the four of

them back to On sailed from Waset. Kaptar stood at the prow with one arm around Nefernehi, the other hand on Khode's shoulder, and gazed out at the Nile.

For the first time in years, the great river was truly carrying him home.

Life in On went more smoothly than Nefernehi had expected. She was forced to see Sheshonk from time to time, of course, and her belly clenched in revulsion and remembered outrage every time she set eyes on him. She saw terror in his eyes the first time he faced her and Kaptar, and she knew he feared that she had told Kaptar about what he had done to her. When it became obvious she had not, Sheshonk relaxed somewhat, but he was always nervous in her presence.

That was good, thought Nefernehi. It was fitting that he be tortured by worry and guilt.

As for her, when she was away from the royal palace she was happier than she had ever been. Kaptar had been rewarded with an estate of his own on the edge of the city, and the family quickly settled in. The best tutors in the land came to instruct Khode, who continued to grow at a seemingly impossible rate. The lad would be quite a warrior when he was grown, according to Nestor, who visited them as often as his duties as a mercenary captain in the army allowed.

"The boy is a Child of the Lion," Nestor declared, "and always have they been great fighters. Khode will be as strong as his uncle and his cousin in the land of the Israelites . . . not to mention his father, of course."

"Of course," Kaptar agreed dryly.

"I am not certain I want my son to be a warrior," said Nefernehi. "But he will be whatever his fate leads him to be, I suppose."

Life was good, she found herself reflecting often. She was able to put all the sadness of the past behind her and look only to the future. But her serenity was disturbed one day when Kaptar strode into the house, a troubled look on his face. He had been at the palace, Nefernehi knew, and she wondered if Sheshonk had done something to disturb him. She found out almost immediately.

"My brother is planning to invade the land of the Israelites," he said heavily as he sat down.

Nefernehi dropped to her knees beside him and caught hold of his left hand in both of hers. "You are certain of this?" she asked.

He nodded. "He has begun making plans with the generals of the army. He will wait until the time is right, he says, but it is inevitable. Sheshonk is determined to restore Canaan to its former position as a vassal state of Egypt."

"The people who live there now—the Israelites— what will they do if they are invaded?"

"The same thing they have always done," replied Kaptar grimly. "They will fight."

"And your brother and his son?"

"Both of them would give their very lives to defend their land."

Nefernehi rested her head against her husband's knee. "Kaptar, I am sorry. What . . . what will you do?"

He sighed. "I promised my uncle Kemose that I would support my brother and assist him in any way I could to make Egypt stronger. But if Sheshonk invades Israel, then Eri and Sunu and the rest of my family there will be in great danger. I wish there was some way I could help them."

Nefernehi felt herself being pulled in different directions, and she knew that Kaptar was torn between his loyalty to Egypt and his brother, and his love for his kin in Israel.

She took a deep breath. Loyalty to Egypt was one thing, but Kaptar's continued support of Sheshonk and the young pharaoh's ambitions was another. If Kaptar was to make a wise choice, he had to know the truth . . . about everything. She was going to have to break the vow she had made to herself that he would never learn of her entanglement with Sheshonk.

"Kaptar, there is something I must tell you," she

said slowly. "Something about your brother . . . and your wife."

He looked at her with a frown. "What are you saying, Nefernehi?"

It would be best to do this quickly, she decided. "While you were gone to the land of the Israelites, Sheshonk . . . forced me into his bed and took me . . . many times. He threatened to kill you and my family if I did not submit. I feared that the child I bore would be his, but I prayed to the gods it would not be." She managed to smile faintly. "They answered my prayers. The mark of the lion's paw proves that Khode is your son, not Sheshonk's. But still, he defiled me, and his guilt at doing that was what made him send me away to Waset and then lie to you about the reasons for my leaving."

His face had hardened as the words tumbled out of her mouth. Her breath caught in her throat when she saw the hatred blazing in his eyes. Was it directed at her?

"This is a true thing you have told me?" he asked.

She nodded shakily. "I swear that it is. I did not want to ever tell you—"

"No, my love, it is good you did." His expression softened, and he reached out to brush his fingertips over her cheek. "I am sorry, Beautiful One. I have been wondering why you seem so uneasy in Sheshonk's presence. Now I know. What he did to you is unforgivable. I should never have allowed it to happen."

"No!" she exclaimed. "It was not your fault, Kaptar. It was your brother—"

"I have no brother in Egypt," he said simply. "My only brother's name is Eri, and he lives in Israel." He took her arms and stood, bringing her to her feet. "We will go to him, you and I and Khode. Or perhaps you and the boy should stay here in Egypt. It is your homeland, after all—"

Nefernehi stopped him by pressing her lips hard to his. When she took her mouth away a moment later, she said quietly, "I have been separated from you once, my husband. I would not have it so again. If you go to Israel, then Khode and I will go as well."

"My love," he murmured. "My Beautiful One."

He had reached the decision she wanted him to. True, it would be difficult to leave Egypt, but Kaptar had been wrong about one thing.

Wherever he was, *there* was her homeland.

Once the decision had been made, plans proceeded quickly. Kaptar bought a boat and hired a crew to take them to Israel. He swore the sailors to secrecy because he did not want Sheshonk to know he was leaving. If Sheshonk was capable of what amounted to the rape of his own brother's wife, what else was he capable of? Perhaps, fearing that Kaptar would warn the Israelites of the impending Egyptian invasion, he might not hesitate to have Kaptar and his family killed. Kaptar could not take any chances. He had to get his family out of Egypt quickly.

One last matter was yet to be resolved, and Kaptar took care of that the next time Nestor came to visit them. Kaptar explained the situation, then concluded by saying, "You have made a place for yourself here in the army of the pharaoh. In time you might become commander of the entire army. I would not have you give up that opportunity just because my family and I are leaving Egypt."

Nestor looked at him intently for a long moment, then threw back his head in a booming laugh. "Think you that I would continue to serve a dog like this Sheshonk?" He drew his sword, a sword Kaptar had made for him, and fingered the edge of the blade. "The Hebrews are valiant warriors, but they will need more good fighting men when Sheshonk gets around to attacking them. I have never given up my dream of one day returning to my own homeland, my prince, but for now my place is with you."

Kaptar clasped his arm fervently. "Thank you, my friend. Truly, it would not have been an adventure without you."

Several days later, on a morning when the sky was clear and a good breeze sprang up not long before dawn, the boat carrying Kaptar, Nefernehi, Khode, and Nestor set sail from On. The vessel made its way through the delta and out into the open waters of the Great Sea, sailing east toward Israel.

East toward home. Kaptar smiled at the thought.

In Jerusalem, three women sat in a luxurious apartment in the palace of the king. Young Leah had grown lovely indeed, although she thought of herself as quite plain compared to her two companions, Bathsheba and Mara.

"I have news," said Bathsheba with a coy smile. "I am with child once more."

"That is wonderful!" Mara exclaimed. "You are blessed, Bathsheba."

The king's favorite wife nodded. "I pray it is so. After what happened before . . ."

Eyes downcast, she fell silent. Mara and Leah both knew she was remembering the child that had died after the prophet Nathan had pronounced God's curse.

Forcing herself to smile again, Bathsheba said, "This time will be different. I feel certain that God will look with favor on this child." She turned to Leah. "It is said that you have certain powers, my young friend. Mystical powers."

Leah looked down at the floor, remembering Jerioth's urgings that she not be too quick to display her special abilities. "I have no control over what people may say, my lady," she murmured.

"But is it true? You must tell me."

Mara said, "It is all right, Leah. You can trust Bathsheba."

"Well . . ." Leah looked up and met the eyes of Bathsheba, who was gazing intently, almost urgently, at her. "Sometimes I can see things. . . ."

"Visions?" Bathsheba asked eagerly.

"Some might call them visions," Leah admitted uneasily.

"You must foretell the future of my unborn child. I must know!"

"I cannot control what I might see," Leah began hesitantly.

Bathsheba leaned forward and caught hold of both her hands. "Try," she implored. "Please try. I . . . I could not stand another tragedy."

Leah took a deep breath and nodded. Already she could feel more than warmth flowing from Bathsheba's hands to hers—she could feel the tides of fate.

Several minutes passed while the three women sat in silence, Bathsheba anxiously watching Leah's face. Leah's eyes closed, and her expression was unreadable, even to Mara. But finally she opened her eyes again and smiled.

"I see great glory for your son," she said. "He will be a wise king, loved by all the people. I see, too, a magnificent temple, which will be a joy to God. Your son will build this temple."

"Yes," Bathsheba breathed. "Oh, yes . . . Is there more?"

Leah shook her head and released Bathsheba's hands. "That is all. I see only good things for your son."

Bathsheba threw her arms around the young woman. "Thank you, thank you. You have eased the burden on my mind, Leah. Your powers are remarkable!"

"Yes," said Leah quietly. "Remarkable . . ."

She fell silent. Bathsheba might have felt differently had she seen the *other* visions that had come to Leah: visions of turmoil and tragedy, of death and weeping. Leah could not predict the future exactly, but before those wondrous times she had foretold would come to pass, great sorrow would plague King David and his family. She murmured a name. *"Absalom . . ."*

"What did you say?" asked Bathsheba.

Leah shook her head. "Nothing, my lady. Nothing at all."

She would speak no more of it. After all, she reasoned, she could not know if her visions had foretold the real future . . . or only what *might* be. The ways of the Lord, the workings of fate, were mysterious indeed. Who could truly tell what would come?

As for her own life, Leah thought, in the end, despite her powers, she could do only what everyone else had to do. Accepting whatever God had in store for her, she would face the future with faith and courage.

And the knowledge that she was a true Child of the Lion.

Epilogue

~~~~~~

"That is all," said the old man. "There is no more to tell."

"No!" exclaimed one of the youths sitting at his feet. "There must be more. What of Kaptar? Did he return to our land?"

"And Nestor?" put in another of the lads. "Did he ever go back to his home?"

A third youth said, "I would hear more of Leah."

One of his friends laughed and said, "Aye, you would be most interested in the pretty young maid in the story, but if you met her, the thoughts in your head would likely cause her to smite you across the face!" The young men laughed at the gibe.

The old man peered up at the sky, which had grown dark while he was talking. The sun had long since set, and the street was dense with shadows. With despair he realized that he still did not know where he was or how to find his way home.

Still, the time had not been wasted, not by any means. It had not escaped the old man's notice that, as he had spun his web of words, the young men's attitude had changed from surly resentment to keen interest. Not for the first time, he realized the power he wielded, the power that belonged to all who told the wondrous tales of the Children of the Lion.

The swordsman uncoiled lithely from his cross-legged position on the ground. "Thank you," he said. "Your story means a great deal to me. I wish there was time for more, but I suppose that is in other hands."

"The hands of fate," murmured the old man as he stood up.

"Yes. May I escort you to your home, my friend?"

Something about the man made the Teller of Tales trust him. He coughed once, then said, "I, ah, am not sure how to go about finding it."

"Do not worry," said the swordsman with a confident smile. "We shall find it together."

The old man nodded. "Yes. Yes, we shall."

The youths moved off down the street, calling their farewells. Forgotten was the hostility that had led them to confront the old man earlier. It would return, surely, but for now their heads were full of a tale of adventure and high drama. The storyteller had done his work well.

The swordsman rested a hand lightly on his companion's shoulder. In a quiet voice he asked, "There really is more to the story, is there not?"

The old man shook his head. "It is not for me to say."

But as he moved down the street with his new friend, trailed by the faithful spotted dog, he thought of all the days yet to come and knew one thing with absolute certainty.

The story would never truly end, so long as there lived someone like him to tell the tales.

From the Producers of WAGONS WEST

THE CHILDREN OF THE LION

Extraordinary tales of epic adventure. A saga that creates anew the splendor and sweeping panorama of desert kingdoms aflame with the excitement and passions of the world's earliest legends.

____26912-7 **THE CHILDREN OF THE LION** $4.99/$5.99 in Canada

____56145-6 **DEPARTED GLORY** $4.99/$5.99 in Canada

____56146-4 **THE DEATH OF KINGS** $4.99/$5.99 in Canada

____56147-2 **THE SHINING KING** $4.99/$5.99 in Canada

ACROSS UNTAMED LANDS THEY FORGED A LEGACY THAT TIME WILL NEVER FORGET!

- -